Smart Girl Summer

OTHER TITLES BY KRISTIN ROCKAWAY

Life, Unscheduled
She's Faking It
How to Hack a Heartbreak
The Wild Woman's Guide to Traveling the World

Young Adult

My Epic Spring Break (Up)

Smart
Girl
Summer

Kristin Rockaway

 Montlake

Published by Montlake, Seattle

www.apub.com

Amazon, the Amazon logo, and Montlake are trademarks of Amazon.com, Inc., or its affiliates.

ISBN-13: 9781542026307 (paperback)
ISBN-13: 9781542026314 (digital)

Cover design by Caroline Teagle Johnson
Cover images: © Betsie Van der Meer / Getty; © deimagine / Getty

Printed in the United States of America

For anyone who's ever had to start over

CHAPTER ONE

There are two kinds of people in this world: those who believe in treating others with respect and decency, and those who have zero qualms about backstabbing their way to the top. I used to think, perhaps naively, that the former far outnumbered the latter. That while a few snakes would always linger in the grass, most everyone I'd encounter in my day-to-day doings would be conscientious, fair, and trustworthy.

Now I know better.

The truth is, you can't really trust anybody. Integrity's hard to come by. Honesty's a myth. And odds are, even the people who are supposed to be on your side care more about protecting the status quo than standing up for what's right.

It's enough to make a woman scream obscenities at the top of her lungs. I won't do that now, of course, because I'm standing in the middle of a crowded subway car and I don't want to end up on some viral video as the woman who inexplicably flipped out during rush hour. So I swallow my rage, forcing it past the lump in my throat until it settles in the pit of my stomach. It sits there like a bowling ball, hard and heavy, for the entire thirty-five-minute subway ride from Lower Manhattan to Astoria, Queens.

The doors open at Steinway Street, and I step out onto the platform through sheer force of habit, allowing myself to get carried away with the crowd. Up the stairs, through the turnstile, up another flight of stairs, and out onto street level, where the late-afternoon sun makes me squint. Half the city is out enjoying this beautiful summer day. There's a line for Mahmoud's food truck, and that trendy new bar with the sidewalk café is packed with smiling patrons. I don't understand how everyone can be this happy when the world is so profoundly unfair.

With clenched fists, I march down Forty-First Street toward my boxy brick apartment building, silently stewing over the injustice of it all. I've worked so hard for so long, poured all my time and my effort into this singular pursuit, only for the fruits of my labor to be shamelessly stolen from me. Nick was my mentor, someone I trusted, and he turned around and stabbed me in the back. The worst part is, he's getting off scot-free.

There must be some way for me to fight this. Maybe I can file a formal appeal with the dean of the graduate school. I'm sure she'd be horrified to hear about the blatant theft and collusion that's occurring in the university's otherwise esteemed physics department.

I stomp up the stairs to my third-story walk-up, each footfall landing heavier than the last. I unlock the front door and storm inside, where Arpita is sitting on the couch, her laptop nestled in the center of her crossed legs. She takes one look at my face and says, "I'm guessing it didn't go well."

"No." I chuck my purse onto the hallway floor with an angry thud. "It did not."

"Tell me what happened. No, wait." She sets her laptop on the coffee table before disappearing into the kitchen as I kick off my shoes and drag myself to the couch. A moment later, she returns with two canned margaritas, one of which she deposits in my hand. "Now tell me."

We crack open our cans and I start to chug, eager to quickly and thoroughly numb my emotions, of which there are many. Beneath the surface-level rage, there's a thin layer of disgust floating atop a bottomless well of despair, regret, and bone-crushing disappointment.

Yet only a few hours ago I'd been feeling so confident, so convinced that Philip would rule in my favor. As the head of the physics department, he had the power to put Nick in his place. Instead, he pulled me into his office and said, "We don't see any evidence of theft."

His response caught me so off guard all I could think to say was "What?"

"You said you conducted this research on dark energy in Professor Bauer's laboratory, correct?"

"Yes." Of course I did. Nick Bauer was my doctoral adviser, the person who was supposed to support my journey through the PhD program. All my research was performed in his lab. That didn't give him the right to steal it. "But the idea for this project was mine."

Philip leaned back in his desk chair, hands clasped firmly across his potbelly. "Ideas have no ownership, Ms. Atkinson."

"Fair enough, but I did all the research, all the data analysis. I made the initial discovery. And Nick published my findings without giving me any credit whatsoever."

"Professor Bauer says he's been working on this specific project for years, and you're simply overstating your contributions."

I shook my head vigorously. "No, that's not true at all."

"Is there documentation to back up your statements?"

"I already showed you my notes and figures."

"They're vague. No dates, no signatures. Nothing to prove they were yours."

Damn. All along, I thought my only responsibility was to collect compelling and accurate scientific data. I didn't realize I should've also been collecting evidence for a potential fraud case. "At this point, I think it's up to Nick to prove he's been working on this project for as long as he says he has."

Philip sighed wearily, like I was the world's biggest pain in the ass. "Science is a collaborative effort, Ms. Atkinson. You'd do well to understand that if you wish to have a successful academic career."

"I understand science is a collaborative effort, but my effort wasn't acknowledged at all. Additionally, a successful academic career requires publications, and this publication was supposed to have my name on it." Not to mention, it was the basis for my dissertation. If I didn't get the credit for this work, then I couldn't use it for my PhD. Which meant I'd have to start over from scratch with a new proposal.

His beady eyes narrowed behind his horn-rimmed glasses. This wasn't the way he'd expected the conversation to go. After all, academia has a hierarchy. Who was I, a lowly graduate student, to be challenging the decision of a department head with decades of experience? Bad enough I'd already accused a tenured professor of academic theft. Of which there was no proof, apparently.

"As I stated," he said, "we've found no evidence of misconduct."

"So that's it? I have no recourse?"

"Recourse assumes wrongdoing. In this case, there was none." He sat forward and shuffled through some papers on his desk, as if he had something important to do and I was very much in the way. "Now, if there's nothing else you need to discuss—"

"There is, actually." Ignoring his withering look, I continued, "I haven't received my summer teaching assignment yet, and the semester begins in less than a week."

"You haven't been given a teaching assignment."

"But I requested one." Teaching assignments were dictated by seniority, which meant I definitely should've received one. Usually, they had to beg people to stick around and teach undergrad summer classes, but I always cheerfully volunteered because I always needed the money. Never before had they turned me down, not even when I was a first-year. "There must be some mistake."

"I assure you there is no mistake."

I didn't understand. It didn't make sense . . . until suddenly, it did. Because if there wasn't a mistake, it must've been intentional. "Was

I purposely denied a teaching assignment because I filed a grievance against Nick? Is this some sort of punishment?"

With an offended grunt, he patted what was left of his thinning gray hair. "Ms. Atkinson, please. I think you've made enough baseless accusations for one afternoon."

I supposed this particular accusation *was* baseless, since there was no hard evidence to back up my claim—not that evidence mattered much to Philip, anyway. But I knew in my gut that this was a retaliatory move. Payback for disrespecting the hierarchy. For not sitting down and shutting up.

It was also a crystal clear warning: *Play by our rules, or we'll make your life miserable.*

"Wow," Arpita says now. "I can't believe Nick's gonna get away with it."

"He isn't." My fingers clench, denting the empty can in my fist. "I'm gonna keep fighting."

"How? You already escalated to Philip."

"I'm gonna go to Dean Stanhope next."

"Really?"

"Of course! These are ethics violations; she needs to know. Plus, if Nick stole from me, there's no telling who else he's stolen from over the years. Who knows if he even earned his PhD fair and square? It could open a whole can of worms that impacts the credibility of the school."

Arpita nods and sips her margarita in silence, which annoys me. I want her to be as outraged as I am, but she simply seems resigned to this ruling.

"You think I'm wrong?" I ask.

"No. I think you're very much in the right. But I also think you need to be smart about this."

"What does that mean?"

"It means don't do anything rash. Take some time to think it through before you bring this to the dean."

"There's nothing to think through. Nick stole from me, Philip is covering for him. It's an open-and-shut case."

"This is academia, Abby. You know as well as I do that politics are just as important as empirical data. Maybe even more so. Have you ever spoken to Dean Stanhope before?"

"No." She doesn't even know me. I'm too low down on the academic food chain for her to be aware of my existence.

"So do you really expect her to take your side?"

My stomach gurgles, margarita mixing with that overpriced salad I had for lunch. It'll be a miracle if I manage to keep it down. I slam the empty can on the coffee table. "That's it, then? I'm just supposed to move on and pretend like this never happened?"

"Not necessarily, but you should definitely press pause before you decide what to do next. You've been obsessing about this for weeks; it's not good for your mental health. Give yourself some time and space to rest."

"Resting isn't my forte. And I don't have time to rest now, anyway. I've gotta find a new adviser, develop a new topic for my dissertation. I'm basically starting over with nothing." Four years into the five-year program, and it's like I'm right back at the beginning. Actually, I'm worse off than I was at the beginning, because back then I had the advantage of anonymity. Now the head of the department sees me as the troublemaker, the loudmouth, the one who refuses to play by the rules. I wonder if word's gotten around to the other physics professors. Would any of them want to be my adviser now, or am I considered damaged goods? Maybe it's not worth it to keep fighting.

There's a hollow in my chest that seems to be growing by the millisecond, a black hole threatening to turn me inside out. Being swallowed up by the universe sounds pretty appealing, to be honest. Then I won't have to worry about what to do next.

I bury my face in my hands and moan. "My life is over."

"That's not true." Arpita scoots closer to me and wraps her arm around my hunched shoulders. "School doesn't define your whole life."

"Doesn't it?" I've been in school for the past twenty-two years. Elementary to middle to high to college, then straight to one of the most competitive graduate programs in the country. My entire life thus far has revolved around being a student, and as soon as I get my PhD, I'm hoping to settle into a career as a university professor. School is my past, my present, and my future. It's everything.

Arpita doesn't agree. "No. You need a break, Abby. Why don't you spend the summer away from campus? You're not teaching, so you don't need to be there. A little distance might help you to get some perspective before you go diving into another research project."

I glance around our living room at the threadbare couch and the disorganized bookshelves. The window offers an unobstructed view of the adjacent building's redbrick wall. "I'm not sure what perspective there is to be gained from staying at home."

"I don't mean staying home. I mean getting out of New York. Wouldn't you love to travel around a little bit? I know I would."

Traveling could be fun. "Where would we go?"

"Oh, I can't go anywhere. My study is running continuously through the end of August." Arpita's getting her PhD in psychology. She has an amazing adviser who would never in a million years steal from her. "If I were you, though, I'd totally take advantage of this break. It's a unique opportunity for you to do something completely different. Step out of your comfort zone, see the world. Get lost to find yourself and all that good stuff."

Going on a solo travel expedition with the intent of "finding yourself" is a tired cliché, but I can't deny that the idea is tempting. I've only traveled outside the United States once—junior year spring break in Cancun: let us never speak of it again—and it would be cool to see some more of this planet. I close my eyes, and I'm whisked away to England, sitting in one of those private train cars and gazing out the window as the countryside whizzes by. Flash forward and I'm at a bistro in Paris, sipping a glass of red wine with the Eiffel Tower in the background. Another flash and I'm in Rome, tossing coins into the Trevi Fountain. Then I'm jumping into the fountain to retrieve that coin, because I can't afford to waste it.

The sad truth is, an international adventure is way out of my budget, especially now that I'm losing my summer teaching income. At least I still have my private tutoring work, even if it's only part time. I suppose I could request more hours, but with summer break in full force, that's a big ask. Worth a shot, though.

I pull out my phone and compose a quick email to the head of the placement agency:

Hi Dianne!

I was wondering if you had any other clients who are in need of a math or science tutor for the summer? I've got some time on my hands and could stand to make some extra cash.

Thanks!
Abby

As I hit send, Arpita asks, "What are you doing? Looking up flights?"

"No. I can't afford a trip right now. I emailed Dianne to ask for more work."

"That's what you're going to do with your free time? Tutor more bratty middle schoolers?"

"Arpita, I have fourteen dollars in my bank account and six figures of student debt. I need the money. Unless you're planning to cover my half of the rent for the foreseeable future?"

She doesn't have a comeback for that.

"And they're not bratty," I add. "I know you have your own assumptions about what these kids are like, but for the most part, my students are super sweet and well mannered and responsible. I like tutoring them."

Also, I like the pay. The families I work for are some of the wealthiest in the city. They live in penthouses on the park, and their kids go to exclusive private schools. Only a few hours of tutoring a week are enough to supplement my meager grad student stipend so I can afford to live in New York. Without it, I'd probably have to drop out of school. Which I might have to do anyway, if I can't find another adviser.

I moan again, this time louder, prompting Arpita to retrieve another round of margaritas. I'm already buzzed, so I'm sure I'll regret a second drink at around two in the morning when I'm hugging the toilet, but somehow that situation seems preferable to the pain I'm feeling right now.

I'm rapidly slipping into an anxiety spiral when my phone buzzes with an incoming call. *Prestige Tutoring Center* flashes across my screen, and I rush to answer.

"Abby? I just got your email." Dianne's always energetic, but there's a frantic edge to her voice now. Hopefully that means she's got work for me.

"Yes. I'm looking to pick up some more hours."

"How many more hours?"

"As many as I can." I take a deep breath and add, "I've decided to take the summer off of school."

She gasps. "That's perfect. Are you willing to travel?"

If someone else is paying? "Sure."

"Do you have a passport?"

"Um . . ." Do I? I haven't used it since that trip to Cancun, so I'm not sure if it's expired. Regardless, I say, "Yes."

"Great. I received a last-minute request for a full-time math tutor. The family wants the tutor to travel with them until mid-August, but everyone on my roster was either unqualified or unavailable. I was freaking out, but then I got your email. I'm so glad you reached out."

"I'm glad I reached out, too." At least something's going right today. "How old is the child, and what do they need help with?"

"It's confidential. Client's very high profile, so I can't discuss it over the phone, but if you come into the office first thing tomorrow, I can give you all the info, have you sign the paperwork, get you all ready to go. Oh, one more thing: You don't get seasick, do you?"

"Uh . . . no." Not that I know of, anyway. I don't spend much time on boats.

"Good. You start Monday morning. Well, technically you'll need to be available starting Sunday night."

That's four days from now. "Would I be getting on a boat then, or—"

She sighs. "I told you, I can't discuss it over the phone. All I can say is the job will last six weeks. You'll get a salary plus all travel expenses paid. Is that gonna work for you?"

"Yes, of course." How could I say no? For six weeks, I'll get paid to see the world and get my mind off the disaster my life has become. Hopefully, by the time I return, I'll have some clarity on what to do next.

Arpita returns with my margarita as Dianne and I say our goodbyes. "Who was that?"

"Dianne. She has a job for me." I crack the can open with a snap and a hiss, then slurp the tangy, cold liquid that collects on the rim.

"Great." The tone of her voice implies she does *not* think this is great. "More math tutoring?"

"Yeah. I need to find my passport, though." At this, Arpita knits her brow, and as the tequila hits my bloodstream, I can't help but smile. "Turns out I'll be traveling after all."

CHAPTER TWO

My passport was buried under a ton of papers in a plastic file box I'd shoved in the back of my closet. It took me two days to find it, but now it's tucked safely in my purse, along with my phone, my Kindle, my earbuds, a sleep mask—everything I need to keep me comfortable on this eight-hour flight to Barcelona. It's a red-eye, so I'm hoping to get at least a little bit of sleep. Don't want to show up to my new job all groggy and incoherent tomorrow morning.

As Arpita and I sit on the couch saying our final goodbyes, she tells me, "I want pictures. Lots of them."

"I'll be updating Instagram on the daily." My phone dings, alerting me to the Uber waiting at the curb. "That's my ride."

My whole body vibrates as I wheel my suitcase to the door. Arpita follows closely behind. "I'm so excited for you," she says. "This trip is going to change your life."

"Change my life? That's a tall order for six weeks of tutoring." Not that I'm not excited, but I'm also trying not to get my hopes up. I figure if I keep my expectations low for this trip, I'll reduce my odds of being disappointed if it doesn't live up to the hype.

But Arpita's been hyped up ever since I told her all the admittedly astounding details. "Are you kidding me?" she shrieks. "You're about to sail around the Mediterranean on an enormous yacht owned by one of the richest people in the world. You're going to see new places, have new experiences, meet new people. It's your hot girl summer! You brought condoms, right?"

"Yes." Even though I'm keeping my expectations low, I'm nevertheless preparing for the unexpected.

"Good." She wraps her strong, slender arms around me and squeezes the air out of my lungs. "You're going to have the best time."

"I hope so."

She releases me from the hug and looks me in the eye. "I know you're still working through your emotions about everything that's happened at school, but don't let it cast a shadow over your whole trip. Live in the moment, soak it all up. Who knows when you'll get an opportunity like this again?"

It's safe to say the answer to that question is "never," which means Arpita is right, as usual. I give her a grateful kiss, then hurry down the stairs and out the door.

The driver rolls down his window. "Abby?"

"That's me." I hoist my suitcase into the trunk and climb into the back seat.

He confirms our destination as JFK and asks, "What airline?"

"Iberia."

"I've never heard of that one."

"It's Spanish."

He nods. "Going to Spain on vacation?"

"Something like that." I don't feel like getting into the logistics of my summer plans with the Uber driver. The way Dianne described it, though, it'll be a lot like a working vacation. I'll be tutoring five days a week, four hours per day, and the rest of the time I'll be free to see those new places and meet those new people that Arpita was going on about. Of course, I'm not sure where I'll be going or who I'll be meeting if I'm stuck on a boat the whole time, but from what I gather, it's a really big boat.

Presumably, we'll be docking places, so I can take excursions ashore, but Dianne didn't know anything specific about the travel itinerary. "He's keeping it confidential for obvious reasons," she said.

He referred to Richard Vale, billionaire venture capitalist, single dad, and my new employer. I'm assuming the obvious reasons were the countless search results that turned up when I googled his name. The gossip rags are all over him, and not in a good way. Photographers follow his every move, snapping stealth photos as he walks down the street. None of the photos are flattering, either; he's always hunched over or scowling, sometimes both. They describe him as a gadabout, flitting around New York City, leaving a trail of brokenhearted women in his wake, all of whom are more than happy to spill the details of their tawdry affairs with him to the tabloids.

From what I can tell, he wasn't always a womanizer. According to the "Personal Life" section of his Wikipedia page, he was married for several years to a woman named Veronica. Then he cheated on her, dragged her through the divorce from hell, and tried to weasel out of paying child support for their only daughter, Bijou. The same daughter who I am tasked with tutoring this summer. Perhaps if her father spent more time helping her study and less time chasing skirts, she wouldn't have failed math this year.

But my job is not to judge. It's to help Bijou master sixth-grade math concepts before September rolls around so she can advance to seventh grade with both competence and confidence. Why I will be doing this on a yacht in the Mediterranean is a mystery, but I'm assuming it's because Richard Vale doesn't want his daughter's studies to interfere with his efforts at international philandering. Though I do wonder what her mother is up to these next six weeks. The way these articles are written, I get the sense Bijou normally lives with her mom, but given her acrimonious relationship with Richard, I can't imagine Veronica will be tagging along with us on this trip. Even if she is, though, it's none of my business. Like I said: my job is not to judge.

We're moving along at a snail's pace here, snarled in inexplicable Sunday-evening traffic. Hopefully, we won't be late. I pull out my phone to check the time. 4:59, which is a relief. My flight's not until 7:45, so there should be plenty of time to get to the airport, pass through security, find my gate, and pace around nervously until they call my boarding group.

Yes, I'm a bit anxious. This is the longest flight I've ever taken. My first trip across the ocean, and the first time I've ever flown by myself. I know I'll be fine, but I can't shake this persistent, low-level sense of dread. Like anything can go wrong at any time.

The dread intensifies as I watch the time on my phone flip to five o'clock. I've forgotten something important, haven't I? I dig through my purse again, confirming the presence of my passport, my Kindle, my earbuds, my sleep mask. Everything's accounted for. Then my phone buzzes with an incoming video call, and I realize exactly what it is I've forgotten: to talk to my mother.

She's tried to reach me twice so far today. The first time I missed it because I was in the shower. The second time I was packing, so I declined it with a text: Busy rn. Call you in a few. But I wasn't exactly looking forward to calling her back, so I kept putting it off and putting it off until I completely forgot about it. Now I'm going to have to break the news to her in the back of an Uber.

See, I haven't gotten around to telling her that I'm going on this trip. I haven't told her about what happened with Philip, either. I've been avoiding it, because I know it will lead to a frustrating conversation—a conversation I don't really want to have on the way to the airport—but at this point I have no other choice.

I slide my thumb across the screen, force a smile, and start the chat. "Hi, Mom!"

She's already scowling. "You're avoiding me. What's going on?" There is no hiding anything from my mother.

"Sorry I forgot to call you back. I've been super busy all day."

"Doing what?"

Here goes nothing. "Well, I got this really cool opportunity to—"

The driver lays on his horn, spewing a string of what can only be swear words in a language I don't recognize.

"Where are you?" Mom asks. Her image is grainy on my phone screen, but those frown lines are coming through clearly.

"In a car." I swallow hard before completing the thought. "On my way to the airport."

She shakes her head, confused. "Are you going somewhere?"

"Yes. I've accepted a tutoring position for the summer. It pays extremely well, and I thought it would be a good idea to—"

"Whoa, whoa, whoa. Slow down. Where exactly are you going?"

"Right now? Barcelona. But I'll be sailing around the Mediterranean for the next six weeks with the family I'm working for." She opens her mouth to speak, but I cut her off. "I'm so sorry I didn't tell you about this earlier, but I literally just found out. It was a last-minute offer from the agency."

"What about school?"

"I've decided to take the summer off. I think it'll do me some good to take a break, considering everything that's been happening lately."

"But you haven't heard back from Philip yet. Don't you think you should be there when he makes his ruling against Nick?"

"He already made his ruling," I say. "And it wasn't against Nick."

Mom's mouth falls open at the same time the driver blasts his horn. It's a funny visual. I'd laugh if I wasn't mentally preparing myself for the inevitable argument that's about to ensue. Starting with Mom's highly predictable response: "You should appeal this decision immediately!"

"Well, that's the thing, Mom. I'm not so sure I want to appeal it. I don't have a whole lot of evidence to back up my claim, and I doubt the dean's going to side with me over the head of the physics department."

"Your father wouldn't have given up so easily."

I want to scream *I'm not Dad!* Instead, I stare silently at the screen as she launches into her fourth retelling of how my father discovered a university colleague was falsifying scientific data. "The dishonesty and corruption he experienced during his time at the university was absolutely atrocious, but he never stopped fighting to stand up for what's right. If he were here, he'd be absolutely furious for you."

"I know." She mentions this every time we speak. If only she'd warned me about his experiences before I'd enrolled in this program, then maybe I would've been prepared instead of blindsided. "Look, I'm not saying I *won't* keep fighting. I'm saying I need some time and space to think about whether I will. That's why I'm taking the summer off. To get some perspective."

"You're running away from your problems. You should be facing them head-on."

"I'm not running away from anything. I'm taking a job, which I need, since my teaching assignment was taken away as punishment for filing this grievance. And beyond that, I'm an adult, and I'm capable of making my own decisions. It would be nice if you supported me."

"I'm only looking out for your best interests. People will walk all over you given the chance, and I didn't raise you to be a doormat."

"I'm not a doormat, and it's really insulting of you to imply that I am."

As she tries to walk back her statement, the driver eases up to the curb in Terminal Seven, providing the perfect excuse to end this train wreck of a phone call. "I just got to the airport, Mom. I've gotta go."

"When do you land in Madrid?"

"Barcelona. And I'm not sure. I'll text you as soon as I find Wi-Fi there so you know I'm safe."

"Okay." She looks a little nervous now, which I'd feel guilty about if I had the emotional bandwidth. "I love you."

"I love you, too. I'll be fine. It's only six weeks. Please don't worry."

I toss my phone back in my purse and step out onto the crowded sidewalk. The airport is mobbed. Between summer vacationers and Sunday-night commuters, it takes me nearly forty-five minutes to get through the security line. I'm engulfed in cacophonous chaos—the screaming of toddlers, the beeping of scanners, the clatter of plastic bins as they're slammed onto conveyor belts and thrust into x-ray machines—but rising above it all is a voice in my head, one that sounds vaguely like Mom's, asking questions to which I have no answers.

Why did you really take this job? It's because you're running away, aren't you? When you come home at the end of the summer, what are you going to do?

I wish Dad were still alive so I could get his take on the whole situation. Mom insists he would've been furious, but I'm not so sure that's the case. Dad wasn't the type of guy to get furious. He always faced challenges with calm, reflective rationality, a trait I wish I'd inherited instead of the hotheadedness I got from my mom. I can't help but wonder if Dad's even-keeled approach to life would've rubbed off on me if only I'd had more time with him.

When I get to the metal detectors, I'm randomly pulled aside for additional screening. Normally, this would annoy me, but tonight I'm grateful for the distraction. It's hard to ruminate on my problems while a TSA agent has her hand in my cleavage.

Cleared for departure, I gather my belongings and head down the long corridor toward my gate. I pass by other flights in various stages of the boarding process, destinations as varied as Brussels and Lima and Taipei. So many people setting off on so many grand adventures. It makes my problems seem small and insignificant. Who cares about getting a byline on one research paper when there's a whole huge world out there for me to explore?

Admittedly, I care. A lot.

My gate's at the tail end of the concourse, across from a restaurant selling overpriced salads and pints of watery beer. I order one of each, then roll my suitcase over to an empty table and whip out my Kindle. Last night, I loaded it full of scholarly papers on a wide variety of topics, from molecular nanotechnology to microfluidics. I'm planning to read them all this summer in the hopes that something will spark an idea for a new research project. It'll have to be a topic that's groundbreaking and awe inspiring, something that will earn me the respect of physicists everywhere.

Arpita said this trip is going to change my life, and she was right. These next few weeks away will be like hitting a reset button on my academic career, allowing me to step away from the politics and the noise and refocus my energy. I'll return stronger than ever, find a new adviser for my dissertation—this time, an honest person with integrity—and twenty-five years from now, when I'm accepting the Nobel Prize onstage in Stockholm, Nick and Philip will rue the day they crossed me.

Mom's wrong. I'm not a doormat. I'm a strong, smart, badass woman, and I will not let these thieving men get away with this. But revenge is a long game, and there's no better revenge than being a whopping success.

CHAPTER THREE

Two hours into the flight and halfway through an article on space dust, I'm beginning to rethink my revenge strategy. Starting from scratch with a brand-new research topic is going to be a lot of hard work. Not that I'm averse to hard work; I did a hell of a lot of it in Nick's lab. But that's exactly what's bugging me. I did all the hard work; Nick got all the credit.

It's completely unfair. I can't give up the fight so easily.

I set aside my Kindle, then take out my phone to cough up $19.99 for the in-flight Wi-Fi. I've decided to shift my research from scientific to legal—as in, what legal rights do I have to ensure I get proper credit for my work? As I nibble on a sad airplane sandwich (is this supposed to be turkey or ham?), I tumble down an internet rabbit hole, bouncing from Reddit to Stack Exchange to College Confidential, where anonymous grad students have posted tale after tale of professional betrayal.

Apparently, academic theft is a common occurrence in almost every field of study. Lots of people are dealing with dishonest, deceitful, and occasionally abusive advisers. Some of these stories make me feel like I don't have it that bad; Nick may have stolen my research, but at least he never screamed at me in a room full of my peers.

So I'm not alone. That's good, I guess. On the other hand, none of these stories have a satisfying ending. Most people don't fight back because they don't want to make waves, and those that do have a hard time proving their cases without lengthy and specific trails of documentation. The few that succeed say they've been ostracized from their academic community, which doesn't exactly seem like a triumph.

The takeaway here is that this situation sucks and I am screwed from every angle.

With that uplifting thought floating around in my head, I spend the rest of the flight in a state of anxious despair. Sleep never comes, even with my eye mask and earbuds firmly in place, so I arrive in Barcelona with a puffy face and a scattered brain. If it weren't for the adrenaline coursing through my veins, I'd probably pass out on the luggage carousel. Instead, I hoist my suitcase off the conveyor belt and head for the exit.

Dianne said there'd be someone waiting for me at pickup. Fortunately, I don't have to go far to find the good-looking man with a handwritten sign that says *Atkinson*.

He smiles and says, "Abigail Atkinson?"

"Yes," I say. "Are you with Richard Vale?"

He nods and lowers the sign, then directs me toward the parking lot, where a shiny black Town Car awaits. All those terrible feelings that plagued me on the plane disappear the moment he starts the engine. This is really happening. I'm really here, in Barcelona, being driven around by a smoking-hot Spanish guy! I wonder if he'll be joining us on the yacht.

"Do you work for Mr. Vale, too?" I ask. A dumb question with an obvious answer, but I need an entry point to a conversation, and my brain's not firing on all cylinders at the moment.

He shrugs his broad shoulders and shoots me an apologetic look in the rearview mirror, which I'm guessing means he doesn't speak English. I consider whipping out some of my high school Spanish before I realize I'm too tired and disoriented to make small talk in any language right now.

Instead, I glance out the window, taking in the sights of this new-to-me city. Nothing exciting to see, though. Just a wide highway flanked by billboards and buildings. I hold my breath, waiting for something more interesting to come into view. Soon, there are shipping containers and cranes, and then a sliver of blue that grows wider the longer we drive. That must be the Mediterranean Sea. My home for the next six weeks.

We drive through a downtown area dotted with palm trees. To the left are shops and restaurants, rows of mopeds parked at the curb. To the right is a waterfront esplanade crowded with pedestrians. There's a lot going on here—street vendors, storefronts, really cool architecture—but we're driving too fast for me to take it all in. Suddenly, I'm restless; I want to hop out of the car and explore. Hopefully we'll spend some time in Barcelona before the yacht departs for . . . wherever it is we're going.

I'm quivering with anticipation as we pull into a parking lot at the end of the road. There's a clear view of the water here, dozens of boats bobbing in their berths. The driver parks, grabs my suitcase, and leads me toward a security checkpoint, where the man at the desk waves us onward. We walk wordlessly past several docks housing smaller boats until we reach what is clearly the yacht section of the marina. They're lined up in size order, from baby yacht to superyacht. With my heart pounding, I search the decks for that hunched-over scowling man I saw in the gossip rags, but he's nowhere to be found.

The last yacht in the lineup is set farther apart from the rest, like it's the outcast none of the other yachts want to play with. It's certainly bigger than the others, both in height and length, so if anything, those other yachts are just intimidated. Frankly, I'm intimidated, too, but I try not to show it as I follow the driver up the narrow boarding ramp.

A woman appears on the deck, looking elegant yet casual in a white sleeveless button-down and pink capris. Her light-brown skin glows in the midmorning sun as she smiles at me. "You must be Abigail."

"Yes, but please call me Abby."

"Nice to meet you, Abby. I'm Colette, but you can call me Coco. I'm Richard's personal assistant."

"Nice to meet you, too." I step aboard and shake her outstretched hand as my gaze sweeps across the deck. It seems even bigger up here than it did down below; this one little section is twice the size of my entire Astoria apartment. It's outfitted like an upscale beach club, with a massive white sectional that could comfortably sit twenty people, and a long glass-top bar lined with brightly upholstered stools.

"So," I say, "this is the yacht." *Astute observation, Abby.*

Coco chuckles, but in a way that doesn't make me feel stupid. "You've never been on a yacht before, have you?"

"Is it that obvious?"

"Don't worry, that was me when we arrived a few days ago. You're gonna love it. Come, let me show you around." She motions toward my bags. "You can leave your stuff here; a crew member will take it to your room in a bit."

The driver has disappeared without so much as an *adiós*, so I place my purse beside my suitcase and hurry to catch up with Coco, who's already walking inside.

"This is the saloon," she says as we pass through a large space resembling a living room. There are plush sofas, armchairs with matching ottomans, and the largest flat-screen TV I've ever seen. "You can hang out here whenever you'd like. Dining area is back there"—she points across the room, toward a large circular dining table—"and kitchen is through those doors behind it."

I follow her up a flight of stairs to an outdoor area designed for lounging with daybeds and chaises and . . . "Is that a hot tub?"

"Yes, and you're welcome to use it anytime." She continues inside, where there's an office with two desks positioned beneath opposite windows and a longer table for collaborative work. "Here's a dedicated study area for you and Bijou, though you can obviously work where you two are most comfortable. Laptops are in the top drawers; I've configured them already so you should be able to hit the ground running. The ship has full wireless internet capability, too, even when we're out to sea."

That's good; since I don't have an international calling or data plan, at least I'll always have reliable Wi-Fi.

We step into a short hallway where there's a closed door on either side. "These are our staterooms. This one's yours"—she points to one, then the other—"this one's mine."

"Where does everyone else sleep?"

"The yacht crew has their quarters below deck. Richard and Bijou are one floor above us."

"Is that it, then? Just the four of us and the crew?"

"Yes. Were you expecting someone else?"

"No. It's just that the boat is so big, I thought there might be more people coming."

Her lips curve into a wry smile. "Richard's renting this yacht from an acquaintance. He didn't realize exactly how big it was until we got here. It's definitely more yacht than he needs."

"It's nice, though. More than nice. It's . . ." I struggle to find a word that conveys its grandeur without sounding insulting. Extravagant? Ostentatious?

Coco finishes my sentence. "It's completely over the top, but he's committed. And Bijou said she wanted a yacht like this, which is the important thing. They don't get much daddy-daughter time together, so he really wants to make this trip special for her."

"That's sweet." There's a gooey feeling in my chest, like my heart's a melting chocolate bar. When I was a kid, there was nothing I loved more than spending one-on-one time with my father. Of course, our daddy-daughter trips involved car camping in the Adirondacks as opposed to sailing on a megayacht in the Mediterranean, but the general sentiment is the same.

"It is." There's a hint of sadness in Coco's smile. "She's a sweet girl, too. I think you'll really like her."

I glance down the hallway toward the glass door that leads to the back deck. "Is she around? I'd love to meet her."

"Of course. Follow me." Coco leads me outside and up another flight of stairs, calling over her shoulder, "This is the Vales' deck. It's basically just their staterooms and Richard's office. Nothing too interesting up here."

Coco must be quite accustomed to yacht life already if she considers this uninteresting, because the first thing I see as I step onto the deck is a helipad—a giant circle with an *H* painted in the center of it, right at the pointy front end of the ship. There's no helicopter, though. Maybe Richard has taken it out for the day.

"Bijou, there's someone here you should meet." I turn toward the sound of Coco's voice. Behind us is a spacious, sunny area with a wide array of seating and an actual, honest-to-god swimming pool.

Floating in said pool is a bright-pink inflatable flamingo. Lounging on said flamingo is a fair-skinned preteen who I can only assume is my new student. She tips her head to one side and squints in my direction. "Are you my tutor?"

"Yes, hi." I wave awkwardly. "I'm Abby."

"We're not starting today, are we?"

Are we? I look to Coco for clarification. "You start tomorrow," Coco calls over to Bijou, then turns to me. "That's okay, right? If you think you need another day to rest or whatever, just let me know."

"No, no. Tomorrow's great." That'll give me plenty of time to poke around the office, familiarize myself with the laptops, and sleep off this jet lag.

"Coco, when are we going to Mallorca?" Bijou asks.

So that's our next stop: Mallorca.

"I'm not sure; I'll have to ask your dad."

"Ask your dad what?" A tall man emerges from inside the cabin. I recognize Richard Vale from the photos I saw on the gossip blogs, but there's something different about him now. Maybe it's the odd outfit. From the waist up, he's all business: neatly combed dark hair, crisp white shirt buttoned up to the collar, wireless earbuds firmly in place. From the waist down, he's in vacation mode: rumpled khaki shorts and bare feet. The standard uniform of a person who spends their days in virtual meetings.

As Coco explains that there's limited berth availability across the Mediterranean all summer, particularly for yachts this enormous, Richard's brown eyes slide over to me. The side of his mouth quirks up into a bashful half smile, and instantly I realize what's different. He's not scowling or hunched over like he is in all his photos. In fact, he seems positively pleasant.

"Taking all of this into account," Coco says, "the earliest berth I could score is for arrival late Friday night. Are you okay with that?"

"That's fine." He calls to Bijou, who's drifted over to the other side of the pool. "Sound good to you, B?"

She shrugs one shoulder and spins the floatie so all we can see is her back resting against the flamingo's oversize neck.

Richard clears his throat. "Let's just go with it. Thanks, Coco." His eyes light up as he looks at me again. "And you must be Abigail."

"Yes, but please call me Abby."

He puts his hands in the pockets of his shorts and rocks back on his heels. "Well, Abby, you came very highly recommended from Dianne. She said you're a fourth-year PhD student?"

"I am." My stomach clenches as I think about the current state of my academic affairs. Best to change the subject. "But I'm taking the summer off of school, and I'm looking forward to getting to know Bijou. From what I understand, our goal is to get her up to speed on the core concepts of the sixth-grade math curriculum. Dianne specified an emphasis on third- and fourth-quarter topics such as algebra and geometry, is that right?"

"Yes. And, um . . ." He inches toward me, softening his voice. "She failed her last semester. Barely passed the semester before that. She's been struggling quite a bit, and we don't want her to get left behind."

"Of course not. I'll see to it that she's more than adequately prepared for the seventh grade in September."

"Wonderful." With an exhale, he steps back, long limbs loosening a bit. "And how was your flight over? Everything go smoothly?"

"As smooth as can be."

"Are you all settled in? Did Coco get you your access key?"

"We're getting there," Coco says, her tone a tinge impatient. A glance down at her watch and she adds, "Don't you have a call with Nat now?"

"Oh, right." As if on cue, a ringing resonates from within his shorts. He pulls his phone from his pocket and stabs at the screen, answering the call with a harsh, "Talk to me, Nat."

Coco and I watch as he retreats inside, sliding the door closed behind him. "So, that's your new boss," she says. "He's a good guy. Great to work for. A little scatterbrained, but he's got a big heart."

Big heart, huh? I wonder if all those women who told their stories to the tabloids would agree with that assessment. Though I'm having a hard time picturing this guy as a womanizer. He's polite and approachable and good looking, but not exactly what I'd call charismatic. Maybe billionaires don't need charisma. An ultrahigh net worth is seductive in itself, I suppose.

"Let's get you situated," Coco says. "I'll show you how to work that access card he was talking about."

"Okay." As I follow Coco toward the stairs, I shoot a glance toward Bijou. She's leaning back on her flamingo, eyes skyward, lips curved down in a gentle frown. I call out, "See you later!" but she doesn't acknowledge me. Hopefully she'll be more responsive in our tutoring sessions.

CHAPTER FOUR

Richard Vale is bonkers rich. This isn't new information, but I don't think it really sank in until I toured the yacht with Coco. So many luxuries on a single vessel, reserved solely for one man and his daughter. And his staff, of course.

Even though Coco said I was more than welcome to take advantage of the amenities on board, I do feel kind of awkward about it. I envision myself reclining in the hot tub or sunbathing on deck, only to have Richard stroll by and try to strike up a casual conversation. Not that he's not a nice guy, but I don't feel like answering a bunch of questions about my personal life. I especially don't feel like talking about school.

I'm used to keeping these parents at arm's length. This is admittedly easier to do back in New York, where I only see my students for forty to sixty minutes per week and maintain my own residence in a different borough. So I'd like to establish some boundaries while I'm living with the Vales this summer, to at least create the illusion of privacy and independence from my employer.

This shouldn't be too hard, since I plan on spending most of my free time on dry land, exploring whatever city we're docked in. There's so much I want to see here in Barcelona—the art and architecture are supposedly unparalleled. I was hoping to hit the ground running with my sightseeing, but as soon as Coco finishes my new-employee orientation, a fresh wave of jet lag overtakes me. I head straight for my stateroom, where my luggage is neatly placed inside the door.

Being on a boat, I expected cramped quarters, but this is spacious. Stylishly appointed, as well. There's a queen-size bed adorned with royal blue pillows that match the upholstery of the love seat situated against the far wall. Dove gray drapes hang on either side of a big rectangular window through which I can clearly see the marina. This is so much nicer than the view of the redbrick wall back in Astoria. Imagine what the views will be like when we're out on the open sea.

As I unpack my suitcase, it quickly becomes clear that there's way more closet space than I need. I packed light, assuming I'd have limited storage in some tiny cabin, but now the half-empty drawers are practically begging to be filled. Maybe I'll go clothes shopping later, when I'm feeling more energetic. There must be plenty of cute boutiques in Barcelona, and I'm certainly getting paid well enough to buy myself a few unique European outfits. After giving Arpita enough money to cover my share of the rent and utilities for the next six weeks, I've still got a lot left over. Way more than I would've made if I'd stayed in grad school all summer.

So there's one good thing about this whole disaster with Nick. I'm raking it in.

Once I'm unpacked, I shove my empty suitcase in the corner of the closet and plop down on the bed. I don't remember falling asleep, but a few hours later, I wake up with a sour taste in my mouth and a ravenous gurgling in my stomach. I haven't eaten since that sad airplane sandwich who-knows-how-many hours ago. Judging by how dim the light is, it's dinnertime, or possibly well past. Coco told me we have full access to the kitchen, and the chef will make us anything we'd like, but I'd rather grab a bite to eat in town. If we're leaving for Mallorca on Friday, that only gives me four nights to enjoy all that Barcelona has to offer.

I slip into a summery dress and sandals that are both cute and comfy enough to carry me through the cobblestoned streets. As I step out of my stateroom, I consider asking Coco to join me, so I knock on her door, wait a few seconds, then knock again. No answer. I make my way toward the back of the ship and head down the stairs toward the exit ramp, but I don't see her anywhere. I don't see anyone else, either.

No matter. There's lots of new people to meet in this town. I charge down the ramp and out of the marina, intent on hunting down a tapas bar overrun with friendly tourists. I'm sure it won't be hard to find; this city is vibrating with energy, even on a Monday night. Couples, families, groups of friends, all crowding the sidewalks and filling the air with lively chatter.

As I'm crossing the street, a guy with bleached-blond dreads whizzes by on a skateboard, which makes me do a little double take. He looks just like Eitan, a postdoc in my lab. Or I guess I should say my *old* lab, since I won't be working with Nick anymore.

I can't believe I have to start all over again with a new adviser. All that time and effort, wasted! If only I'd done a better job of guarding my ideas and keeping a paper trail, instead of naively assuming everyone would have my back. Honestly, this whole mess could've been avoided if I'd just been a little more careful, a little less trusting, and a whole lot smarter about everything . . .

You know what? I'm not going down this road. I am here on this trip to hit the reset button and refocus my energy. To move forward toward the future, not to dwell on the past. What's done is done, and nothing can change it.

Instead, I will focus on the good things happening in this present moment, like the warm summer breeze rustling my hair, and the winding wonder of these side streets. The narrow alleys pulse with activity, bright signs advertising flamenco and pinchos and beer. Patrons spill out of restaurants, their happy chitchat echoing down the street. The scent of grilled meat mingles with cigarette smoke and hangs heavy in the air.

I duck down a dimly lit lane and emerge in a bustling, airy plaza filled with sidewalk cafés. They're all packed, but my stomach's demanding food, so I make my way around the inner perimeter, searching for a spare seat. Finally, I find an empty table for two at the outer edge of a tapas restaurant. I sit down, taking note of a big rowdy group right beside me, all of whom are probably around my age, in their midtwenties. They've pushed three or four tables together so they can share their food and wine. Laughter flows off them in waves. I scoot my chair a few inches closer and hear they're speaking English.

This is how travelers meet, right? They just kind of happen across each other in a crowded town square and strike up a conversation, don't they? I've never done any traveling on my own before, but I'm assuming that's how it works. All I've gotta do is make eye contact with one of them. Of course, that's proving difficult since nobody's looking my way. Eventually, one girl turns her head in my direction, so I smile but she doesn't seem to notice me. Makes me feel kind of invisible.

At least the server sees me. He gives me a cordial nod as he takes my order, a glass of tempranillo and a couple of small plates.

Once he's gone, I give up on trying to befriend these people next to me and direct my attention toward the center of the square. A street musician is playing the drums—quite well, might I add—and a few people are dancing around him. One guy shimmies out of the crowd and starts wandering in my direction, his eyes searching the sea of tables around me. He's good looking—tall, slender, shoulder-length hair pulled back in a ponytail, jawline that could cut glass.

When his gaze lands on me, I instinctively smile. "Hola," I say.

His brow crinkles slightly as he responds, "Hola."

I used to know how to say *sit down* in Spanish. My ninth-grade teacher was always yelling it if we got up without asking permission, but I can't seem to remember it now. Maybe this guy speaks Catalan, though. Should I just ask in English? Or maybe I could use Google Translate? If I wait any longer, it's going to get awkward, so I simply gesture to the open seat at my table, the one directly across from me, and say, "Por favor."

He glances down at the chair as if the blue wicker were covered in slime, then gives me this apologetic little smile—one that says, *Sorry, but no*—and continues on his way.

Meeting people is a lot harder than I thought it was going to be.

I've never been particularly great at making friends outside of a school environment. I've never had to because school always came pre-loaded with ready-made friendships. No matter how different you may have been from your classmates, you at least had this one huge thing in common to connect you: you were both freshmen in high school, or you were both majoring in chemistry, or you were both searching for an apartment in New York City whose rent you could afford on a grad student stipend.

That's how I met Arpita: on a campus message board called "ISO Roommates." It's also how I met every guy I've ever dated, crushed on, or hooked up with. I don't know how to make friends—or romantic connections—any other way. But if I want to have a hot girl summer, I'm gonna have to learn.

The thought of it makes me sleepy. Or maybe that's the jet lag. Either way, I'm two seconds from putting my head down on the table when the server returns with my order. The smell of fried potatoes and garlicky shrimp perks me right up. As soon as the warm wine hits my soft palate, I forget all about how lonely I'm feeling. I only feel gratitude for the opportunity to be here, savoring these incredible flavors, basking in this beautiful scene.

I joyously inhale my meal, and while I'm tempted to order another glass of wine and sit here enjoying the atmosphere for hours on end, it wouldn't be prudent. Work starts at nine o'clock tomorrow morning, and I don't want to be groggy or hungover for my first tutoring session. There'll be plenty of time to party on this trip. Right now, I need to focus on winning Bijou over.

∼

Despite my intention to get a good night's sleep, I'm up until two thirty. Partially because I'm still on New York time, but mostly because I'm prepping our first lesson. I spend several hours choosing examples and crafting problem sets, trying my best to make the work rigorous yet engaging. By now, I could tutor sixth-grade math in my sleep, but I have to admit, I'm nervous about working with Bijou.

Coco said I'd like her and that she was a sweet girl, but she didn't strike me as especially warm or friendly. During our brief ten-minute interaction, she remained aloof, almost bored, floating around in her pink flamingo like a princess on a palanquin. I didn't expect her to jump for joy or anything—I'm the math tutor, after all—but a polite "Welcome aboard" would've been nice.

My biggest fear is that she doesn't want me here, that she's not down with the whole "summer tutoring" thing her dad's forcing upon her. If so, then I'll be fighting an uphill battle for the next six weeks—assuming I last that long. So I need to prepare some top-notch content, stuff that will captivate a disinterested student. Plus, I've gotta get myself in the right headspace.

I'll acknowledge my anxiety is fueled, in part, by the fact that Richard Vale is a billionaire. The kids I tutor all come from rich families—their parents are investment bankers on Wall Street or plastic surgeons on Park Avenue—but at best they're solid multimillionaires. This is my first experience working for someone worth ten figures (or more), and I can't help but wonder how being ultrawealthy will impact Bijou's behavior toward me. Will she be more demanding than my average student? Less tolerant? Totally entitled?

What exactly have I gotten myself into here?

By nine o'clock, I've worked myself into a real lather. As I wait in the office for Bijou to show up, my hands are trembling so hard I have to clasp them tightly together on the desktop to steady them. When it comes to tutoring, I'm usually so confident; I can't believe a twelve-year-old is making me feel so unsure of myself.

Then again, ever since my ill-fated meeting with Philip, I've been riddled with self-doubt. Like I'm not really as smart as I always thought I was.

Two minutes past nine, the cabin door slides open and in walks Bijou. She's wearing a bikini top and short shorts, which I suppose is perfectly appropriate attire for yacht-tutoring.

As she plops into the chair across from me, I say, "Good morning."

"Good morning." Her voice is small and timid, so different from the assertive shouting she displayed yesterday at the pool. She sits on her hands, looking to me for direction.

"As you already know, my name is Abby, and I'm here to help you with math. Our goal for the next few weeks is to strengthen your skills so you're ready to tackle the seventh grade." I tap a few keys on my laptop to pull up her online grade book, then swivel the screen around so we both can see it. "I've reviewed some of your assignments from last year to figure out what areas we'll need to focus on."

She groans and covers her face.

"You okay?" I ask.

"I don't wanna see this."

I swivel the laptop back to me. "Okay. I can just tell you."

"I don't wanna hear it, either." She drops her hands to her sides. "I already know my grades suck. That's why you're here. Because I'm a failure."

"You're not a failure," I say. "You only got one F."

"What do you think F stands for?"

"Failing a single class doesn't mean you're a failure."

She rolls her eyes. I'm itching to tell her that one semester of sixth-grade math won't define her, but when you're twelve years old, it's hard not to feel like *everything* defines you. I don't want to be dismissive of these big feelings, either, because they're perfectly valid! But to succeed this summer, she needs to believe she's capable of succeeding.

"Don't dwell on the bad grade," I say. "I know it felt terrible to fail. Believe me, I understand what failing feels like."

"Did you ever fail math?"

"No." She rolls her eyes again, so I quickly add, "But I've failed in other ways."

"Like how?"

"Well, I recently lost several years' worth of research. Which definitely feels like a huge failure, especially because I'm going to have to start all over again. From scratch." Before I fall into a pit of despair, I shake my head and slap on an encouraging smile. "But a clean slate holds a lot of potential. And you're starting seventh grade with a clean slate. Last semester is history. The work we're going to do together will help you to feel prepared and confident when September rolls around. Okay?"

"Okay." She gives a hesitant little nod, but I'm not sure she's convinced that what I'm saying is true. I'll just keep moving forward in the hopes that eventually she'll hop on board.

I lay out a road map for the next six weeks, then dive straight into our first lesson on basic algebraic expressions. While I wouldn't describe her as enthralled, she's a good listener, receptive to instruction, and responsive at all the appropriate times.

So there was no need for me to be nervous, after all. Bijou's a model student. She clearly struggles a bit with her self-confidence, but who doesn't? And that's something we can work on as time goes by. For now, everything's going along great.

Then Richard appears.

At first, I don't see him. My gaze is pointed down, focused on the number line I've printed out on a sheet of paper, when I sense a shift in Bijou's energy. She sits forward abruptly and balls her hands into fists. I look up in time to see her father sliding open the office door, an affable grin on his face. He's wearing that same "business on the top, party on the bottom" getup, which sounds like it'd be completely ridiculous, but for some reason it works on him. Business casual, but make it on a yacht.

"Hey there," he says. "Hope I'm not interrupting."

"Of course not," I say. Truthfully, he *is* interrupting, but as the person who signs my paychecks, he's allowed to interrupt whenever he pleases.

"My ten o'clock meeting got canceled, so I have some time on my hands. Figured I'd stop by to see how things are going." He strolls up behind Bijou and rests a hand on her shoulder. "Are you learning a lot, sweetie?"

"We literally just got started." There's an icy sheen to her words.

Richard retracts his hand and jams it in his pocket, his smile faltering slightly as he turns to me. "Do you have everything you need, Abby?"

"Yes." I gesture to the elaborate setup behind me: wireless printer, scanner, document camera. Not to mention the abundance of office supplies in the cabinets. I'm not sure why anyone would ever need this many Post-it Notes on a boat. "The office is incredibly well stocked. Thank you."

"I can't take credit for that. Yuri provided everything on this ship as is. Worth every penny we're paying for it. Don't you think, Bijou?"

She rolls her eyes. "Dad, we're kind of in the middle of something."

"Right." He tugs at his shirt collar, his smile completely flattened now. Bijou is so thoroughly dismissive of his fatherly overtures it almost makes me feel bad for him. More than anything, though, I'm still wondering how this guy is the same heartbreaking Casanova that the gossip blogs love to post about.

He's definitely attractive; the more I see him, the more attractive he becomes. From the breadth of his shoulders and the definition in his calves, I'd say he works out, too. But he's sort of awkward, with the constant throat clearing and the way he can't quite settle on a stance—hands in his pockets, then on his hips, then back in his pockets before he rocks back on his heels. He's a geek, and I love geeks, but generally speaking they don't have reputations as lotharios.

"Real quick before I go," he says to me, clearing his throat yet again, "I want to make sure you'll be covering polygons on the coordinate plane."

"Yes, we'll have a significant review of coordinate geometry."

"And specifically polygons? Prisms, cuboids—"

"Dad, she said yes." Bijou's attitude has gone from ice to liquid nitrogen.

"I'm simply double-checking because you've always had a tough time with geometry. That's the unit you failed, and I promised your mother that—"

She cuts him off with a nasty growl. "Can you please go away?"

The office is a vacuum chamber. There's no air, no sound. My gaze drops to the desktop, and I'm holding my breath, waiting for someone else to make the next move. It's always uncomfortable being trapped in the middle of another family's squabble, and it's even worse being a stranger who's known them for all of twenty-four hours. I'd like to fold into myself and disappear until it's all over, please.

Finally, I hear the pads of Richard's bare feet shuffle toward the door, hear it slide closed behind him. I glance out the window and see his legs disappearing up the outside stairs.

I exhale, relieved the unpleasant moment is behind us. Bijou's cheeks are flushed bright pink; her lips are pursed into a tight frown.

"Are you okay?" I ask.

She nods sharply. "Now that he's gone, I'm fine."

She does not seem fine. She looks like she might cry, or possibly screech at the top of her lungs. It doesn't take a family therapist to understand that there's a whole lot of tension between her and her father, which makes me feel bad for all sorts of reasons. I always had a completely different relationship with my dad; we were buddies, honestly. I couldn't imagine kicking him out of the room, or being annoyed at him for asking about my well-being, or speaking to him with such vitriol in my voice. Even thinking about that makes me sad.

Coco said this is a special daddy-daughter trip, but their daddy-daughter vibes are all the way off. I'm tempted to ask her what's going on, to see if there's any way I can help. But I don't. Because I never get involved in my students' personal lives, and I certainly never get between them and their parents. Boundaries, remember? I need to maintain them, even though we're all living on the same boat.

I'm here for one purpose and one purpose only: to tutor math. So I turn my attention back to the number line, and that's exactly what I do.

CHAPTER FIVE

Our next couple of tutoring sessions go better than I expect them to, and Bijou and I have established a pretty good rapport. During our lessons, she's engaged and upbeat, and thankfully Richard doesn't make another appearance. In fact, I've hardly seen him around the boat at all, though that's probably because I'm not spending much time hanging out there.

When I'm not in the office with Bijou, I'm off exploring Barcelona on my own. I haven't met any fellow travelers yet, but I've gotten used to sitting at a table for one, and frankly, there are some plus sides to navigating the city by myself. I don't have to make compromises on where to go or what to eat. I can simply hit the streets and do exactly what I want to do.

I've managed to cram a lot of sightseeing into a short period of time. I strolled through Ciutadella Park, admiring the sculptures and the monuments and the magnificent Cascada fountain. I did a self-guided tour of the Picasso Museum, and climbed to the top of the Sagrada Familia basilica. I learned how to say, "One glass of red wine, please" in Spanish *and* Catalan, which are both official languages here.

On Thursday, I brave the crowds on La Rambla for some shopping, buying a Gaudi-inspired pendant and some turrón for Arpita and a gauzy minidress for myself. That night—our final night in Barcelona—I treat myself to paella and a flamenco show and return to the boat ready for bed by ten o'clock.

Yes, I am aware that ten o'clock is incredibly early, especially in a city where it's not unheard of to eat dinner at midnight. But it's important for me to show up to work each morning on time and full of energy. I never want to give Richard a reason to doubt my competency, because that could put this trip in jeopardy. And the longer I'm here—the more sights I see and experiences I have—the more I realize what a gift it is.

I also realize how fleeting it is. Six weeks is not all that long, and it'll be over before I know it. So while I'm spending as much time as I can living in the moment—"soaking it all up" as Arpita implored me to do—I haven't forgotten about what's happening back in New York. To that end, I've established an evening ritual of reading one scientific paper before bed. Once I find a topic that inspires me, I can start working on a research proposal. Then hopefully, I'll return in the fall ready to find a new adviser and get on with my life.

Tonight's selection is from the *American Journal of Physics*, titled "The Edge Profile of Liquid Spills." It's fascinating stuff, really, but for some reason I can't concentrate. I must be overstimulated from that flamenco show. Even now, the clacking of castanets still echoes in my ears.

Rat-tat-tat, rat-tat-tat.

Oh wait, that's someone knocking at the door. Who could it be this late at night? What if it's an emergency? The ship could be sinking or something. That iceberg scene from *Titanic* flashes through my brain as I throw back the covers and crack the door.

Coco's smiling in the hallway. "Did I wake you?"

"No, no." I smile back and open the door a bit wider. She's wearing a one-shoulder romper with ankle strap heels, her long hair twirled up in a topknot. "You look great. What's going on?"

"Wanna celebrate our last night in Barcelona? I've got an extra guest pass for this new club. It's right around the corner on the water." She glances at my PJs and adds, "I'll wait for you to change."

You know that feeling when you're in high school and the cool kids ask you to sit at their lunch table? I don't—the cool kids never liked me—but I'm assuming this is what it feels like. Because even though I've been having a good time seeing Barcelona by myself, I've also been feeling pretty lonely. Sure, I can do exactly what I want, but experiences are always so much richer when you have someone to share them with. I'd been hoping to connect with Coco and get to know her a little better, but she's been so hard to nail down, either darting around the ship on a mission for Richard or completely MIA—she's never once answered when I knocked on her door.

Now that she's standing here, inviting me out for a night on the town, I'm dying to say yes. There's one little problem, though. "I've gotta work with Bijou in the morning, and I don't wanna show up all tired."

She shrugs, like it's no big deal. "I'll reschedule her tutoring session for the afternoon."

"You can do that?"

"I'm the keeper of the calendars at Chez Vale—of course I can. Besides, we're gonna be sailing all day tomorrow; there'll be nothing else for her to do."

"Are you sure Richard will be okay with that?"

"Uh, yeah." She looks like she's stifling a laugh.

That settles it, then. "Give me five minutes."

I race to the closet to survey my options. Damn, I wish I'd bought some club clothes while I was shopping today. The new dress might work, though, if I pair it with my rhinestone slides. After a simple swipe of shimmery lip gloss, I'm ready to hit the floor.

Coco's waiting for me out on the back deck. "I love that dress," she says.

"Thanks, I got it at a boutique on La Rambla today."

"Nice. I meant to go shopping, but then I got caught up in work. I've been so slammed all day. Really looking forward to letting loose tonight." As we walk down the ramp and through the marina, she asks, "How have things been going with Bijou?"

"Great," I say, conveniently omitting that unpleasant altercation between her and her father. "You're right, she is sweet. And she's got a good grasp on the material so far. She's not bad at math; I think she just needed someone to explain things to her one-on-one."

"Oh, fantastic. I know Richard was worried about that F she got."

"Yeah, he mentioned that the other day." Should I ask Coco about the status of their daddy-daughter relationship? I know I need to maintain boundaries, but it couldn't hurt to get some insight into what's happening here. I'll be casual about it. "He came into the office during one of our sessions, and there seemed to be some tension between them."

She inhales sharply. "You can thank her mother for that. She likes to badmouth him in front of her."

Yikes. If Richard had dragged Veronica through a miserable divorce and tried to shaft her on child support, I couldn't blame her for harboring some lingering resentment. But it sucked to have it spill over onto Bijou's shoulders.

"What's Bijou's living arrangement like? Does she live with her mother or do they split custody or—"

"They're *supposed* to split custody, but Veronica hasn't respected the visitation schedule in months. She has me rearranging it every other week; then half the time she keeps Bijou on Richard's days anyway. It's ridiculous."

"I thought visitation schedules were mandated by a judge."

"They are. What she's doing isn't legal, but Richard doesn't want to bring her to court. Then it'll be a whole thing in the press, and he doesn't want Bijou to go through that. If you ask me, he's too nice."

There's a deep V in Coco's brow. Safe to say she's not a fan of Veronica Vale.

We pass by the security booth, throwing a friendly wave to the guard on duty before making a right onto the main street, at which point she continues her rant. "Now, after causing all these problems for so long, she tells him she needs him to take Bijou for the whole summer.

Doesn't ask, just demands it. Naturally, he's happy to do it—that's why he set up this trip, so he can make the time special for her—but it still pisses me off."

"Where's Veronica this summer?"

"Being thirsty in LA, trying to worm her way into a season of *Real Housewives*. For someone who claims to hate Richard so much, she sure likes to use his name to get what she wants." She snorts. "Let me stop. Once I get started on that woman, I can go for hours."

I kind of wish she'd keep going because I want to know all the dirt, but she seems really worked up about it, and this is meant to be a chill, celebratory evening, so I change the subject. "Thanks for inviting me out tonight."

"Of course! I'm happy we're finally getting to hang out, you and me. This club is supposed to be amazing, with beautiful views of the city and the sea."

"Where'd you get these guest passes?"

"Richard, where else? It's one of the perks of this job. Everywhere we go, we're VIP."

I don't go to clubs all that often and when I do, I'm certainly not a VIP. I'm not even sure what VIP treatment entails, but when we arrive, I learn quickly. First, we've got a separate entrance, so there's no standing around in a long line. Instead, Coco says one word—*Vale*—and a burly guy in a blazer ushers us to a private elevator, which promptly whisks us up to the twenty-sixth floor.

The doors open, and I'm instantly enveloped in a swirl of sound. People are chatting, glasses are clinking, the bass line's going thump thump thump. A tangle of bodies undulates on the dance floor. Our escort leads us around it toward a roped-off platform on the other side of the club. In front of a wall of windows, an empty banquet with a *Reserved* sign awaits.

A server appears with a smile on her face and the biggest bottle of vodka I've ever seen. "Is that whole thing just for the two of us?" I ask.

"Sure is," Coco says. "Would you prefer something else? We can order some Dom Pérignon, too, if you want."

"No, no. This is good."

Another server appears, rolling in a cart full of mixers, including a whole tray of fresh garnish—scored citrus peels, pineapple wedges, thin strips of cucumber. "Good evening," she says, in perfect English. "My name is Paula. I understand you're special guests of Richard Vale. Will he be joining you this evening?"

"Unfortunately, no," Coco says, "but he sends his best regards."

She nods and hands us a drink list. "These are our specialty cocktails, but we can prepare anything you'd like."

Without looking at the menu, Coco says, "I'll have a vodka tonic, please."

"Very well. And you?"

"Same." I'm not a huge fan of vodka, but I don't want to seem fussy. On the other hand, VIPs are practically obligated to be fussy, aren't they? Maybe I'll eventually grow accustomed to this kind of lifestyle; for now, I'm feeling slightly overwhelmed and out of place.

Coco fits right in, though. She exudes confidence, lounging back on the banquette, one arm slung over the back of the couch, one long bare leg crossed over the other. When the server hands her her drink, she graciously accepts, then waits patiently for me to get mine so we can toast.

"To adventures abroad," she says, raising her glass.

"To adventures abroad," I reply. We clink and sip. This is the smoothest vodka I've ever tasted. So unlike the turpentine I'm used to drinking from the well. Another one of these and I'll become accustomed to this lifestyle pretty quickly.

Frankly, it won't even take another drink. This unobstructed view is enough to convince me that VIP is the only way to go. The whole city is on display, an expanse of twinkling lights that sweeps toward the horizon. Directly below, the land meets the sea at Barceloneta Beach.

Waves lap against the shore as the lamps from the boardwalk cast an ethereal glow out over the water.

"You weren't kidding about the beautiful views," I say. I've got to yell a little to be heard over the music.

"Right? This is the hottest club in Barcelona right now, and I totally understand why."

"I'm surprised Richard didn't want to come with us." Though we'd probably cramp his style in a place like this, with so many eligible women to choose from. Between the gorgeous scenery and this gargantuan bottle of booze, he wouldn't need charm to win anyone over. The atmosphere is seductive in itself.

Coco laughs. "This is *so* not his scene. Like, at all. When we're in New York, he barely even leaves the apartment unless it's to go to work. That's why every time he gets an invite like this, he hands it off to me. Like I said, job perks."

Interesting. If Richard barely leaves the house, then how do the paparazzi manage to get so many photos of him? I found countless images of him walking down the street, hunched over and scowling. Come to think of it, those were the *only* kinds of photos I saw. There were no candids of him clubbing in the city or canoodling with any of those scorned women who poured their hearts out to the gossip rags. He must be stealthy in his sexual conquests.

I'm sipping my cocktail, silently trying to reconcile the Richard Vale I've read about in the tabloids with the geeky homebody who's always dressed for an impromptu Zoom meeting, when Coco turns to me and asks, "So you're in grad school for physics, right?"

I suck back the rest of my drink in one anxious slurp. "Yeah."

"How much longer until you're done?"

If she'd asked me this question a week ago, I'd have confidently said, "At most, two years." Now, I have no idea. I don't even have a dissertation topic anymore. I can't bring myself to speculate out loud, but in my head, I'm thinking, *Four to five years? Maybe more?*

As if sensing my need for liquid courage, the server hands me another vodka tonic. I take a sip and say, "I'm not sure. I've recently encountered a bit of a setback."

She nods empathetically. "I feel you. Grad school sucks."

"Are you in grad school, too?"

"I used to be. I finished my degree two years ago, but I wish I hadn't wasted my time. All I have to show for it now is this enormous pile of debt that I'm going to be drowning in forever. MFAs don't pay off." She sighs and takes a long drink. "At least I lucked into this job. Richard compensates more than fairly—as you well know—and I've got plenty of free time to write on the side. Plus, he always cuts me slack if I've got a deadline. But the truth is, I'm doing exactly what I've always wanted to do—writing my heart out and living my best life in New York—and I didn't need that degree to get here."

"That's not the case for me. I mean, my goal is to become a college professor and I can't do that without a PhD."

"Oh, that's cool. Why a college professor?"

"My father was a physics professor. I've always wanted to follow in his footsteps."

She smiles fondly. "That's so sweet. Continuing the legacy?"

"Exactly." My father has been the single most influential figure in my life. He sparked my interest in science at an early age, taking me on private tours of his university's labs and observatories, and going on exploratory hikes with me in nature. He always encouraged me to ask questions and be curious, to think like a scientist. Devoting my life to science is a way for me to stay close to him.

At first, I thought I'd accomplish that by being a teacher. I loved the idea of running hands-on science experiments in a classroom full of wide-eyed kids; I wanted to spark their interest early on, the same way my father had for me. My mom, however, persuaded me to "think bigger."

"You're too smart for that," she said. "With a brain like yours, you should get a PhD just like your father. It would be such an honor to his memory."

And of course I wanted to honor my father's memory. But if I'd just stuck with that teacher idea, I'd be so much further along in life by now. I'd already be working full time, enjoying job security, maybe even building a savings account with more than fourteen dollars in it. I certainly wouldn't have had the last few years of my professional life stolen out from under me. I wouldn't be starting all over again from scratch.

"Well," Coco says now, "I admire you for going after what you want."

"Sometimes I'm not so sure it's what I want. Academia's rougher than I thought it would be. There's a lot of drama."

"There's a lot of drama everywhere," she says. "You can't avoid it. You just have to try your best to ignore it and go about your business."

"You're probably right." Surely, I'm idealizing the life of a teacher. Lord knows they have their fair share of struggles—they're overworked, underpaid, and constantly being criticized. I'll bet the gossip in the teacher's lounge is brutal, too. "Anyway, it's nice to have a few weeks off so I can step away from it all."

"Good for you. Ignore the drama! And what better place to do it?" She gestures around to the unobstructed view of Barcelona and the crush of people writhing on the dance floor. "Look at where you are. VIP in an exclusive club overlooking the Mediterranean Sea. And when the party's over, you're going to sleep on one of the most luxurious superyachts in the world. Did you ever think you would end up here?"

I answer honestly. "No."

"Me neither. The way I see it, if this is possible, anything is."

I'm just tipsy enough to believe her words could be a prophecy. *Anything is possible.* Like maybe I could move on from this whole research-theft debacle without it being a whole dramatic thing. Maybe I'll simply enjoy the hell out of this summer, then go home and find a new topic with a new adviser and everything will work out just fine. No drama!

The music shifts from a booming bass to a heavy synth, and Coco hops to her feet. "Let's dance," she says as she grabs my hand and pulls me past the velvet rope. We snake through the crowd until we find a vacancy in the center of the dance floor, just big enough for the two of us.

With the rhythm as our guide, we bounce and sway, pop our hips and roll our shoulders. I can feel the vodka in my veins, warming me up, making me sweat. I don't know how long we dance for. All I know is that my cheeks ache from smiling. At one point, I even find myself feeling thankful that Nick stole my research. If it hadn't happened, I wouldn't be here, enjoying this rare and implausible moment of bliss. And if this is possible, anything is.

CHAPTER SIX

Vodka was a terrible choice. With the music and dancing and general dreamlike nature of the evening, I lost track of how many times the server refilled my glass. It was so smooth going down that I just kept drinking. And now I'm in a world of hurt.

I have no idea what time we got back to the yacht. I have no memory of putting on my pajamas or getting into bed. All I know is I forgot to draw the curtains, because I am awoken by the sun blazing directly on my face. I bury my head beneath the covers and attempt to slip back into unconsciousness when the room suddenly lurches to one side. Usually if I lie very still, I can stop the spins, but it's not working this time. It takes me a second to realize that the vertigo I'm experiencing isn't because I'm hungover. It's because the ship is in motion.

We must be on our way to Mallorca already. Coco said we were leaving at around nine o'clock and it would take about eight hours to get there. I crack one eye open and check my phone for the time. Already eleven fifteen? Dear Lord.

Coco's a saint for moving my tutoring session to noon. Hopefully Bijou doesn't mind. I need to get going, scrub the smell of cigarettes and spilled drinks off my skin. Sitting up is a special kind of torture, and I'm pretty sure a fissure has formed down the center of my skull. As I set one foot on the floor, the boat lurches again. Oh wait, those are the actual spins.

Hangovers at sea are the worst hangovers in existence.

Get it together, Atkinson. I am dying to lie back down, but under no circumstances can I show up late to a tutoring session I've already delayed, particularly since I delayed it for the express purpose of going out and getting hammered. Fortunately, Past Abby was smart enough to set a giant bottle of water and a packet of Advil on the nightstand, so I gulp it down like a desperate, dehydrated animal.

Somehow, I manage to haul myself into the shower and get dressed without incident. In the kitchen, the chef graciously fries me an egg and peels me a banana, and after I wolf them both down, I'm finally feeling halfway human.

Apparently, though, I'm not looking so hot. As soon as I step foot in the office, Bijou grimaces. "What happened to you?"

There's no sense in lying. "I went out with Coco last night and we kind of overdid it."

"You look like a zombie."

"Thanks." She's not wrong, though. Last I checked, my face had a sickly green tint, and my eyes were carrying some heavy bags. "I'm sorry I started our session late."

"Don't worry about it. It's not like there's anything else to do today. We're stranded in the middle of the ocean."

She's joking, right? This is a luxury yacht with every amenity under the sun. There's a swimming pool, for crying out loud. But from the way she's sneering, as if this trip were a burden as opposed to the greatest blessing a twelve-year-old could ever receive, it's clear she's 100 percent serious.

"It's the sea, not the ocean," I say.

"Same difference." Her sneer disappears, and her blue eyes light up. "You know, if you're not feeling well, I'm totally fine with skipping today's session."

"Not a chance. I may look like death, but my brain is still very much alive. I'm required to tutor you Monday through Friday, four hours per day, and that's exactly what we're going to do."

Her face falls, and she huffs out an irritated sigh. "Fine."

"It's not that bad. It's almost the weekend, so you'll get the next two days off." I flip open my laptop and pull up our current lesson. "If we get started right away, we'll be done by the time we dock in Mallorca."

A half hour later, I've chugged another sixty-four ounces of water and Bijou has mastered the concept of combining like terms in algebraic expressions. We're flying through these lessons at a much faster rate than I'd anticipated. She's an ideal student, attentive and inquisitive, and she seems to have a natural aptitude for math. I'm genuinely shocked that she failed her last semester, but if there's one thing I've learned in my years of tutoring, it's that grades don't necessarily reflect an understanding of the course material. Maybe something else was going on. She may struggle with test anxiety, or she could've been distracted by some drama with her friends. It's also possible the situation with her parents was contributing to her poor school performance. But it's not my job to psychoanalyze her. Boundaries!

We're about to switch gears and launch into our next lesson, equivalent expressions, when Bijou lets out an agonized groan. She's looking out the window, and I follow her gaze to see Richard peering in at us from outside on the deck. He offers a dorky little wave, which I awkwardly return, all the while thinking, *Please do not come in here. I am still too hungover to deal with a tense interaction between you and your daughter.*

It's like he can read my thoughts, because he suddenly shoves his hand in his pocket and walks away. Bijou and I simultaneously sigh. As soon as he's gone, though, I feel a pang of guilt. Or maybe it's pity. Richard looked so defeated as he gazed at his daughter. So sad.

"He is beyond annoying." She tears off a corner of her scrap paper and rolls it between her fingertips into a tiny little ball, which she then flicks off into a far corner of the office. I wonder if she'll pick it up later or leave it for a member of the yacht crew to take care of.

"I think he just wants to make sure you're doing okay."

"Yeah, right. My dad doesn't actually care about me."

"Of course he does." I say it with conviction, but how can I be so sure? It's been less than a week since I met these people, and everything I know about Richard Vale I've gleaned from either shady gossip blogs or his personal assistant. I haven't talked to the man for more than five consecutive minutes, and that's a generous estimate.

Thing is, I've been unduly influenced by what Coco told me about Veronica, that she messes with the visitation schedule and badmouths Richard to Bijou. As Richard's employee, Coco is undoubtedly biased, but there'd be no reason for her to lie about it to me. Plus, she seems genuinely concerned about Bijou's well-being—not to mention, genuinely pissed off at Veronica.

Whatever happened between the Vales in the wake of their divorce, it isn't fair for Bijou to have to suffer the fallout. Romances fade, relationships crumble. People make unforgivable mistakes that may cause a marriage to fail. But most kids only get one father. As a child, I cherished every moment with my dad, and Bijou deserves that, too. I would hate for her to grow up and look back on this summer with resentment or regret.

"I know for a fact that he wants to make this summer special for you," I say. "That's why he chartered this yacht. Didn't you want this?"

"Yeah, I did. But it's not as fun as I thought it was going to be."

"Why not?"

She shrugs and tears off another corner of her paper. "Dad's always working."

I picture his videoconference attire, those wireless earbuds always at the ready. "Aren't you guys spending time together after our tutoring sessions are over?"

Another shrug. "Yeah, but it sucks. Like, yesterday he took me to that park with all the weird-looking buildings."

She must be talking about Park Güell, the tremendous green space designed by Antoni Gaudi that houses all sorts of whimsical sculptures and structures. I ducked in there on Wednesday, and it was like strolling through a fairy-tale village.

"What was so bad about that?"

"He was on his phone the whole time, and right when we were getting to the good part of the tour, he made us leave because he had to take an emergency meeting in his office."

Well, that doesn't sound like special daddy-daughter time. "Does he do that a lot?"

She nods without elaborating, and I'm not going to push her to say more. After a few seconds of silence, she quietly adds, "It's like he has no idea who I am."

"What do you mean?"

"The things he plans for us to do are not things I'm into at all. Like, I'm fine with going to *one* museum. But the other day he arranged for us to tour five museums in a row. Do you know how boring that was?"

I'll bet it was the swankiest five-museum tour anyone's ever been on. Private car escorting them from site to site. Dedicated docent giving them behind-the-scenes access. After all, everywhere Richard Vale goes, he's a VIP. Hardly sounds boring to me.

I get it, though. Bijou is twelve. When I was twelve, I wouldn't have been thrilled about a five-museum tour, either. Unless, of course, they were science museums. But half the fun of that was hanging out with my dad, asking him questions and learning from him. He was always enthusiastic about spending time with me. Richard just seems checked out. "What are some things that you're into, then?"

"I don't know," she says. "Fun stuff. Adventurous stuff. Not following someone around a bunch of buildings for hours while they give me some boring art lecture."

"Have you told your dad how you feel?"

She shakes her head. "He won't care."

"Yes, he will."

"You don't know my dad."

Her eyes narrow to piercing blue slits, and I realize she's right. I don't know her dad. I don't really know her, either. And it's not my place to go messing around in their relationship.

I need to stick with what I do know, which is math. "Okay," I say, turning my attention back to the lesson displayed on my laptop. "Equivalent expressions. Let's get started."

~

Sometime after I'm done tutoring Bijou and before we arrive in Mallorca, a fresh wave of hangover misery descends upon me. My headache comes roaring back, and there's a bonfire burning in my stomach. I know I said I wouldn't take advantage of the amenities on board, but there is no way I can stay in my stateroom while this boat is in motion. Each time we crest a wave, I can feel my brain jostling around inside my skull. I need fresh air on my face. And maybe some hair of the dog.

Actually, a soak in the hot tub sounds excellent. I change into a swimsuit and head outside, where the deck is blissfully empty. It's like a mini resort back here, with a basket of freshly rolled towels and a cooler full of chilled water. I grab a bottle and chug half of it before lowering myself into the tub. Ah, that's nice and warm.

My muscles instantly turn to jelly. I sink into the lounge seat, stretching my legs out as far as they'll go. The tips of my toes peek out from beneath the surface, and I rest my head back against the edge of the tub, exhaling a heavy, happy breath. The only thing that would make this perfect is if the massage jets were on full blast, but I've only just realized the button to activate them is at the other end of the deck.

A poor design choice, to be sure. Not worth getting out of the water to turn them on, though. Not when I'm feeling so relaxed. I close my eyes and feel the sun beat down on my face, the cool breeze ripple through my hair.

"Abby."

At the sound of my name, I open my eyes to find Richard standing over me. It's jarring, like my boss just caught me slacking off on the job. I jolt upright, ready to apologize, before realizing I've already put in an honest four hours of work today. Even if I did start late on account of my raging hangover.

"Richard. Hi."

"I'm so sorry to interrupt you," he says without a hint of sarcasm. "But do you have a quick moment to chat?"

"Sure." Oh no. It's about the late start, isn't it? Coco told me he wouldn't mind, but maybe she was wrong. Now he thinks I'm a slug who can't do the one simple thing she's been hired to do. "It'll never happen again, I assure you."

His forehead wrinkles. "What won't happen again?"

"Bijou and I didn't start our session until noon today. It was all my fault; I went out last night and stayed out way too late."

"Oh, right. Coco said you two went to that club with the great views. Did you have a nice time?"

"Yes, thank you for the passes." I probably should've thanked him earlier. "But I shouldn't have let it interfere with my work."

"It didn't interfere with your work. You still tutored Bijou today, right?" I nod, and he says, "She and I didn't have anything planned for this afternoon, anyway. I'm glad the passes didn't go to waste."

He crouches down beside me, and all at once, I'm aware of how tiny my bikini is. It's not one of those sporty ones with the high waist and the full cups; it's a few triangles held together with flimsy string. Not that Richard's being creepy about it—his gaze hasn't wandered south of my eyes, not for a split second—but when meeting with parents, I tend toward conservative, professional attire. Not bikinis. Then again, these conversations usually don't take place in or around hot tubs.

He clears his throat and continues. "I'm here because I was hoping you could provide some feedback on Bijou's academic performance. How she's progressing through her lessons. If she's facing any stumbling blocks."

"She's doing really well," I say, hugging my arms across my chest. "Much better than I expected, considering her grades the last two semesters. She's developed a solid understanding of algebraic expressions, aced all the quizzes I've given her. She's also very enthusiastic; she shows up to each session full of energy and ready to work. I'm impressed with the level of effort she puts in."

"That's great to hear." He breaks out in a big smile, radiating Proud Dad energy. But it only lasts a moment before the corners of his mouth begin to droop. "I'd been hoping to pop in on your lessons and see for myself, but I know she doesn't want me in the office while you're working. I've asked her how it's going several times, but she only ever gives me one- or two-word answers."

"That's a twelve-year-old for you." Not all twelve-year-olds are like that. I just want to say something supportive, because right now he's looking pretty sad.

"I'm trying to give her some space, respect her boundaries. Maybe that'll help her open up to me. I had high hopes for this summer, but I'm not sure she's happy to be here."

There are so many ways I can respond to this. I can tell him what Bijou said during our tutoring session—how she's not having fun, how she's convinced he doesn't care about her—but I don't want to betray her confidence. I can play dumb, act like what he's saying couldn't possibly be true, but that wouldn't do either of them any good. They're both unhappy, which is painful to witness, especially knowing this was meant to be a special daddy-daughter vacation.

Perhaps the best course of action is to ask some leading questions and drop some subtle hints, then let him come to a conclusion on his own. "Have you tried asking her what might make her happy?"

"Yes, and her answer was 'whatever.' I didn't have much to go on, so I asked Coco to research the most popular sites in Barcelona and arrange for some private tours. Museums, parks, cultural sites. She hated them all."

I have to clench my teeth to keep from mentioning the trip to Park Güell that got cut short on account of his emergency meeting. According to Bijou, that wasn't an unusual occurrence. If he'd prioritized his time with her, remained present in her presence, she might be having a better time.

But I can't suggest my boss not do his work. Presumably, working all the time is how he makes his billions. And I'm certainly in no position to be telling anyone how to manage their career, given that my career is in a tailspin and I'm in debt up to my ears.

He rakes his hand through his neatly combed hair, mussing his dark curls. They stick out at all angles and fall across his forehead. He suddenly seems younger now, more vulnerable. Less like a powerful billionaire.

"I don't know how to fix this," he says. The anguish in his voice cracks my heart wide open.

"You know, when I was a kid, I liked to do stuff with my dad that was a little more . . . adventurous."

I hope I haven't insulted him. After all, I'm insinuating that his ideas are tame and uninteresting. Fortunately, there's a hopeful gleam in his eyes as he asks, "Adventurous how?"

"We spent a lot of time outside together." We'd taken so many day trips, went away for so many long weekends. Mom was never big on the outdoors, so for the most part it was just the two of us exploring the natural world. Now, memories crash over me in waves. "We'd go camping in the Adirondacks, near a river where we'd go tubing and white water rafting. He taught me how to fly-fish; I was never very good, but I loved doing it all the same. In the winter, we'd snowshoe and cross-country ski. Sometimes, we'd go out on the back roads with ATVs. At night, we'd stargaze, and he'd show me all the constellations. I always thought he was this bottomless well of knowledge."

I stop myself short because I realize I'm rambling. Richard's looking at me with wide, wondering eyes. My cheeks burn.

"Sounds like your dad is an amazing man."

I nod. I don't want to say my dad *was* an amazing man, because I don't feel like getting into all that. Richard's gaze is focused, like he wants me to keep talking, but I think I've already said too much. This man's my boss. I'm in a bikini. What happened to those boundaries, Abby?

I decide to shift the focus back to Bijou. "By the way, I'm not suggesting you take her camping." Camping would probably be a nightmare for a girl who's used to living the cushy life on a luxury yacht. "But she might like something that's a little more hands on and interactive than a tour of an art museum. Something a little more daring and off the beaten path."

Richard opens his mouth, draws in a breath, as if he's about to say something. Then he presses his lips together and stands upright, smoothing his hair back into place. The noncompliant curls fall back across his forehead. He clears his throat. "That's great advice. Thank you."

"You're welcome."

"I'll let you get back to your soak now."

He walks away, but at the edge of the deck, he pauses and turns to me. I hold my breath as he points toward the button that activates the jets. "Want me to turn these on for you?"

I exhale. "I'd love that. Thank you."

"Of course." One tap of his finger and the hot tub swirls to life. Streams of water massage my back. The splash and gurgle of bubbles drown out all other sounds. Richard smiles at me, and it feels warm like the sun. He disappears up the stairs, and I sink back into the lounge seat again. I close my eyes, feel the cool sea breeze ripple through my hair. Now *this* is perfect.

CHAPTER SEVEN

I'm still in the hot tub when Mallorca comes into view. First, it's a faint outline on the horizon. Soon, it's dense trees and craggy cliffs. From the edge of the deck, I watch it grow larger and lusher. Before we pull into the marina, I duck into my room to shower and change before dinner.

Coco and I grab a bite to eat in town. We're in the capital, Palma, where there is no shortage of dining options. We settle on a tapas restaurant with views of the coastline, splitting plates of grilled octopus and ham croquettes as we watch the sun go down. I order one glass of white wine, sipping it slowly. My headache's finally gone, and I'm not interested in back-to-back hangovers.

That's why I politely decline Coco's invitation to go to another club. "Come on, it's Friday night," she says. "And we're VIPs."

"You got guest passes again?"

"I always have guest passes. If you change your mind, let me know."

But I'm not going to change my mind. Just the thought of working my way through another big-ass bottle of vodka sends a wave of nausea through my entire body. Instead, I take a leisurely seaside stroll back to the ship. The evening air is warm and salty. Waves crash like rhythmic thunder against the rocks. I swipe my card at the marina and make my way to the private berth where the yacht is docked. No sign of Bijou or Richard on board.

What do those two do at night? Maybe Bijou holes up in her room and texts her friends or something. Which would give Richard plenty of time to conduct his sexual affairs. Though I get the sense he's on temporary hiatus from those shenanigans. I haven't seen him sneaking out on his own, nor have I spotted any strange women hanging around.

Back on the ship, I return to my stateroom to find a message from Arpita on my phone: why no IG update??? I've been posting to Instagram religiously, but I forgot today on account of the hangover. I plop down in bed, then scroll through my camera roll to search for a good one. Finally, I select a sunset photo I'd snapped during dinner, all orange sun and purple clouds and sapphire sea. I upload it with the caption *Mallorca views* and send it off to Arpita.

She replies with a heart-eye emoji and asks, are you going out tonight?

No, I reply. Still nursing last night's hangover.

can u talk?

A minute later, Arpita's smiling face is flashing on my phone screen. I didn't realize exactly how much I missed her until this moment. "It's so good to see you," I say. "What time is it there?"

"A little after four in the afternoon. You?"

"Just past ten. What are you up to tonight?"

"I'm gonna hit up the beer garden."

"That sounds fun." The beer garden is the usual Friday-night hang-out, popular among the grad students at our school.

"I wish you were here," she says. "But I'd rather be on a yacht in the Mediterranean, to be honest. How are things going with the billionaire's daughter?"

"Fine. She's the perfect student. Easy to work with, eager to learn. She's doing really well."

"That's good. And what about the billionaire?"

I flash back to our conversation by the hot tub, the warmth of his smile when he turned on the jets, the way his curls fell lazily across his forehead. "What about him?"

"I've been checking the gossip blogs every day, but there haven't been any updates on him. Figured you could give me the inside scoop."

"There's nothing to report."

"Really? No one doing the walk of shame off the boat at five in the morning?"

"No." Granted, I haven't been monitoring the premises twenty-four seven, but I can't imagine that's actually been happening. "I don't think he's doing that kind of thing with his daughter around. To be honest, he doesn't seem like the type. He's good looking, but he's kind of a dork."

"A dork with an ultrahigh net worth. Trust me, he's the type."

"I wish you could meet him; then you'd understand what I mean. He's got this super sincere vibe going on. And I'm really surprised by how handsome he is. Nothing like the photos we saw online where he was all hunched over and scowling."

She narrows her eyes at me. "Abby, do you have a crush on your billionaire boss?"

"No! I mean, I like him, but not like that. He's just not what I expected him to be, that's all. He's way nicer. And better looking."

"Okay, that is the third time you've mentioned how good looking he is. You totally have a crush on him. Am I gonna have to fly out there and rescue you before you wind up in the tabloids?"

"Don't be ridiculous." To be honest, she's not being all that ridiculous. I have to admit I may be developing the teeniest, tiniest crush on Richard Vale. I can't help myself; he's exactly my type—a good-looking geek! But it's completely harmless, and I would never act on it. "He's my boss, Arpita. It would be totally inappropriate. I have boundaries, you know."

"I know, I know. I'm just teasing. So what do you have planned for Mallorca?"

"I'm not totally sure. I wanna do a little research tonight, figure out a plan for the week." If we're even staying here for the whole week. Coco hasn't told me when we're leaving, or where we're going next.

63

Arpita and I chat a few minutes longer about mundane stuff, like a new podcast Arpita's been bingeing and whether we think our landlady's going to raise the rent when our lease is up in September, before saying our good nights. Then, after getting ready for bed, I google "things to do in Mallorca by yourself" and scroll through the list of results until I fall asleep.

I wake to the sound of frantic knocking. This is it. We're sinking, aren't we? I knew I should've slept with a life jacket on! I leap out of bed in a half-conscious frenzy and open the door to find Bijou standing in the hallway, wearing a sporty swimsuit and a radiant smile.

"We're leaving in ten minutes for the other side of the island. The car is almost here."

"What?" I scrub the sleep from my eyes and blink until my vision clears. That's when I realize we are not, in fact, sinking. We're floating safely in our assigned berth, on the surface of the water, with the early-morning sun streaming through my window. "Where are you going?"

Her smile falters. "What are you talking about? Dad said this was your idea."

I'm lost. At no point in our brief conversation did Richard and I discuss a cross-island expedition. Unless he took my advice to heart and planned his own daddy-daughter adventure. "Is your dad taking you somewhere fun today?"

"He's taking us both. Get your bathing suit on."

"I'm sorry, what? No." I shake my head, wondering if maybe this isn't some weird lucid dream. My subconscious is clearly still anxious about the whole string-bikini-in-front-of-the-boss incident.

I'm very much awake, though, and now Bijou's pulling a face, sticking her lower lip out in a petulant pout. Or it could be that she's genuinely hurt by my rebuff, because her voice is small when she asks, "You don't want to come with us?"

"It's not that I don't want to come. It's that I don't want to intrude."

"You're not intruding, I promise."

"Your dad may disagree. He probably wants some alone time with you."

"He's the one who told me to invite you along. And I really want you to come." There's an urgency in her eyes, a sudden desperation. "Please. We have a private guide who's gonna take us to this secluded beach, and we're gonna go out to lunch afterward. But it's an hour-long drive to get there, and I'm sure Dad's gonna be on his phone the whole time. It'll be so much more fun if you're there."

Considering the bulk of our time together is spent reviewing math problems, I'm surprised Bijou thinks of me as someone who'll bring more fun to this already fun-sounding experience. Then again, we crack jokes all the time, and we've got an easy rapport. Much easier than the one she's got with Richard, that's for sure.

He asked her to invite me, so he obviously wants me there, too. Probably to act as a buffer or a babysitter, but either way, I'd be stupid to say no to a private tour and a free lunch. It's Mallorca, VIP-style.

"Give me a minute to change."

Bijou hops up and down, clapping her hands together like a circus seal. "I'll meet you outside."

Why did I only pack string bikinis? I should've brought a one-piece, something with a bit more coverage, but I didn't think I'd be spending so much bathing suit time with my boss. I don't know why I'm so worried about this, anyway. Like I said, he's perfectly respectful and not the least bit pervy. It's just that when he's around, I feel this heightened awareness of my skin, specifically all the bare parts. Even if his mind isn't in the gutter, mine is, no matter how inappropriate it might be.

I throw on my least skimpy (though still quite skimpy) swimsuit along with a billowy dress and a pair of flip-flops. Then I grab the essentials for a day at the beach—sunglasses, sunscreen, my phone to take some pictures—and toss them in a bag before heading out the door.

Bijou is waiting for me near the exit ramp. She chatters excitedly as we walk toward the parking lot. "This is supposed to be the prettiest beach on the island. At least, that's what Dad said."

"I'm sure it is." According to my research, there's no shortage of beautiful beaches on Mallorca. I'd been planning to explore a few closer to the marina, but I'm thrilled to get the opportunity to see one on the opposite end of the island.

A Range Rover with tinted windows is idling by the curb. As we approach, a man in a suit opens the back door and waves us inside with a "Bon dia."

Damn, it's roomy in here. We ease ourselves into the third row, like we're the bad kids sitting at the back of the bus. Except I've never been in a bus quite like this, with unblemished white leather seats and soft music playing on surround sound speakers. We buckle ourselves in and adjust our personal air vents as we wait for Richard to join us.

"He's always late," Bijou mutters.

"He's a busy guy." I can't imagine how busy. I don't know what the day-to-day responsibilities of a venture capitalist entail—probably lots of networking and negotiations—but he clearly puts in a lot of hours.

"My mom said when she went into labor, he showed up late to the hospital and almost missed me being born."

"Is that so?"

"Yeah. It's like I've never been his number one priority."

As Bijou anxiously twirls her hair, I wonder if there's any hope of salvaging their father-daughter relationship. I want to believe there is. At least Richard took my advice and booked a more adventurous excursion today. Maybe that'll show Bijou he cares about her.

Though it'd be a lot more convincing if he weren't late. Ten minutes pass, then fifteen. The chauffeur leans on the hood of the car, occasionally checking his watch. Finally, he makes a phone call, and two minutes later Richard's jogging our way in flip-flops and board shorts and a T-shirt that appears to have been put on backward.

"Sorry, sweetie." He ducks into the Rover with a guilty smile. "I got stuck in a meeting."

"Of course you did." There's not a trace of sympathy in Bijou's voice.

He sits in the middle row and swivels to face us. "Are you excited?"

She shrugs and turns away, her attention focused on the city passing by as we pull out of the marina and onto the street. Richard's smile withers.

"Well, *I'm* excited," I say with all the enthusiasm I can muster. I'm determined to have a pleasant day, and there's nothing pleasant about watching these two dance around their insecurities. It's time to get hyped. We're in Mallorca, for crying out loud. "What's the name of the place we're going to?"

"Uh . . . let me check." Richard pulls his phone from the pocket of his shorts and scrolls through until he finds the answer. "Cala Varques. Says here it's one of the best cliff-jumping beaches on the entire island."

A bubble of nervous laughter escapes me. "You're going cliff jumping?"

"Heck yeah," Bijou says. She's excited now, no doubt about it.

"Is that safe?" I turn to Richard. "I mean, aren't there age restrictions? I just worry about Bijou getting hurt."

I can see her scowling in my peripheral vision. Straight ahead, Richard just looks confused. "There's an experienced guide meeting us there. He said kids as young as five do this all the time."

"See? It's fine," Bijou says. "I thought this was your idea, anyway, Abby."

"No, it wasn't. I only suggested something adventurous."

"And what's more adventurous than jumping off a cliff?" Richard's beaming, so proud of himself for this novel idea. "They assured me it's extremely safe."

"Can we do backflips?" Bijou asks.

"I'm not sure. Personally, I won't be attempting a backflip, but maybe Abby will."

"Oh, I'm not gonna jump." No way, no how. Not happening.

They both give me the same incredulous stare, and the genetic ties are immediately apparent. Bijou is fair and Richard is dark, but they have the same arch to their eyebrows, the same prominent cheekbones, the same deep Cupid's bow in their upper lips.

"What do you mean, you're not gonna jump?" Bijou asks.

"You said you liked adventurous pursuits." Richard looks as if I've betrayed him somehow. His mouth is agape, and there's a frustrated line in his forehead.

"Yeah. Why won't you do it?"

Geez, it's not like I'm lying. I *do* like adventurous pursuits. The kind that are closer to the ground. All those activities I mentioned yesterday—the water sports, the winter sports, the camping in the woods—none of it involved steep inclines or sheer drops. There's a reason my dad and I went cross-country skiing instead of hitting the downhill slopes. I'm terrified of heights, and I always have been.

It's not something I'm proud of, either. It's embarrassing to have an irrational fear like this, and I don't feel like discussing it with the Vales. If I'd known we were heading off to a day of standing on the edge of a cliff and flinging ourselves into the sea, I'd have politely declined this invitation. Now we've merged onto the highway, speeding toward my worst nightmare, and suddenly this soft music sounds suspiciously like the soundtrack to a horror film. I'm trapped.

And they're still staring at me, like they want me to explain myself. I'd rather tuck and roll out of this Range Rover than have an earnest chat about my long-standing phobia, so instead I just say, "I'll see what it's like when I get there."

This doesn't appear to satisfy Richard, because the furrow in his brow only deepens. Why is he so concerned about it, anyway? I never said I wanted to go cliff jumping, and I certainly didn't ask to tag along on this outing. I'm the math tutor, not the activities coordinator, and this is supposed to be my day off.

Mercifully, the awkward moment is interrupted by the shrill beep of Richard's phone. He glances down and sighs gruffly. "I gotta take this," he says, before swiveling back around and answering the call firmly but discreetly.

Bijou pats my knee and says, "It's okay. You don't have to jump if you don't want to. I didn't mean to make you feel bad."

"You didn't." It must be obvious how agitated I am. My fists are clenched and so is my jaw. I open my mouth and sigh out a breath to release all the built-up tension. "This whole thing caught me off guard, that's all. I didn't realize exactly what your dad had planned."

She glances at the back of his head, which is bowed in concentration. Then she turns to me and, with a hushed voice, says, "Thanks for convincing him to do something fun."

"You're welcome. I want you two to have a good time together on this trip." I almost add, *Because you may never get the chance to do this with your dad again*, but then think better of it. There's no need to remind her of her father's mortality. Besides, with her family's wealth, she'll be able to return to Mallorca whenever she wants. That is, if she hasn't been here already. "Do you travel a lot with your parents?"

She shakes her head. "Not really. I've been to Saint Barts and Cabo a few times. Hawaii, too, of course. My mom and I usually spend Christmas in Aspen. And last summer she took me to London for a Harry Styles concert, so we went to Paris for a few days, too. That's all."

Oh. That's all?

"I really wanted to go to LA with my mom this summer," she continues. "But she said she'd be too busy working so I needed to stay with my dad. As if he's not busy working, too." She gestures to Richard, who's still engrossed in his phone conversation.

"I'm sure your mom had very good reasons to tell you to be with your dad." Didn't Coco say Veronica was trying to get on a season of

Real Housewives in LA? I believe her exact words were "being thirsty." Probably not the best environment for a twelve-year-old.

We ride to Cala Varques in silence, save for the soft music and the commentary from Richard's one-sided phone conversation. The scenery is pretty but not particularly interesting. Lots of flat land and open sky, green hills off in the distance. Eventually, the road narrows and the flat land around us gives way to dense shrubbery. We turn left onto a single-lane gravel road that's so bumpy I have to grip the seat to stay upright.

The driver pulls off the main road and parks in a gravel lot. That's when the nerves I've managed to bury in the pit of my stomach come gurgling back to the surface. Richard removes his earbuds and places them in the side console, along with his phone, then slams it shut. I guess jumping off a cliff is the one thing to get him to take a break from work.

"Let's get this party started!" He whoops as he leaps out of the car.

Bijou covers her eyes. "He is so embarrassing."

"Oh, come on," I say, nudging her gently with my elbow. "He's just happy to spend time with you. It's cute."

She drops her hand and cringes. "Please don't call my dad cute ever again."

"What? No, you misunderstood." There's no point in trying to explain, since she's already hopped out of the car, but I feel an urgent need to clear this up. I follow behind her, saying, "I didn't say *he* was cute; I said *it* was cute."

"Who's cute?" Richard asks, and before humiliation can cause me to evaporate into a fine mist, he points across the lot to a youngish, shirtless guy. "Him?"

That guy's got a thick black beard and a six-pack you could grate cheese on. I suppose he's objectively cute, but he's not my type. He is, however, running toward us while waving both hands in the air.

"Hola!" He shouts despite the fact that we're now less than six feet apart. "My name is Leo. I will be your guide to the cliffs today. Are you ready to do some jumping?"

"Totally." Bijou's got hearts in her eyes for this guy. It'd be endearing if I wasn't on the verge of passing out from fear.

"Wonderful," Leo says. "Now, Cala Varques is a hidden jewel of a beach, so it will be a short walk to get there. But I promise you, it will be worth it."

"Can't wait," Richard says. As he looks down at Bijou, he's beaming with that Proud Dad energy again.

The driver hangs back with the Range Rover while Leo hoists a well-worn backpack onto his shoulders and leads the rest of us through a rusty gate and down a rocky path. I go slow so I don't turn an ankle. I should've worn sturdier shoes.

After a few minutes of walking, we come to another gate, this one accompanied by a big red sign that reads *Propiedad Privada*. I'm no Spanish scholar, but I get the sense we shouldn't be walking here. The wall beside the gate has been smashed to bits, leaving a large person-size hole. Leo climbs through it and gestures for us to follow. I glance sideways at Richard, assuming he'll be just as freaked out as I am, but he looks giddy as he guides Bijou through the wall. I guess we're doing this.

The path is rockier on the other side, with lots of thick vegetation and underbrush. Parts of the path are blocked by felled trees that we have to climb over. This whole situation seems less than legit and definitely not VIP. If a cliff jump doesn't kill me today, it's entirely possible Leo will. How did Richard even find this guy?

"Um, Leo?" I call. "What's the deal with the private property signs? We're not trespassing, are we?"

He barks out a short, sharp laugh. "Oh no. The beaches are public here. The people who own the land around it do not like that and try to keep people away. But nothing can keep us away. Not even a brick wall!"

We're definitely trespassing. And now I have one more thing to worry about: being arrested. Or maybe even murdered by the owners of this property. Why doesn't Richard look concerned about this? Maybe there's an invincibility that comes with being a billionaire. The feeling that no matter what terrible predicament you get yourself into, you'll always get out of it unscathed because you're too big to fail.

I'm beginning to doubt the existence of this hidden jewel of a beach when a cool breeze passes over my skin. It's light at first, like a salty whisper, but it's undoubtedly a sign that the sea is nearby. Sure enough, we round a corner, and there it is. The shimmering turquoise water, the pristine white sand. I breathe deeply, letting the fresh air rejuvenate me before I exhale my fears.

The beach itself is a small cove surrounded by trees and—of course—cliffs. Most people are sunbathing on blankets or swimming in the shallows. It's all very calm here. As we make our way over to an empty stretch of sand, I feel that sense of impending doom dissipate and float away with the receding tide.

"You can leave your things right here. No one will bother them," Leo says. He drops his backpack in the sand and points to a steep pebble-strewn path off to the left. "That is the way to the cliff tops."

"Let's go!" Bijou says before racing up the hill.

We're getting right into it, huh? No settling in or lazing around. Just going straight for the jump.

"Wait up, B!" Richard calls. He takes his shirt off and tosses it onto the sand, and wow, I was *not* expecting him to be quite so ripped. Casting an unsure glance in my direction, he asks, "Will you be okay here by yourself?"

"Of course. Go on, I'm totally fine."

Leo frowns. "You are not going to jump?"

I shake my head. "It's fine, though. I'm fine."

"What is the matter?" Leo's smile isn't friendly. It's condescending, like he's teasing me. "You are not afraid, are you?"

"No." I'm not sure why I feel the need to even acknowledge that question. Probably because Richard's looking at me like he wants to know the answer.

I gaze up, toward the top of the cliff, where someone's balancing precariously at the edge. My heart pounds against my ribs, so afraid they're going to fall. Then they launch themselves out into a swan dive, flying gracefully through the air like a fearless superhero, before splashing down into the water. I hold my breath until they resurface, which they do rather quickly, grinning from ear to ear.

Leo persists. "The view is beautiful up there, you will see. It is a very low cliff. There is nothing to be scared of."

There *is* something to be scared of, even if it makes no sense to him. My hands are shaking at the mere thought of it. I watch another person jump with ease and curse myself for being such a wimp. Because it does look fun, in a terrifying sort of way.

"Come now," Leo says. "Make the climb. Even the twelve-year-old girl, she is jumping. Don't be the chicken."

Richard cuts in. "If she's not comfortable, she's not comfortable. Let her do what she wants to do." His tone is decisive, like the high-powered businessman he is. I can only imagine the way he takes charge in meetings.

It's enough to make Leo back off, but it also makes me realize that I want to go with them. No one's forcing me to do anything, and no one's shaming me into it, either. I can make my own decisions based on what I'm comfortable with. There's no reason I can't climb to the top of the cliff to take in all the beautiful scenery he mentioned, then walk back down the path instead of leaping off the edge.

"Actually, I think I'll go."

"You sure?" Richard asks.

"Yeah. I want to see the view."

"That is the spirit!" Leo says and charges up the hill behind Bijou. I go at a slower pace, taking careful steps to make sure I don't trip. The stones are rough on the soles of my feet. I think a pebble just lodged itself under my skin.

When Leo and Bijou are far ahead, out of earshot, I ask Richard, "This guy is intense. Where did you find him?"

"Coco booked him. Apparently, he came highly recommended. I'm sorry, by the way. If I knew you weren't comfortable cliff jumping, I would've planned something else."

"Why? Bijou's absolutely thrilled. That's what's important. You planned this for her, not me."

"Of course." He clears his throat. "It's just that you helped me so much. If not for your advice, I wouldn't have known what to do to make her happy. The way she smiled at me this morning when I told her we were coming here? It was better than the sunrise. It's like you gave me a little window into her brain. I wanted to find a way to thank you, and since you said you enjoyed adventure, I hoped this would be fun for you."

"This is fun." This is such a thoughtful gesture; I don't want him to think I'm ungrateful. "The beach is beautiful, and I'm excited to see the view. But you didn't need to thank me. It was honestly my pleasure to help."

"Well, I appreciate it," he says, turning back and holding out his hand. "Easy on this last rock, it's a steep one."

"Thanks." I place my palm in his, allowing him to steady me as I climb the final step to the top of the cliff.

The view up here is magnificent. Clear sky stretches for miles in every direction. Sunlight dances on the surface of the sea. The rocky coastline is dotted with caves and crags. In the distance, there's a natural arch.

"This is beautiful," I say.

"Just wait until you jump," Leo says. "It is even better on the way down."

Maybe I *could* do it. I inch closer to the edge and peer down into the water. Instantly, my stomach bottoms out. That's a no.

"I wanna go!" Bijou yells, but Leo holds his hand out to stop her.

"I will go first. I will wait at the bottom for you to make sure you're okay when you land. Most important thing to know: feet down. Hug your body like this"—he holds his arms by his sides, straight as an arrow—"and press your legs together. Point your toes when you get to the bottom. Any questions?"

"Can I hold my nose?" Bijou asks.

"Of course. Anything else?"

Richard looks to me with concern in his eyes, but I wave him off and mouth, "I'm fine," even though I'm pretty sure my knees are about to give out.

"Okay. Here I go." Leo glances down to ensure there's no one swimming below, then yells something unintelligible as he hurls himself outward. Gravity does its work, and suddenly he's gone. I hang back while Richard and Bijou look over the edge. A loud splash confirms his landing, at which point Bijou yells, "My turn!"

All at once, Bijou holds her nose and jumps with a squeal. My heart lurches at the sight of her suspended in midair, and instinctively I hurry toward the edge, arriving just in time to see her body make contact with the water. Leo swims toward her immediately, ensuring her safety. She waves up at us with an ebullient smile.

"Wow," Richard says, watching in awe as his daughter swims to shore. "My brave girl did it."

"She's pretty fearless." Unlike me and my trembling legs.

He turns to me. "Are you going to walk back down now?"

"I don't know." Yes, I'm terrified, but I also realize that there's no logical reason to be afraid. Bijou jumped ten seconds ago, and she's already climbing back up the hill for more. And I'm curious about what it would feel like to take a running leap off this cliff. It must be exhilarating to experience a free fall, knowing the water will provide a safe place for you to land.

"It's okay if you don't want to jump," he says.

"I *do* want to jump, I'm just really scared. But I'm also scared that I'll regret it if I don't. I can't leave here being known as 'the chicken.'" Maybe there *is* an element of shame involved. I'm pissed at myself for letting that guy's judgy attitude get to me. I'm shaking, too. At this point, it's a whole-body tremor, from my wiggly feet to my chattering jaw.

Richard puts his hands on my shoulders, gives me a firm yet tender squeeze. "Forget about what Leo said. Whether you walk down or jump down, it's not for anyone else to judge. I certainly won't judge you. You have nothing to prove to anyone."

His voice is gentle, soothing, and as his deep-brown eyes search mine, the trembling in my body slowly subsides. I no longer feel embarrassed or cowardly. I feel witnessed. Like even if he can't understand my fear, he respects it as valid.

"I don't know what to do."

He squeezes my shoulders again, almost like a reflex. Like comforting me is the most natural thing in the world. "When I don't know what to do, I try not to overthink it. Admittedly, that's hard for me, because I have a tendency to overthink things."

"So do I." For example, right now I really wish I could google statistics for cliff-jumping injuries. "How do you move past it? The overthinking, I mean."

"Well, usually I clear my mind as best I can, and I close my eyes, and I ask myself what I want the outcome to look like. It always appears quickly, like a bolt of lightning. And it's always the right answer."

It sounds too simple, but I might as well try it. It's better than standing here, marinating in my own indecision. So I close my eyes, and I ask myself what I want the outcome of this excursion to look like.

In my mind, I'm flying. Sailing out over the water. Then I'm falling, but instead of feeling afraid, I feel empowered. Like the strong, smart, badass woman I know I am. As I splash down, I welcome the cool embrace of the sea, the gurgle of water in my ears. I break the surface, filling my lungs with fresh air before swimming toward Richard, who awaits me with a smile like the sun.

I open my eyes. Richard's waiting patiently, his gaze like a gentle caress as he stands beside me in all my fear and uncertainty.

Now I know. This is how women fall head over heels for him. It's not about being smooth or charming or rich. Okay, I'm sure sometimes it's about being rich. But right here, in this moment, it's only about how attentive he is. The way he looks at me like my feelings are more significant than the cliffs or the sea or the sun. The soft pressure of his fingertips on my bare skin. It makes me feel like anything is possible.

"I'm ready," I say.

He drops his hands from my shoulders and steps out of my path. "Go for it."

I breathe in. I breathe out. And I take a running leap.

CHAPTER EIGHT

I regret this. The moment my feet are in the air, I wish I'd stayed on solid ground. But there's no fighting momentum, no defying gravity, so I close my eyes and surrender to physics. There's a peace that comes with letting go, and as I plummet toward the water, the panic pulsing through my veins unexpectedly turns to a giddy pleasure. I open my eyes to see the sea rushing to meet me, and even though it's hard to think straight, my brain somehow conjures those instructions from Leo—legs together, point your toes—before I splash down.

It's funny to think that I've been floating on the Mediterranean for almost a week now, but this is the first time I've made skin-on-skin contact with it. It's cool and clear, like the world's biggest saltwater swimming pool. I stay beneath the surface for a moment, savoring the white noise and the sensation of weightlessness. When I come up for air, the first thing I see is Richard's smile as he waves down at me from the top of the cliff.

"You did it!" he calls.

I *did* it. And I am pretty damn proud of myself. I'm aware that, in the grand scheme of life, this jump is a minor matter. All told, it took less than three seconds. But those three seconds felt transformative. I swim to shore with a renewed sense of purpose, hoisting myself onto the rocks with a strength I didn't know I had. The joy of triumph courses through my veins. I want more.

So I climb back to the top, and I jump again. This time, I keep my eyes open from the get-go. I jump again and again, eventually losing count. At some point, Richard taps out, but Bijou and I press on, eager to take advantage of every second we have in this magical place. All the while, Leo treads water a few feet away from our landing spot, keeping an eye out to make sure we're safe. We don't need him, though. As far as I'm concerned, we're invincible.

When we finally decide to call it quits, we head back to the sand, breathless and limp limbed, where Richard's sitting on a blanket fussing with his watch. As I get closer, I see it's a smartwatch, into which he's dictating what I'm assuming is an email. Has he been wearing that thing the whole time? So much for taking a break from work.

As soon as he sees us, he quickly wraps up whatever he was attending to. Then he stands and holds out a fresh beach towel in each hand. "How was it?"

"Amazing!" Bijou grabs a towel and scrubs it down her face.

"And you, Abby?" When he speaks my name, all the tiny hairs on the back of my neck stand on end. "It looked like you were having fun, too. I could see your smile from all the way back here."

My skin tingles at the thought of him watching me from afar. "It was more than fun. It was exhilarating."

Our eyes lock, and all at once the rest of the world falls away. We're the only two people on this beach now. The Mediterranean Sea belongs to us and us alone.

"I'm gonna walk down the beach." Bijou's voice snaps me back to reality.

"You cannot go by yourself," Leo says. "I'll come with you."

"I'll come, too," Richard says, then turns to me. "Coming, Abby?"

"Uh . . ." I look from him to Bijou, who's already started racing across the sand. "I think I'll stay here."

His brow twitches. "Are you sure?"

"Yes. I just want to relax and dry off." I turn away quickly, focusing all my attention on spreading my towel smoothly across the sand. If I look at Richard any longer, I'll change my mind and tag along, but what I really need right now is some breathing room.

See, this teeny, tiny, harmless crush is expanding into something potentially huge and unwieldy. I need to get a handle on it, because lusting after my boss is not smart. It's unprofessional, it's distracting—not to mention, it's completely pointless. I'm expressly forbidden from fraternizing with the parents of the children I tutor. It's written into every contract I've ever signed. This is the first time it's ever been a problem, though. Usually, I have better boundaries than this.

Anyway, this trip is supposed to be a daddy-daughter bonding experience—one I shouldn't be horning in on with my lingering stares and lecherous thoughts. So I sit on my towel and watch the two of them walk away with Leo hot on their heels.

Soon, they disappear among the crowd. It's a lot busier than it was when we first arrived; obviously, having to trek through private property isn't much of a deterrent to the public. Leo was right. Nothing can keep Mallorcans from their beaches.

With his billions of dollars and exclusive connections, I'm sure Richard could've easily gained access to a more sparsely populated beach with an easier means of entry. So what exactly made him decide to come here? And why did he trust this shady tour guide with the scruffy beard? Part of me wonders if he's going to kidnap us and hold us for ransom.

Regardless of what Leo may or may not be plotting, this moment right here is pretty spectacular. I lie back and close my eyes, feeling grateful for so many things: my skin is warm, my muscles are satisfyingly sore, and my heart is full because I've conquered my greatest fear. I still can't believe I flung myself off that cliff. And I wouldn't have done it without Richard's gentle encouragement. Coco was right when she said he was a good guy. I'm grateful for him, too. Probably more than I should be.

I'm in a half-waking state of sunbaked bliss when I hear Bijou's voice echoing from across the beach. I sit up in time to see the three of them approach.

"How was it?" I ask.

"Not as good as jumping off the cliffs." She stretches her arms above her head and yawns. "I'm starving. When are we going to eat lunch?"

"Our reservations are in an hour," Richard says.

"Where are we going to eat?" I ask.

"A Basque grill," he says, and Bijou chimes in with "There's a gelato place right next door, and the website looked *amazing*."

Richard smiles in his daughter's direction. "Bijou loves her ice cream. Just wait until we get to Italy, B. You'll be in heaven."

"We're going to Italy?" A sudden tingle travels up and down my spine. So far, I've been practicing living in the moment, enjoying the current locale without thinking too much about our future destinations, but after this morning of serendipitous adventure, I'm curious about what else is in store.

"Yep," he says. "But first we're going to France."

Wow. France. My mind whirls as I envision myself strolling down the Champs-Élysées and sipping wine at a Parisian sidewalk café. "I've always wanted to see the Eiffel Tower in person."

"Oh." He looks caught out. "We'll actually be in Saint-Tropez, which is well south of Paris. But we can always fly up for the day. I was actually thinking about that myself. Bijou, want to see the Eiffel Tower?"

She sneers. "No. I already saw it with Mom."

He's about to respond when Leo says, "If you want to be on time for your reservation, we need to go now. It will take some time to get back to the car."

No fooling.

The walk back is a lot more strenuous than the walk out was. Not only am I physically spent, but it's about fifteen degrees hotter than it was this morning. Nobody talks as we drag ourselves along the path, dodging downed branches and climbing through that hole in the wall. By the time we make it back to the lot, every inch of my body is covered in sweat. The Range Rover awaits, and when the chauffeur opens the door for us to enter, Leo waves goodbye with a casual "Ciao!" before he disappears down the road.

"He was a little weird," Richard mutters as we climb into the back seat.

Again, no fooling.

The air conditioner is on full blast in here, and it feels like absolute heaven. Bijou and I aim our personal air vents directly at our faces, while Richard dives for his phone. Seconds later, he's engaged in what sounds like a tense, terse conversation. I can't hear exactly what he's saying, but the tone of his voice is troubling. I keep thinking about the tour of Park Güell, how he cut it short to take an urgent private meeting back on the yacht. If he decides to skip lunch today, Bijou will be so disappointed. Especially if she misses out on that gelato.

He remains on the phone for the entire ride back to Palma, but at least he doesn't cancel our lunch plans. We dine at a beautiful seaside restaurant, on our own private veranda. It's fancy here, but no one seems to mind our beach attire. Servers bring us plate after plate of incredible food—spicy sausages, grilled artichokes, a cheese plate with walnuts and figs—and we devour every last morsel. Then we head next door to the gelato shop, where Bijou orders an enormous bowl, half chocolate and half tiramisu. Richard and I opt for single-scoop cones—his lemon, mine almond.

We're enjoying our dessert on a long stone bench overlooking the water when Richard asks Bijou, "What else would you like to do while we're in Mallorca?"

She shrugs. "I dunno. What else is there to do?"

"There's a whole sea cave system to explore. Or we can go kayaking. Or take a hot-air balloon ride."

"Yes, yes, and yes!" Her face explodes into a smile, her cheeks glowing bright pink. Richard smiles back, and the whole exchange is so pure and so tender that I'm convinced everything is going to be okay between them. Their relationship may be strained, but it's salvageable. This daddy-daughter trip will be the bonding experience they need to heal.

We finish our gelato, and the driver brings us back to the yacht, where the Vales retreat immediately to the top deck. I'm lingering below, contemplating a soak in the hot tub to soothe my sore muscles, when Coco appears from inside the cabin.

"Hey," she says, sliding the door closed behind her. "Did you all have fun today?"

"Yes, it was amazing. The beach was in this beautiful cove that was hidden away from everything. We actually had to hike through private property to get there."

"Yeah, I told Richard it was gonna be a trek, but he insisted on having a 'daring, off-the-beaten-path' experience. I don't know where he got that idea from."

My cheeks warm at the familiar words. I know exactly where he got that idea from.

"Anyway," she continues, "that's why I hired Leo to go with you guys."

"Where did you find him? Richard said he came highly recommended, but to be honest, he was kind of a sketchy tour guide."

"He's not a tour guide—he's an elite bodyguard trained in like five different kinds of unarmed combat."

"What?" I picture his thick beard and his six-pack abs, the way he was scanning the beach with such intensity in his eyes. He was never plotting to kidnap us. He was there to prevent us from getting kidnapped.

"Do you honestly think I'd send the Vales out into the wild like that without protection? Richard is one of the richest men on the planet. I tried to talk him into going someplace a little more secure, like a private beach club, but he said he wanted something more adventurous. It was really important to him to make sure Bijou had a good time. Do you think she did?"

"Absolutely." I think of her wide smile, her pink cheeks, the dribble of chocolate gelato on her chin. "And it was for sure an adventure. Why didn't you come, too?"

"I had some writing to do today. Besides, adventure is not my thing. I prefer a chill vibe and a drink in my hand." She snaps her fingers. "Which reminds me: Club tonight?"

"Definitely."

But first, I need to sneak in a late-afternoon catnap, because all that swimming and sun has worn me out. I return to my room and pass out quickly. When I wake up, it's dark and quiet, and according to the clock, it's one in the morning. I just slept the entire night away. Jet lag's a hell of a drug.

There's a slip of paper on the floor just inside the door, a note from Coco:

Knocked but you're not answering so I assume you're asleep.

Headed out now. If you want to meet me at BCM,

tell the doorman you're with Richard Vale.

—C

Technically, it's not too late to go to the club—they're open until sunrise here—but I'm not in the mood to go dancing now. I am, however, wide awake and extremely parched, so I head to the kitchen to pour myself a tall glass of ice water. Then I head down to the main deck to take in the nighttime view of Mallorca from our spot at the edge of the sea.

The landscape is dominated by a large cathedral bathed in bright white light. It looks otherworldly up on a hill, surrounded by smaller, earthier structures—short square buildings, sprawling palm trees, yellow streetlamps. There's not much activity on the streets, at least none that I can see from here. I wonder how Coco's night is going.

"Abby."

The tiny hairs on the back of my neck stand on end. I spin around to find Richard sitting in the center of the sectional, his long legs crossed ankle over knee. For once, he's not dressed for a videoconference, looking casual in joggers and a simple white T-shirt. He's as handsome as I've ever seen him.

Somehow, I find my voice. "Richard, hi. I didn't realize you'd be out here. Sorry to interrupt."

"You're not interrupting." He gestures to a book in his hand, his index finger holding his place between the pages. "I couldn't sleep, so I decided to sit outside and read for a bit. Please, join me."

I take a seat on the opposite end of the sectional, eyeing the cover of his book. "What're you reading?"

"A fantasy novel. Ordinary people discovering powers they didn't know they had and doing extraordinary things with them. I think this is the fourth time I've read it."

"Must be a really good book."

"It is. Mostly it's a good form of escape. No better way to get my mind off the stress of real life than escaping into a world of make believe." He sets the book on the table beside him and asks, "What are you doing up so late?"

"I actually fell asleep early and just woke up. I was supposed to go out with Coco tonight, but I was so zonked that I didn't hear her knocking on my door."

"All the excitement we had in Cala Varques really tired you out, huh?" Richard sits forward, uncrossing his legs and resting his elbows on his knees. There's this little half smile on his face, and his curly hair's all ruffled. I wish I could reach out and run my hand through it.

"Yeah. Thank you for convincing me to jump off that cliff."

"I didn't convince you of anything. You convinced yourself."

I suppose that's true. "Well then, thank you for encouraging me. I think it's safe to say my fear of heights has been properly conquered."

"Good. Then you can come with us on our hot-air balloon ride."

His half smile swells to a full-blown grin. The idea of flying high above the Mediterranean with Richard Vale is like something out of a fairy tale. So beautiful, so romantic. So not what I'm here for.

I deflect. "Bijou had a good time today, didn't she?"

"Oh yeah. I don't think I've ever seen her laugh like that. So technically, I should be the one thanking you. I never would've thought to bring her somewhere off the beaten path if it wasn't for your advice."

"It was off the beaten path, all right. I have to admit, there were a couple of times when I wasn't sure we were going to make it out alive. Like when we had to climb through that broken brick wall?"

"That was exciting, wasn't it? I'm so used to going to these exclusive, private spaces where everything is so curated and safe and sterile. Walking down that torn-up path to the beach was invigorating. It made me feel alive. I've already asked Coco to book another tour for tomorrow. We're going kayaking up north, near the mountains. Another off-the-beaten-path situation."

"Oh, I love kayaking. I haven't done that since I was a kid."

"With your father?"

"Yeah. He had one of those two-person kayaks, and we took it out every summer, to Lake Placid and Taylor Pond. It took me a while to get the hang of paddling in tandem, but Dad was always so patient with me, no matter how many times I sent us spinning around in circles."

"Do you two still spend a lot of time together?" Richard asks.

I shift in my seat, scratch a nonexistent itch on the back of my neck. "He died, actually. When I was in high school."

"Oh." His mouth drops open; his eyes soften. "I'm so sorry."

"Don't be. I was lucky to have the time I did with him."

"It must've been wonderful to have such a close relationship with your father."

I nod. "He was so fun. So smart. Just the best dad ever."

His gaze is compassionate as he allows space for reverent silence. Then he says, "I want to be that kind of father to Bijou."

"There's no reason you can't be."

"Sometimes I feel like I've screwed things up irreparably between us."

"That can't be true. I saw the joy on her face today. She loves being with you."

"I'm not so sure about that." He takes a deep breath, blows it out slowly. "Back in New York, she barely comes over to see me anymore, even on the days when she's technically supposed to."

"Is that legal? I mean, don't you have a custody arrangement with Veronica?"

"Yes, but if Bijou doesn't want to spend time with me, I'm not going to force her to. And I can't blame her, honestly. I think she's lost faith in me. Up until about six months ago, I was working eighteen-to twenty-hour days, traveling nonstop, always on the phone. I kept rearranging our visitation schedule at the last minute to accommodate my business trips, and if I couldn't, I'd end up leaving her with Coco, which nobody was very happy about. Eventually, Veronica threatened to bring me to court, and I didn't want to drag Bijou through that whole mess. The tabloids would've had a field day, and they can say what they want about me, I don't care. But to involve my daughter . . . that's another story.

"Anyway, that's when I started to change. I cut the travel way back and implemented some strict *Do Not Disturb* hours to coincide with Bijou's visits, but by then I think the damage was done."

This provides a bit more context for what Coco told me. Veronica isn't some evil woman who's pointlessly giving her ex-husband a hard time; she's a mother who wants to provide stability for her daughter. And if Richard's really serious about improving his relationship with Bijou, there's a lot more he could do. Like implementing those *Do Not Disturb* hours on this trip.

"Well, is there any way you can take off of work this summer? If you give her your complete and total focus, maybe you can turn things around."

"I'd been hoping to do exactly that. When Veronica said she needed me to take Bijou for six weeks, I immediately put everything else on hold. Told my staff I'd be unavailable, worked up contingency plans. I was all set. Then we got this last-minute once-in-a-lifetime opportunity to invest in an incredible new technology that's going to change the world for the better, and I couldn't say no. But that means I have to work. My team needs my input, my leadership. I can't hang them out to dry."

He rakes his hand through his thick curls and stares vacantly out at the coastline. I recognize the specific sort of torment in his eyes. It's the realization that your life is spinning out of control.

But it's not like he's some grad student who's had her research stolen out from under her nose. He's the one with the power in this situation. The company is called *Vale* Venture Capital, for crying out loud. Not to mention, he's a billionaire. He can choose his own path forward.

"Bijou is a once-in-a-lifetime opportunity, too," I say. He narrows his eyes, like he doesn't quite get it, so I keep pushing on. "She'll only ever be twelve years old once, right? And the older she gets, the harder it's going to be to forge a relationship with her. If you want things to be different, you'll have to act differently."

"It's not that simple."

"Isn't it, though? The most important thing my father ever did for me was make me feel like I mattered to him. He had so many priorities competing for his attention, but I was always his number one priority.

The choice is clear: prioritize the deal, or prioritize your daughter. It's up to you to decide which one is more important to you."

"My daughter is more important to me," he says without hesitation. "She's more important than anything."

"Then she needs to know that. Because right now, I don't think she does."

He swallows hard, and the crestfallen look on his face makes me wish I could take that last sentence back. In fact, this whole conversation suddenly seems totally inappropriate. Who am I to be giving Richard Vale advice on how to parent his daughter? Once again, I've overstepped my boundaries. I've been having a hard time with that lately.

In an instant, I'm on my feet. "I should get back to bed."

"Oh. Okay." He clears his throat, like he does whenever he's flustered. "Well, thank you for your insight. I appreciate it."

"No problem. I'm happy to help."

As I'm walking away, he calls after me, "Would you like to come kayaking with us tomorrow? Or, I guess, later today. The car will be here at nine."

I freeze in place, my hand gripping the doorknob. Kayaking in the northern mountains of Mallorca sounds like an incredible adventure, one I don't want to miss out on. But now that I know exactly how strained Richard and Bijou's relationship has been, it's clear that I shouldn't tag along. They need time alone to bond, and Bijou needs the full force of his attention. I'd be a distraction from what's really important.

"I can't," I say, turning around. "I promised Coco I'd go sightseeing with her."

"Coco wants to go sightseeing?" He furrows his brow. "I'm surprised. That's usually not her thing."

"Sightseeing on a beach. With a drink in her hand. You know how she is." I smile brightly, hoping to distract from how flagrantly I'm lying. "I'm sorry."

"Don't worry about it," he says, waving it off like it's no big deal. "I'm sure you'll both have a great time."

He says, "Good night," but I'm already headed into the cabin, holding my breath while I speed walk to my stateroom. When I'm safely inside, I lock the door and draw the curtains, then close my eyes and silently remind myself why I'm here with these people on this yacht: to tutor math. I'm not a shrink or a confidante. I'm not even a friend. I'm merely an employee. The help.

So I'm going to put in my four hours of work, five days a week, then I'll go off and do my own thing—away from the Vales. It's time to put my boundaries firmly back in place.

CHAPTER NINE

Sleep is impossible. My mind's whirring, replaying my conversation with Richard over and over again. Memories of kayaking on Lake Placid fade into freeze-frames of Cala Varques. I hear the white noise of the water all around me, the weightless sensation making me feel like I could float right off the bed. Tabloid headlines flash behind my closed eyes, followed by images of Richard with his rumpled hair and his half smile. His bare muscular chest. His dark-brown eyes searing through me. His fingertips stroking my skin.

This is bad. I should absolutely *not* have a crush on my boss. Then again, it's not something I can simply turn off, like a light switch. Feelings are hard to control. The heart wants what it wants—isn't that the saying?

What I can do is keep my distance. The less time I spend around him, the weaker my feelings for him will be, and eventually I'll stop feeling anything at all. At least that's how I'm hoping it'll all go down.

When first light dawns over the harbor, before anyone else is awake, I hop out of bed and run straight off the yacht. I find an adorable café tucked away in an alley, where I stop for a breakfast of ensaïmadas, Mallorcan pastries filled with custard and topped with apricots. Then I wander the streets of Palma without a plan.

It's amazing what wonders you discover when you don't know what you're looking for. The architecture in this city dates back hundreds of years. Gothic mansions with mullioned windows and haunting gargoyles. Courtyards lush with plants and vines that snake up sweeping staircases. French doors with colorful shutters that open onto wrought iron balconies four stories high. I get lost for hours roaming the maze of streets, ducking into art galleries and shopping for handmade trinkets at local boutiques.

I have gelato for lunch because I'm an adult who can make her own decisions. A double scoop of dulce de leche topped with whipped cream, almonds, and an inverted sugar cone, which I eat in a cobblestoned square, sitting on a bench beneath the shade of a fig tree. It's the sweetest, most picturesque lunch I've ever had.

Bijou would love this. I wonder if Richard's getting her gelato today after they go kayaking. I hope he isn't wearing his smartwatch again.

Enough! I need to stop thinking about the Vales. I'm off duty, for crying out loud. I toss my empty gelato cup in the nearest trash bin and set off to continue exploring. I stroll through a sculpture garden and tour a royal palace. I sample Spanish ham and cheese at the Mercat de l'Olivar. I learn all about the history of Mallorca at the local museum. I enjoy a lovely dinner of grilled fish and white wine at a restaurant on Passeig del Born. Whenever I find myself wondering what Richard is doing, I chase the thought away, forcing myself to focus on whatever is directly in front of me: a meal, a painting, a palm tree. Eventually, the thoughts taper off.

By the time the sun starts to set, my feet are throbbing from all the miles I've walked. As I board the yacht, Bijou's lilting voice echoes out from the open saloon window. From this vantage point, I can see her sitting on a couch next to Richard. They're playing some sort of fast-paced game, slapping cards on the coffee table and laughing. Looks like fun.

I duck out of sight and take the long way around the ship to get to my stateroom. It's not that late, only about eight o'clock, but seeing as I've been awake since one in the morning, I'm ready to call it a night. After washing up and changing into my pajamas, I finally snuggle up in bed with my Kindle, hoping this next article will spark an idea for a new research topic.

The screen lights up to reveal the title: "A New Phase for Superfluid Helium."

I cannot think of anything I want to read less.

You know, maybe I'm putting too much pressure on myself. Maybe if I stop reading these articles and let the default-mode network of my brain take over for a little while, the perfect idea will just come to me, like magic. That's supposed to be why I'm taking this trip, anyway. To hit the reset button and step away from it all.

I close down the article and scroll through my digital library for something fun and escapist to read. Unfortunately, all I can find is serious scientific stuff: textbooks, journals, scholarly papers. When was the last time I read anything that wasn't assigned by a professor or required for my research? I'll bet it's been years.

With two taps, I connect to Wi-Fi, where the internet abounds with reading material meant purely for entertainment purposes. I scroll through and download at least a dozen novels in a variety of genres— sci-fi, mystery, romance—anything that looks the slightest bit escapist and enjoyable. Then I pick one at random, and I start to read.

Instantly, I'm sucked into the story. It's historical fiction set in Europe during World War II, all about strong, smart, badass women who spied for the French Resistance against the Nazis. These women had a passion and a purpose. They always stood up for what was right, even if it put their lives in danger.

I'm halfway through chapter 15 when my phone buzzes. It's a text from Mom: Can we talk?

Ugh. I do *not* want to leave my World War II fantasy world to have a frustrating conversation with my mother. Ever since I left New York, we've been communicating solely by text. In my opinion, it's been perfect, because rather than getting into another squabble, I can simply ignore annoying questions like "Have you heard anything else from Philip?" or "Do you think you're going to appeal to the dean?"

I can't very well ignore *this* question, though, and I feel bad telling her no. What if it's important?

She answers the video chat on the first ring. I can't tell if she's sullen or worried, but either way, the frown on her face is unmistakable. "How's Barcelona?"

"I'm in Mallorca now. And it's amazing."

"How long is this trip again?"

"Five more weeks."

Mom purses her lips, and an uncomfortable silence ensues. I can feel her judgment resonating from four thousand miles away.

"Did you want to talk about something, Mom? Because I was just getting ready to go to sleep."

"Yes." She takes a deep breath. "I wanted to apologize for insinuating that you were being a doormat. You are smart and self-assured, and I am proud of you for everything you've accomplished so far."

I take note of the date and time: July 10, 10:42 p.m. The first time my mother has apologized to me in my entire adult life. "Thank you, Mom. I—"

"I'm not done." Of course she isn't. How could she offer an apology without a caveat? "I didn't mean to insult you. I'm simply concerned about your future."

"Obviously, I'm concerned about my future, too."

"Then why did you run away?"

This again. "I didn't run away! I took a job—a *temporary* job."

"And you couldn't find a tutoring job at home in New York?"

"Not one that pays this well." At least, not that I'm aware of. It didn't occur to me to ask Dianne. Once she offered up this opportunity, I jumped on it without thinking twice. "Besides, I told you, I wanted to take some time before I figure out whether to go to the dean."

"Time isn't on your side here, Abigail. You have to strike when the iron is hot."

"It's been one week, Mom. And there's no statute of limitations on academic theft, anyway." I found out that little tidbit during my panicked airplane googling.

"No, but the longer you wait, the less credibility you'll have. Meanwhile, Nick will go around using your research to apply for grants or get published—"

"He already published it, Mom. And he left my name off the byline."

"Well, have you contacted the publication to tell them it's your work?"

"I can't go straight to an international science journal without the backing of the university. I'm just a graduate student; why would they believe me? It's like you have no idea how academia works."

She flinches, and her frown takes on a distinctively sad quality. "You're right. I don't. Academia was your father's domain, not mine. I was just trying to be helpful."

Now I feel bad. Mom's always been self-conscious of the fact that she never went to college. Regardless, she's done quite well for herself as a real estate agent; she's been one of the top earners in the greater Rochester area for the past fifteen consecutive years. Her work ethic is unsurpassed, and I know that's why she has such high standards for me. She knows how to push all my buttons, but she never has anything but good intentions. "I appreciate that, but there's really nothing you can do."

She runs her hand through her hair and smooths it back down into her familiar shoulder-length bob. She's had the same hairstyle since I was in grade school. There's a lot more gray than there used to be, though.

"I can't believe not a single person is standing up for you. Not even your lab mates? Surely, they must have been aware of what happened."

"They know, but they said they didn't want to get involved."

She makes a sound of disgust. "How repugnant."

"I can't blame them for not wanting to be associated with me. Filing this grievance didn't exactly help my reputation in the department. I feel like everyone sees me as the troublemaker now."

"Better a troublemaker than a doormat."

Is it, though? Before this whole disaster happened, my lab mates and I got along really well. We weren't best friends or anything, but we talked every day, followed each other on social media, and enjoyed our Friday-night hangouts at the beer garden. Once I filed the grievance, things changed. The mail room chitchat tapered off, and my texts went unanswered. It's been over a week since I've been on campus, and no one has checked in to see where I am or how I'm doing. Not a single one of them has liked any of my undeniably breathtaking #travelgram posts, which is frankly just rude. And the only email I've received in my school inbox is the weekly newsletter from Philip, which he sends to the entire department. It's like my absence has gone completely unnoticed. Or worse yet, it's been welcomed.

"Maybe I should just give up."

Her eyes go wide. "Nonsense. You are not a quitter, and you cannot let this keep you from achieving your goals."

"But I'm so unhappy."

"Of course you are; you've been betrayed by your mentor."

"It's more than that. I've been unhappy for a while—I just didn't realize it until I came here." I gaze out the window at the twinkling lights of Mallorca. A week ago, I barely knew this island existed. Now I can navigate the streets of Palma without a map. "I can't explain how much fun I'm having, Mom. There's so much to explore, so many adventures to have. Yesterday, I jumped off a cliff."

"I thought you were afraid of heights."

"Not anymore. I just closed my eyes, and I went for it, and then I suddenly couldn't get enough. Now I'm wondering what I was so afraid of all this time. And what else am I missing out on? There's a whole huge world out here, and I've been spending my life cooped up in a lab with a bunch of people who have no problem throwing me under the bus to protect their own reputations."

"Abigail, you will find that everywhere you go. In work, in school, in life—there will always be people who try to tear you down. The only person you can rely on is yourself."

Funny, I didn't feel that way yesterday. When my body was trembling with fear, it was Richard's supportive hands that steadied me, his encouraging words that inspired me to take the leap. If I'd relied on myself, I would've slid back down that pebbly path without ever knowing what it feels like to fly.

"I've never felt this happy before."

"Of course you're happy—you're on vacation."

"No, I'm not; I'm working."

She snickers. "Well, it sounds like a pretty cush gig to me. Look, tutoring is a great part-time job to earn extra money, but it's hardly a career. And you can't keep traveling like this forever."

Technically, I could. Dianne told me she had a whole team of tutors on her roster who did nothing but travel the world with her wealthiest clients. Some of them even supplied full-time homeschooling services. When this summer is over, I could easily hop aboard another yacht. Teach chemistry in the Caribbean or coding in Dubai. I'd make great money, have amazing experiences, and never see Nick or Philip again.

But then it would no longer be a temporary summer job. Then I'd really be running away. It's scary how appealing that sounds.

"It's getting late here, Mom. I should go."

"Okay. Keep in touch. I love you."

"I love you, too."

The moment the call ends, I feel a palpable sense of relief. Talking to my mother is exhausting, because I'm always on the defense. She loves to poke holes in my arguments and challenge my assertions. It's particularly frustrating when she's right. And I think she might be right about one thing.

See, I keep saying this summer is about "stepping away from it all," but what's the difference between stepping away and running away? It's only a matter of semantics. The truth is, I accepted this job because I didn't want to deal with the problems I had in New York. Instead of sticking around and fighting for what's right, I'm hiding out on a luxury yacht, disappearing into novels and lusting after Richard. This crush I have on him? Now I know it isn't real. It's a form of escapist fiction where the main characters are me and my billionaire boss.

If I'm fantasizing about him, then I don't have to think about reality. If I'm enjoying a novel, then I don't have to read a science paper. And if I'm jumping off a cliff, then I don't have to worry about how to handle this horrible mess that's waiting for me back home.

Mom's right, I can't do this forever. Not because it's not possible, but because I refuse to give up. I'm not a quitter.

I set my phone back on the nightstand and pick up my Kindle. I know I should read that article on superfluid helium, but I really want to find out what happens next in this spy story. It's not necessarily the smart thing to do, but I dive back into chapter 15, anyway.

To be clear: This doesn't mean I'm giving up. It means I'm taking a break. In five weeks, it's back to reality. For now, I just want to be happy.

CHAPTER TEN

I stay up until two o'clock reading. The book is so good I can't put it down until I'm done. In the end, the strong, smart, badass women win, which is so satisfying that it's worth being a little tired for my morning session with Bijou. I'm in the office setting up our workspace when she comes bounding in, all smiles.

"Hey there," I say. "You're in a good mood. Excited about tackling our math problems today?"

She playfully rolls her eyes. "Can't wait."

"How was your day yesterday? Did you have fun kayaking?"

"So much fun. At first, I had a hard time steering, but Leo helped me out. And I only tipped over once. Dad didn't tip over at all. He's really good at kayaking, I was surprised. My arms got so tired toward the end, but Dad just kept paddling and paddling like it was nothing."

Given how ripped he is, I'm not surprised at all. It's easy to envision his muscles pulsing with each stroke of the oar, his tan skin glistening under the sun. "That's . . . that's awesome."

"We're going to a sea cave this afternoon. It's, like, a boat ride on an underground lake. Doesn't that sound cool?"

"Really cool." There is a teensy-weensy part of me that's feeling kind of sad and left out, especially when I think about all the fun the three of us had together at Cala Varques. But I remind myself: boundaries! I can always visit that sea cave later on, by myself.

"Let's get to work," I say, because that's the whole reason I'm here.

We're halfway through our first problem set when Richard peeks in the window. My spine goes stiff, preparing for the inevitable snide remark from Bijou. But when she notices him standing there, she gives a casual wave and a smile, which he returns just as casually. Then he strolls away with his hands in his pockets, and Bijou doesn't make a single comment about how embarrassing or annoying he is. She simply turns her attention back to her equations.

Maybe they're getting along better now. I'm about to ask her, but I catch myself at the last second. Boundaries!

At the end of our session, Bijou bounces out of the office. I stay behind to tidy up, and as I'm leaving, I spy her stepping off the yacht, hand in hand with Richard. They're probably heading out to the caves now. Likely stopping for lunch first. That's nice. I'm glad they're having a good time together and I am not experiencing FOMO at all.

Why would I, when I've got exciting plans of my own? This afternoon, I'm doing a self-guided audio tour of Bellver Castle. It's not as adventurous as, say, a boat ride on an underground lake, but it's interesting in its own way. I have to hike for a while up a very steep hill to get there, but once I do, it's worth it for the 360-degree views of the island. All rolling green mountains and expansive blue sea. The castle itself is impressive, as well, with three huge towers full of artifacts to explore.

I'm there well into the early evening, at which point I trek back down the hill and grab some dinner in town at a quaint little pizza shop. Later that night, I cuddle up in bed with another novel; this time, it's a sci-fi romance about a hunky, horny alien and the woman who loves it. I know it sounds bonkers, but there's something deeply touching about two beings from such disparate worlds who forge this loving and lasting connection.

The rest of the week follows the same sort of pattern: tutor in the morning, sightsee in the afternoon, read another book until I fall asleep. I barely see Coco at all; when she's not working for Richard, she's ironing out the kinks in a short story she wants to submit to a literary journal. So mostly, I keep to myself.

By Friday, Bijou can successfully solve *and* graph single-variable inequalities. I've seen a lot more of the island, touring a traditional fishing village and taking a sunset catamaran cruise along the coast. I've also read a young adult thriller and a sequel to that sci-fi romance that takes place on a different planet with equally hunky, horny aliens. All this escapist fiction has been a refreshing change from my usual regimen of dry, dull academic publications.

On Saturday, I decide to explore those sea caves Bijou was talking about. There are a ton of them all over Mallorca, but I'm really excited to check out the Cuevas del Drach, which is one of the largest underground lakes in the world. That morning, as I step out of my stateroom, Coco opens her door across the hall at the same exact time.

"Hey! Long time no see," I say.

"Yeah, I've been drowning under this deadline but I just turned it in last night. Wanna hang out today? We can celebrate, kick back on the beach with a few drinks."

On the one hand, I've been looking forward to this sea cave excursion for a few days now. On the other hand, I'm starting to feel really lonely again. I suppose the sea caves can wait until tomorrow. "Let's do it."

Mallorca is teeming with beaches, each one more beautiful than the next, but Coco insists on going to this one specific beach in Magaluf, a resort town twenty minutes from the marina. She orders a car care of Richard and, after grabbing two iced coffees to go, we climb into the back seat together.

"What have you been up to all week?" she asks. "Aside from tutoring Bijou, of course."

"Sightseeing. I did a walking tour of Old Town, went to Bellver Castle, did a sunset cruise. I still want to go to the sea caves, but I think I'll do that tomorrow."

"We're leaving for Saint-Tropez tomorrow."

"Oh. Bummer." I guess I'll never see them now.

"What have you been doing at night? Did you hit up any clubs?"

"No." I've been spending my evenings reading in bed. Now that I know we're moving on from Mallorca, though, it feels like I wasted my time. I should've been reveling in the moment, soaking up the scenery. This summer is flying by. Only four more weeks before I'm headed home, and then what?

Coco rests her hand on my knee. "You look upset. Everything okay?"

"Yeah. I've just been thinking." I take a long sip from my iced coffee, while Coco waits patiently for me to continue.

When I don't, she asks, "Is this about the drama back home? Because I thought you were ignoring that."

"I am, for now. But that's only delaying the inevitable. Eventually I'm gonna have to go back to school and face it."

"Not if you quit."

"Quit grad school? No. I'm not a quitter."

"There's no shame in being a quitter. I quit things all the time, especially if they make me unhappy. Lord knows I should've quit grad school. And this is the first job I've stayed at for longer than three months. My motto is: if it doesn't serve you, let it go."

"Grad school is serving me." Could I sound any less convincing? "Besides, I don't even know what else I'd do."

"Didn't I tell you anything's possible?" Her smile is sweet, but her words don't resonate quite as strongly as they did when I was full of vodka tonics.

"For as long as I can remember, my whole identity's been wrapped up in going to school. I'm not sure I'm good at anything except being a student."

"That's bullshit," she says. "Because I know for a fact you're an incredible teacher. Bijou is thriving under your instruction."

"She *is* doing really well." It's been fun working with her, too. Honestly, it's always fun working with the kids I tutor. There's nothing more satisfying than seeing the looks on their faces when they finally understand a complicated concept. It's the light bulb moment, when everything clicks. I feel the same way about my undergrad classes. Come to think of it, my course evaluation forms always feature glowing reviews. "You're right. I am a good teacher."

"Richard agrees, too," she says. "He was gushing to me yesterday about what a good influence you've been on Bijou. Even her attitude toward him has shifted since you started working with her."

"Gushing, huh?"

"Mm-hmm." She waggles her eyebrows at me. "He's very impressed with you."

"Good to know." I turn toward the window so Coco can't see what I'm certain is a goofy smile. I'm sure she means that Richard is impressed with my professionalism and my technical skills, but I allow myself to believe it's more than that. Like he's not just impressed with Abby the Tutor. He's also impressed with Abby the Cliff Jumper and Abby the Conversationalist. That he sees me for who I am, and he likes every bit of it.

Soon we arrive in Magaluf, where our driver drops us off in front of a boxy brown building sandwiched by two high-rises. In the narrow space between them, I spy a sliver of sea. The beach must be on the other side.

Except Coco walks up to the boxy brown building, and as soon as she utters the word *Vale* to the beefcake who's guarding the door, I understand why she was so intent on coming to this specific location. This isn't just a beach. It's a beach club. And naturally, we're VIPs.

We're led through an indoor bar area and out the wide back doors, which open onto an expansive patio. It's barely noon, but you wouldn't know it out here, where people are grinding on the dance floor to pulse-pounding EDM. Down a short flight of stairs is a long, narrow pool flanked by three tiers of lounge chairs and daybeds. A few club-goers sit along the edge dangling their feet in. Others lie beneath open umbrellas, sipping cocktails and chatting.

We stroll past them, toward a roped-off private space directly on the beach with unobstructed views of the water. The host waves us in and asks what we'd like to drink.

"Let's do champagne today," Coco says. "I'm in a celebratory mood."

"Sounds perfect." I set my beach bag on a daybed and collapse onto one of our personal pristine white couches. The sky is pastel blue and cloudless except for a few wisps of white near the horizon. There's a small island not too far off the coast that seems to be uninhabited. I bet it'd be fun to kayak out there and take a look around.

"What are Bijou and Richard up to today?" I ask.

"Horseback riding in the forest. Followed by a hot-air balloon flight over the mountains."

"Wow." I swallow against the bubble of envy forming in my chest. After all, I'm very happy to be here with Coco. This beach, this club, this experience: it's unparalleled. But what must it feel like to get a bird's-eye view of Mallorca? "I've always wanted to ride in a hot-air balloon."

"If I knew that, I would've arranged for you to join them. After the excuse you gave Richard last weekend, I assumed you wouldn't want to." She gives a little laugh. "He asked me how our day at the beach was, and I had no clue what he was talking about. It took me a minute to realize you made up fake plans with me to get out of hanging out with them."

"He knows I lied?" Not that I did such a great job of concocting that sightseeing story, but I don't want him to think I'm a liar.

"No, I don't think so. Once I caught on, I told him we had a great time at the public beach in Palmanova, but it was too crowded. That's when he hooked me up with this." She gestures around to our very private, very uncrowded VIP area.

"Thanks for covering for me. I like hanging out with them a lot, I just needed to establish some boundaries."

"Trust me, I get it. You should've seen the look on his face, though. Like a sad little puppy dog." She sticks out her lower lip and bats her eyelashes.

"Why?"

"He was clearly disappointed that you bailed." With a mischievous smile, she adds, "I think he's got a thing for you."

"Shut up." My cheeks are hotter than the sun. I toss a throw pillow at her so she can't see me blushing, and she bats it away with one hand.

"Seriously! He's always talking about Abby this and Abby that. How smart and kind and clever you are."

"Really?"

"Really." She studies my face, which must be beet red by now. "You've got a thing for him, too, don't you?"

"No. Not at *all*." I've allowed myself to indulge this silly fantasy in my head, but I will never admit it out loud. This *thing* I have for him isn't real, anyway. It's just a convenient distraction. I even force a dramatic shudder to emphasize exactly how *not* attracted to him I am.

"Oh." She sounds disappointed. "Well, don't worry. If he really does have a thing for you, he'd never act on it."

"Why not?" Now I sound disappointed. "I mean, does he have a girlfriend or something?"

"Nope. He doesn't even date. And I run his calendar, so I always know what he's up to. He's so hyperfocused on his work he doesn't have time to maintain a relationship. I doubt he's been out with a woman since he got divorced."

"That's not what the tabloids say."

Her perfectly sculpted eyebrows pinch together. "You don't actually believe any of that bullshit, do you?"

"No, of course not." Not when she's looking at me like that, anyway. "But if it's not true, where do the stories all come from?"

"I don't know for sure, but I've got some ideas."

A server approaches with our champagne, which he presents to us with a flourish before popping the cork and pouring it into two slender flutes. He rests the bottle in a bucket of ice, and as he walks away, Coco lifts her glass. "Let's forget about Richard and toast to us."

"To submitting your story," I say.

"To starting a new one."

"To VIP treatment."

"To our last day in Mallorca."

We clink our glasses and take long, luxurious sips. It tastes like a bit of fizzy heaven, delicious and decadent. I sink back into the couch and rest my feet up on the ottoman, watching the waves gently crest and collapse against the sand.

"How does it feel to be done with your story?" I ask.

"It feels good to have submitted it," she says, "but I don't know if it's really 'done.' I've been rewriting this one for a year and a half now. If it's accepted, I'm sure I'll be asked to make changes before they publish it. If it's rejected, I might do another rewrite."

"That sounds like hard work. Have you ever been published before?"

She nods and takes another sip. "In a few literary magazines. They're all indie, kind of obscure."

"What's your main goal as a writer?"

"What do you mean?"

"Like, are you working on a novel? Or are you trying to get published in a major magazine, like the *New Yorker*?"

"Nah, I don't have a goal like that. I just write the stories I want to write. Hopefully one day something hits big. Until then, working for Richard pays the bills."

She lifts her flute in another toast, then drains her glass. I envy Coco's take-it-as-it-comes attitude. She certainly seems content living in the day-to-day, doing the thing that makes her happy without worrying about achieving some lofty long-term goal. Kinda makes me wanna be a quitter.

The server pours us another round of champagne, and by now I'm starting to feel it. There's a buzzing sensation in my chest, and my fingertips are all tingly. My head bobs in time to the beat of the music. More people have gathered in the pool, swimming and dancing and splashing around.

I turn to Coco, who's reclining on the daybed with her eyes closed. "Wanna go in the pool?"

She answers without opening her eyes. "Maybe in a little while. Right now, I wanna chill. The sun feels good on my skin."

It does, but it also feels hot, and that cool turquoise water is calling my name. I navigate around the velvet rope and descend to the pool deck, weaving through the crowd with a rhythm to my step. I am so ready to dive in, but as soon as I get to the edge of the water, people are leaping out of the pool, screeching and abandoning their drinks. The beach club staff immediately starts herding us away from the chaos. I'm so caught off guard that I lose my balance and stumble backward.

Fortunately, the guy behind me breaks my fall. He grabs my arms to steady me and asks, "Are you okay?"

"Yeah, thanks." He's got an accent of some kind, I think Australian, though I have a hard time distinguishing Aussies from Kiwis. As I regain my footing, I realize he's cute, too. Tall and sort of lanky, with shaggy blond hair and a tattoo of a tall ship on his upper arm. Not my usual type, but not bad, either. "Do you know what's going on?"

"Some guy spewed in the pool."

"He what?"

"He threw up." He points to a man sitting on a lounge chair with his head in his hands. There's a bunched-up towel at his feet, and a group of women is loudly booing him.

"Gross."

"Yep. Now they're shutting the pool down for cleaning."

Another chorus of boos erupts from the crowd, followed by what I'm assuming are swear words in a variety of languages. The staff escorts our queasy hero inside, away from the angry mob, and I find myself face-to-face with the Australian. Or possible Kiwi.

"Now what?" I ask.

"Well, this *is* a beach club. There's a whole sea to swim in over there. I'm Brent, by the way."

"Abby."

"Nice to meet you, Abby. Wanna walk down to the shore?"

"Let's do it."

We push through the crowd, away from the pool and onto the beach. The sand is hot on the soles of my feet, but it cools off as we approach the water. Gentle waves lap the tips of my toes and splash against my ankles. We wade in until we're waist deep, then crouch down so it looks like we're a couple of floating heads.

"So," Brent says, "what brings you to Mallorca? Are you here on holiday?"

"Working holiday. I'm a private tutor."

"Teaching English to the locals?"

"No, math. And I'm working for an American family. We're sailing around the Mediterranean for six weeks."

"What, like, on one of those big yachts in the marina?"

Technically, we're on the *biggest* yacht in the marina. "Yeah."

"Is your boss a millionaire?"

Technically, a billionaire. "You could say he's well off."

"What's your next stop?"

"Saint-Tropez. We're leaving tomorrow."

"Funny, I thought for sure it'd have been the moon." I must look as confused as I feel because he follows up with "It's a joke. Since rich people are always flying into space."

"Oh. Right." It wasn't a very funny joke. I actually find it kind of offensive. Maybe because I don't think about Richard as that kind of billionaire. "My boss is a good guy."

"He owns a yacht," he says with a snicker. "No one gets that rich by being a good guy."

"He doesn't own it; he's renting." As the words pass my lips, I realize how ridiculous they sound. Does it matter whether he owns or rents? Either way, he surely paid an astronomical amount of money for these six weeks at sea. I'm not even sure how he's made all his money; it could've been by nefarious means. So why the hell am I trying to defend him?

Time to change the subject. "What about you? What are you doing in Mallorca?"

"I'm with friends on holiday. Not a working holiday, though."

I almost ask him what he does for a living. It's a natural next question in a conversation like this, where you're getting to know someone new. Then I think: Who cares? I'll never see this guy again, and there are a million other things to talk about. So I ask him what he's done so far in Mallorca.

"The usual. Toured Old Town, laid on the beach a whole bunch, saw the sea caves."

"Oh, man, I wanted to visit the sea caves, but I never got the chance."

"That's a shame, they're impressive. We can go now, if you want."

"You mean, *now* now? Like, leave the club?"

"Sure, why not? Unless you want to stay and swim in the vomit-pool."

It's a tempting offer, but I'm not about to abandon Coco, and I'm absolutely sure sea caving isn't her thing. "I can't."

"Fair enough," he says but doesn't press me for an explanation.

We float around for a while, talking about our respective European itineraries. He's in the middle of a four-week sojourn that started in

London, and it turns out we were both in Barcelona at the same time. After this he's headed to Rome to visit a friend, and he'll end his trip in Paris, which admittedly makes me envious.

We talk about other stuff, too. I tell him I live in Queens, which leads to a minor geography lesson about the five boroughs and the state of New York. He tells me he's twenty-five and lives in Sydney and that his tall ship tattoo was an impulse decision made when he was seventeen, but he just hasn't gotten around to covering it up yet.

By the time we wade back to dry land, I'm completely sober. I also still have no idea what he does for a living. He may not even have a job. Who cares?

Coco's standing on the sand about fifty yards away, shielding her eyes from the sun, staring out at the water. I wave my hands in the air and yell her name, jogging toward her with Brent on my heels.

"There you are," she says, then quickly sizes up Brent from head to toe. "Who are you?"

"I'm Brent."

"Hi, Brent." She offers a polite grin before turning to me. "They shut the pool down. I think someone threw up in it."

"Yeah, that's why we came out to swim in the sea," I say.

"Do you wanna go somewhere else? There's a beach club in Llucmajor that's supposed to be really classy."

"Sure."

"Great, I'll go call a car." With a nod toward Brent, she says, "Nice to meet you," even though they didn't really meet at all.

She strolls away, and I turn to face Brent, who's shifting his weight from foot to foot. "You said you're leaving Mallorca tomorrow?"

"I am."

"I guess this is it, then."

"I guess so."

He looks sort of sad, chewing his lower lip. I consider inviting him to this other club we're going to, then think better of it. Coco didn't seem too keen on having him around. Plus, I've enjoyed talking to him, but I'm absolutely fine with the fact that I'm never going to see him again.

Brent, however, feels differently. "I'd really like to see you again. I'm going to watch the sunset in Palma tonight. There's this lovely little bar on the water, very relaxed vibe. I can't remember the name of it now, but it's right at the west entrance of Can Pere Antoni beach. I'd love it if you joined me."

His smile is so earnest. He's got beautiful blue eyes. He's been kind and courteous and sweet as an ensaïmada. But there is not a single spark flying. The space between us? Completely sparkless.

On the other hand, who's to say that sparks couldn't develop? Especially during a romantic date at sunset, with the sky glowing and the wine flowing. Maybe he and I will have an extraordinary night that will fuel my fantasies for the rest of the summer. And if I'm distracted with thoughts of Brent, that might put an end to this ridiculous crush I have on Richard. Don't they say the best way to get your mind off a man is another man?

"Sure," I say, even though I'm still not so sure. Then I wave goodbye and walk away without looking back.

CHAPTER ELEVEN

In Mallorca, the summer sun doesn't set until nine o'clock, which gives me plenty of time to decide what to do tonight. In the meanwhile, Coco and I go to Llucmajor, where the beach club is indeed a lot classier. It's also a lot less crowded, so even though we have a VIP space all to ourselves, it feels almost superfluous. I spend the rest of my afternoon napping, sipping cucumber water, and swimming in a crystalline, vomit-free pool.

At six o'clock, we pack up our stuff and call it a day. On the drive back to the yacht, my stomach starts doing somersaults. At first, I think it's from all the sunshine and champagne I've indulged in today, but it's less a queasy feeling than a nervous one. I keep thinking back to my conversation with Coco, how she said Richard might have a *thing* for me. I'm flattered, but flustered. How do I even act around him now? Probably best to continue avoiding him, like I've been doing all week.

It's eerily quiet when we arrive. Coco says Bijou and Richard aren't due back until eight o'clock, and the yacht crew is off for the evening, so I head to the kitchen to scrounge around in the fridge for leftovers. Then I shower and change, do my hair, swipe on lip gloss. I'm all ready to meet Brent now. Guess it's time to go. Might as well get it over with.

I should feel more excited about this, shouldn't I? It's a drink at sunset with a good-looking guy, and I'm acting like I'm about to get my teeth cleaned. I wish Arpita were here to talk some sense into me. I grab my phone and send her a text: You around?

She sends back a thumbs-up, so I call her. "Hey there," she says, then scowls, instantly sensing my discontent. "What's wrong?"

"I have a date tonight."

"And why is this cause for distress?"

"I don't know. I'm feeling very ambivalent about it."

"Well, who's it with?"

"Some guy I met at the beach today. He's nice and everything. Good looking. Cute Australian accent."

"I fail to see the problem."

"I'm guess I'm just not that into him."

"Then don't go." She makes it seem so simple.

"But this is supposed to be my hot girl summer."

"Hot girls don't force themselves into situations they're not comfortable with," she says. "You can't make yourself like this guy if you don't. The heart wants what it wants."

That's the issue. I know what my heart wants, and it's not Brent. "Sometimes the heart can be wrong."

"Look, you're clearly on the fence, so if any part of you thinks you'll regret not going, then you should go. The worst thing that happens is you have a boring date and leave early. The best thing that happens is you realize he's the love of your life."

I am 99.9 percent certain that Brent from Australia is not the love of my life, but Arpita's argument is sound. "You're right. Thanks for the advice."

"Anytime. Let me know how it goes."

I end the call feeling no less conflicted.

This is absurd. I am clearly overthinking this, which is exactly what Richard said not to do when faced with a difficult decision. He suggested I clear my mind, close my eyes, and ask myself what I want the outcome to look like. So that's what I do.

Instantly, I'm sitting by the water, a glass of wine in my hand, watching the sun dip below the horizon. I can't see Brent, but I can sense him somewhere off to my side. There's a warmth flowing through my veins, and I feel satisfied and completely at ease.

Well, I guess my gut is telling me to go. And honestly, what's the alternative? Sitting alone in my stateroom, moping and avoiding Richard? That's no way to spend my last night in Mallorca.

There's a spring in my step as I exit the cabin and make my way down to the main deck. I'm determined to make tonight great. Even if there's no romantic spark between me and Brent, we can still have a pleasant conversation while watching the sunset and enjoying a nice glass of—

"Abby?"

Richard's voice derails my train of thought, shattering my interior pep talk into a thousand pieces. I turn around to see him sitting alone at the glass-top bar, his long fingers fondling the stem of a wineglass. He gives me that cute little half smile, and suddenly I have no clue where I was going or why I was going there.

I sound out of breath when I say, "Hi."

"Hi. You look nice. Are you going to another club tonight?"

"No, I'm . . ." What was I doing again? Oh, right, meeting that guy. What was his name? Brett or Brad or something like that. "I was going to watch the sunset."

"That's my plan, too. Perfect view from here." He points out over the water, and I follow his gaze. Nothing but clear sky and blue water and a golden slice of sun.

"It really is the perfect view."

"You're welcome to join me."

"I'd love to." I don't miss a beat. There's no ambivalence or sec-ond-guessing or weighing the pros and cons. I basically leap into the stool right beside him.

"Would you like some wine?" he asks. "The one I'm drinking is a local red blend, some sort of syrah, but I can open a white, if you'd prefer."

"Red is great." The glass trembles when I pick it up. I steady it with my other hand and take a sip.

"I haven't seen you around much this week."

"I've been busy." *Busy hiding from you.* "Where's Bijou?"

"On the phone with her friends back in New York. Well, some of them are in New York, and others are on vacation in various other parts of the globe, but they've all decided that this is the best time for them to get together once a week. Virtually, that is. So on Saturday nights, I'm not allowed to go anywhere near her room. That's her private time with her friends, and I want to respect it."

He clears his throat and looks at me, his dark-brown eyes searching my face. Those tiny hairs on the back of my neck stand at attention, and I hold my breath, waiting for him to say the words I'm longing to hear. Because if he says them first, then maybe it's okay to admit this isn't some farce I've concocted to distract me from the real world. That these feelings I'm experiencing for him are as real as can be.

"Actually," he says, "while Bijou's distracted, I was hoping you could catch me up on her performance."

Oh, so that's what this is about. I mean, of course it is. Parents always want regular updates on how their kids are doing. Usually, I'll hang around after a tutoring session to chat or send a weekly progress report via email, but this summer I've been slacking on that.

"She's doing really well. We finished up our algebra unit this week, and on Monday we'll start on geometry. I know you're concerned about her understanding of coordinates, but I have faith in her abilities."

"And I have faith in your teaching skills, so I'm no longer concerned. She's really flourishing under your instruction. She told me she never understood what an inequality actually was until you explained it to her."

"That's surprising. Makes me wonder what's going on in her math class."

"Well, Bijou told me she's too nervous to speak up in class. That she's too embarrassed to admit to everyone that she can't understand the material."

"She told you that?"

"Yeah, she's actually been talking to me. When I ask questions, she answers in complete sentences. Can you believe it?"

"That's amazing."

"Things have improved immensely this past week, in ways I never could've imagined. We've laughed together more in the past few days than we have over the course of our entire relationship. And I have you to thank for it. Everything changed once I started being present with her. I stopped taking calls, stopped checking my email. I've delegated all responsibilities to my team for the next four weeks and told them not to contact me until I'm back in the New York office."

"Wow. I'm proud of you."

"Thanks." He's suddenly bashful as he peers down into his wineglass. "I think what put it in perspective was when you told me that if I wanted things to be different, I needed to act differently. And it's clear to me now that I wasn't prioritizing her. We've had a lot of long conversations over these past few days. Some of them were really hard. But I hope now she knows, without a doubt, exactly how important she is to me. I never would've done that without you."

My heart swells. If I've accomplished anything significant this summer, it isn't tutoring math. It's playing a part, however small, in helping Richard connect with his daughter. A year from now, Bijou probably won't remember how to graph a single-variable inequality, but she'll never forget the memories she's making with her dad.

He clears his throat again and shifts in his seat. "I'd be lying if I said I wasn't uncomfortable. This company I want to invest in, they've garnered a lot of interest from other firms. I trust my team to get the job done, but I don't like not being in control."

"You're doing the right thing, though."

His forehead wrinkles, but he nods in agreement and wordlessly takes another sip.

"You said this company had some sort of revolutionary technology?" I ask.

"Yes." Instantly, his spine straightens and his eyes light up. If he launches into an impassioned speech about the virtues of cryptocurrency or deepfakes, I'm going to throw myself overboard. "It's a community-based clean energy system that allows owners and renters to subscribe to a shared solar farm in their immediate area."

Well, that's far more beneficial to humanity than virtual money or face-swapping software. As a matter of fact, "That's really cool."

"It's *incredibly* cool." Richard speaks briskly, like he's just chugged a Big Gulp of Mountain Dew. "It has the potential to make solar power accessible, affordable, and ubiquitous."

As he goes on about the importance of energy equity in an increasingly inequitable world, I find myself getting amped up, too. His enthusiasm for the subject is contagious. I don't think I've ever felt this enthusiastic about anything I've ever worked on, and certainly not in the physics lab. Sure, there've been moments when I've enjoyed doing research, but at no point do I remember feeling this bounce-off-the-walls excitement that Richard's exuding right now.

"I'm boring you, aren't I?" he says. "I can tell by the look on your face."

"No, it's not that. I think this is fascinating, really. It's just . . . how did you know this is what you wanted to do?"

"Well, when the company pitched me the idea, I thought—"

"I don't mean this specific investment. I mean venture capitalism, in general. Is it a goal you've always dreamed of pursuing?"

He laughs, like the idea is ludicrous. "Not at all. For a while, I thought I'd spend my life grinding away at a software company. I started out as a programmer."

"Then how did you end up here?"

"Good question. I often ask myself the same thing." He takes a long drink of wine and stares out onto the horizon before he continues. "About ten years ago, I wrote a data-encryption algorithm. Now, it's used in financial and health care systems all around the globe, but back then I sold it to a big tech company for a lot of money. I took that money, made a few careful investments, and turned it into a lot more money. Frankly, it was more money than I knew what to do with, but I knew I wanted to use it to make the world a better place. That's why I launched Vale Venture Capital. We only fund early-stage projects that are committed to using science and technology to tackle problems like hunger, poverty, or climate change. And then we have a separate philanthropic arm that makes grants to nonprofits, schools, public housing organizations, and the like."

So he's a benevolent billionaire. I didn't think those existed. "That's really wonderful."

"It's what I have to do."

"Technically, you don't have to do anything."

"If I didn't, I'd be miserable. The phrase 'money can't buy happiness'? It's a cliché, but it's true. For me, working was never about making money. Not when I created the encryption algorithm and not now. It's always been about creating something useful and sharing it with others. Contributing something of value to this world."

His eyes sparkle in the fading daylight, and my heart feels as if it might burst. All this time, I've been trying to pretend that my feelings for Richard aren't real. But in this moment, I can't deny that I'm absolutely smitten. He's everything I'd ever wanted in a man: confident yet humble, ambitious yet upstanding, geeky yet absolutely gorgeous. This isn't just lust; this is desire in its purest form.

I'm floating on a heart-shaped cloud, finally prepared to surrender to my feelings, when he asks me, "What about you?"

"What about me?"

"Did you always want to pursue your PhD in physics?"

The cloud dissolves to nothing, and I free-fall back to earth. "Pretty much."

"What are your plans for when you finish your degree?"

Richard crosses one leg over the other and rests his chin on his fist, leaning in so he can hear me better. He is genuinely interested in what I have to say and also completely oblivious to my internal struggle. Sweat drips down the back of my neck. I gulp down the rest of my wine in three huge glugs.

"I'm not sure yet."

"Well, I work with some fantastic start-ups, and they're always looking for dedicated, driven scientists with PhDs. If you'd like, I'd be happy to facilitate an introduction."

"Thank you. That's very kind."

"What's your area of research?"

"Um." I bring the wineglass to my lips in an effort to stall, but then realize it's empty and awkwardly set it back down on the bar. "To be honest, I don't know what it is anymore. It used to be dark energy, but my adviser stole my research and published it without giving me credit. It was the whole basis for my dissertation, and now I can't use it, so I've gotta switch gears. I haven't nailed down a new topic, and I'm not sure how long it'll take me to catch up."

"That's reprehensible. Do you have any recourse?"

"I don't know. I've already brought it to the head of the department, and he said there was no evidence of theft. I'm thinking about escalating to the dean, but I need to be smart about how I handle it. There's a lot of politics in academia, especially among the higher-ups."

"Right. People in power are always looking out for number one."

"Exactly. That's why I'm here for the summer. Just stepping away and thinking things through." Or running away and hiding in a fantasy. Same difference.

"That's smart." He reaches for the bottle of red and refills both our glasses. "You know, I admire you for pursuing an advanced degree. I could never get a PhD. I couldn't even finish undergrad."

"You dropped out of college?"

"Flunked out. I planned to double major in econ and computer science. Freshman year, I worked hard and was invited to the honors program, but as time went on, I sort of lost my motivation. There was no good reason why. I just decided I wanted to spend more time coding and less time sitting in class. So I stopped going. And when they put me on academic probation, I withdrew."

"But you at least had this other big goal you were working toward, right? Designing the data-encryption algorithm?"

"No. At the time, I didn't have any idea of what I was building. I was mostly screwing around, trying new things, failing at those things, and trying again. That went on for about a year and a half. My parents were so pissed."

I picture Richard as an insecure teenager, hunched over his computer keyboard, his disapproving parents shaking their heads in the background. I wonder what they think of him now. If they're still around.

"Did they want you to stay in school?" I ask.

"Oh, of course. My father said I was making the biggest mistake of my life. My mother said I was too smart to be squandering my brain."

"That's what my mother said, too."

"You're pursuing your PhD in physics. I wouldn't call that squandering your brain."

"No, this was before I applied to the program. Originally, I wanted to become a schoolteacher, but she said I was 'too smart' for that. As if schoolteachers aren't smart?"

"Of course they're smart." He shakes his head, his mouth hanging open in disbelief. "It's a unique skill to be able to break down complex concepts into ideas that are easy to understand, to engage students and to make them enjoy learning. You're an incredible teacher. And you don't need an advanced degree to prove how smart you are, either. It was obvious from the moment I met you."

I sit up a little straighter, emboldened by Richard's praise. "Lately I've been thinking about quitting school. But I also feel this need to make my parents proud, you know? Both my mom and my dad, even though he's not around anymore."

"You've accomplished so much. You don't think they're proud of you already?"

I know my mother is. She told me so. But she also told me I shouldn't be a doormat, that I should face my problems instead of running away, and that my dad would never have given up so easily. She might be proud of me for what I've done so far, but she wants me to see it through all the way to the end. "I think they'd be disappointed in me for not finishing what I started."

"Funny, I don't think of life as a linear path with only one way to get to the finish line. I think of it more like one of those corn mazes, where you try going off in one direction, and if it leads to a dead end, you just back up and try another one. For me, flunking out of school was a dead end that started me down the right path. I thought I was meant to do one thing, but it turned out I was destined for something else."

"You believe in destiny?"

"Maybe." He sheepishly shrugs a shoulder. "I just think it'll all end up the way it's supposed to."

I never believed in destiny before, but for some reason, I think he's right. Maybe it's his tone of voice, so calm and reassuring, or the sincerity sparkling in his eyes. Richard makes me feel completely at ease. Like there's no place I'd rather be.

His fingertips graze my shoulder, and every nerve ending in my body flickers on. Then he points to the horizon, where the sun is beginning its final descent. "There it goes," he whispers.

For the next few minutes, we sit side by side in silence, watching the center of our solar system slowly slide down the peach-and-purple sky. I sip my wine slowly. Warmth flows through my veins. This is all I wanted from this evening. More than I ever expected.

When the sun disappears below the horizon, I slide my gaze toward Richard to find he's already looking at me. And though his eyes are dark and inscrutable, I think he wants me as much as I want him. In fact, I know he does. I can feel desire radiating off his body in waves.

This is it. We're going to kiss. I can't wait to find out what his lips taste like. *Kiss me, dammit. Kiss me.*

He sits back abruptly and clears his throat. "I'm sorry."

"For what?"

"For talking your ear off. I didn't mean to keep you from wherever you were going."

"I wasn't going anywhere special." My voice is high pitched and embarrassingly hopeful. We were having a moment—a tender, touching moment—but it's slipping away as steadily as the sunset, and I am desperate to get it back.

He stands up and pushes in his stool. It's too late. "Thank you for the delightful conversation, Abby."

I want to tell him that the conversation doesn't have to end. We could keep talking all night. Until the sun rises. But he's already walking away, up the stairs, out of sight. The moment is officially irretrievable.

I should've made the first move. Coco said that if he really does have feelings for me, he'll never act on them, so I've got to be explicit. Next time I get him alone, I'll tell him I want him. And I'll ask him to kiss me, instead of foolishly hoping he can read my thoughts.

Now I'm all by myself with this half-empty bottle of wine. It'd be a shame to let it go to waste. So I pop the cork and refill my glass and count the stars as they appear in the sky.

CHAPTER TWELVE

You'd think all the years I've spent in school would make me a quick study, but you'd be wrong. Because I did not learn my lesson about being hungover at sea. No, I chose to polish off the rest of that bottle of wine, despite knowing we'd be spending the entire next day on the open water, sailing to Saint-Tropez.

In my defense, I had a lot of feelings to drink away. Feelings that were too overwhelming to actually feel. Lustful longing for my billionaire boss. Despair for all the hard work I've lost. Profound fear of what my future will hold. So I numbed my emotions with a Mallorcan syrah blend, and now my skull feels like it's actively shrinking around my brain.

At least I don't have to work today. I struggle to sit up, then choke down two Advil with the water on my nightstand—thanks, Past Abby!—before collapsing back onto my pillow. I close my eyes, fighting through the fog of last night's inebriation to remember the specifics of my chat with Richard. He told me about his passion for investing in companies that do good in the world. He admitted that he flunked out of school. He said he believed in destiny, maybe.

And then we almost kissed. I didn't make that part up, did I?

Regardless, we connected in a very real way. A genuine way. I can't go back in time or pretend that never happened. My boundaries have been obliterated. And I'm kind of glad for that, honestly, because I don't feel like hiding out in my stateroom all day, especially with these rough seas.

A little sun would do me good. Maybe I'll lie by the pool. After the worst of my headache subsides, I throw on a bikini and a cover-up and head to the top deck, where Bijou is floating on her pink flamingo. She waves and yells, "Hey, Abby!"

"Hey! Mind if I hang with you for a while?"

"Of course not!"

I grab a towel from the stack in the corner and set it on an empty lounge chair. Bijou flops off her floatie and swims to the edge of the pool, then climbs out right in front of me. Water drips from the ends of her hair. "Wanna play Uno?"

"Uh . . ." The Advil has only just taken effect, and I'm barely hanging on here. There is no way I'll be able to handle a high-energy card game without my head caving in on itself. "Maybe in a—"

"Found them!" Richard comes bounding out of the cabin holding a slender red box. He slows down when he spots me, his gaze hot and focused. I'm intensely aware of how tiny my bikini is again, but not in an uncomfortable-in-front-of-the-boss kind of way. "Hello, Abby."

"Hello." Maybe I shouldn't be here. This is their daddy-daughter time, after all, and I can't seem to rein in my indecent thoughts.

Richard shakes his head, like he's cleaning out his own dirty mind. Then his eyes go soft as he smiles innocently and holds the box aloft. "Can I interest you in a rousing game of Uno?"

"Come on, Abby." Bijou bounces on the balls of her feet. "It's more fun with three people."

"She's got a point," he says.

There's really no way I can turn down this offer, so it's time to cut this ogling session short. "Sure. Sounds like fun."

Despite my initial misgivings, it *is* fun. Bijou is a strategic player and a master at employing Skip cards to annoy her father. Richard doesn't go easy on her, either, slapping down the Draw Four card with an evil laugh. They're both fiercely competitive in a fun-loving way. It's sweet to witness how similar they are in their efforts to win the game.

It's even sweeter to see how much their relationship has blossomed in such a short period of time. A little over a week ago, she would sneer at the very sight of him, but now she's smiling and giggling. The only time she rolls her eyes is when he tells a very eye-roll-inducing dad joke, and then she does it in a playful manner. For his part, Richard is practically glowing. Being a doting, attentive father looks good on him.

We're sitting around a table, munching on cheese and crackers and sipping icy lemon water between rounds. The sun is warm, the sea breeze is cool, my hangover is a distant memory. This is shaping up to be a most excellent day.

Then a phone rings.

I hadn't noticed it sitting beside the charcuterie board, but now it's impossible to ignore with its screen alight and its speaker blaring. Bijou picks it up, and from the bedazzled case and rainbow-glitter PopSocket, I'm going to assume it's hers. Which is good, because if Richard was interrupting our Uno game to take a work call, I'd have to question how committed he was to taking the rest of the summer off.

"It's Mom," Bijou says.

Richard's neck stiffens, and his shoulders hunch up toward his ears. He sets his hand of cards facedown on the table as Bijou swipes the green button to answer her video call. "Hi, Mom."

"Hello, darling." So that's what Veronica Vale sounds like. She's got this fabricated accent, like a cross between Moira Rose and early-2000s Madonna. It's a fitting voice for the photos I've seen of her online, always dressed in designer clothes and festooned with garish jewelry.

Despite my eavesdropping, I'm trying my best to seem completely disinterested, as if I can't even hear when she asks, "How are you this morning?"

"It's afternoon here," Bijou says, "but I'm good."

"Where are you at the moment?"

"On the boat. We're on our way to France."

"Your father's taking you to France again? We were there only a summer ago." Veronica's voice drips with disdain.

Richard clears his throat. "We're going to Saint-Tropez."

"Was that your father?" Veronica says. "Richard, I can't hear you, speak up."

"I said, we're going to Saint-Tropez," he says, this time much louder. "You took her to Paris, which is much farther north."

"I'm familiar with the geography of France, Richard. I've been to Saint-Tropez before. Bijou, how's the yacht, dear?"

She shrugs one shoulder. "It's okay. My bed's a little uncomfortable."

"I'm sorry, darling. If your father had purchased his own yacht instead of chartering one from his friend, you could've picked out a bed that suited you. Honestly, Richard, I don't know why you're so cheap. You could afford ten yachts."

"I don't need my own yacht," he says. "I'd hardly ever use it. It's wasteful and besides that—"

"Bijou, we haven't spoken in a couple of days." Veronica continues talking as if she hasn't heard him. "How have you been keeping busy?"

"Dad took me horseback riding yesterday."

"Oh, is that right?"

"Then we went up in a hot-air balloon."

"You're not allowing her to neglect her studies, Richard, are you?"

He sighs. "Of course not. Bijou has been studying for four hours a day, five days a week, just like we agreed upon."

"My tutor is helping me so much," she adds, flashing a subtle smile at me over the edge of her phone. "I'm learning a lot. All the stuff I didn't understand makes sense now."

"Good," Veronica says. "We absolutely cannot have another failure on your record. You'll never get into Harvard with a transcript full of Fs."

Well, now I see why Coco can't stand this woman. Her condescending manner and obnoxious accent are bad enough, but how can she be so oblivious to her own daughter's feelings? When Veronica says the word *failure*, Bijou's face falls like a deflated soufflé. And why is she already harassing her about college admissions? Bijou hasn't even started the seventh grade! Maybe she won't even want to go to college. She's got so much time to figure that out.

Thankfully, Richard intervenes. He snatches Bijou's phone from her hands and scowls into the camera. "She's not going to fail again, and if she does, it's not the end of the world. Besides, she's working with an excellent tutor who's thoughtful and supportive. She's an incredibly intelligent and accomplished academic, so you have no reason to be concerned. Bijou's in good hands with Abby."

A thousand butterflies flap their wings inside my rib cage. If Bijou weren't here, I would lunge across the table and kiss Richard right on his beautiful mouth.

Veronica cackles. "Abby? That's her name, is it? Oh, Richard, you sound absolutely smitten."

The tips of his ears turn crimson, the same shade as that syrah blend we shared last night. Bijou furrows her brow, and I stay still as a stone, waiting for his response.

When he doesn't say anything, she continues. "I'm sure she'd love to get her hands on a billionaire, but don't go messing around with the help again, dear. You should know nothing good ever comes of it."

"That's wildly inappropriate, Veronica," Richard says, his voice sharp and sure. "May I remind you that Bijou is sitting right here?"

"Oh, please, Bijou knows all about it already."

Now would be an excellent time for a tidal wave to spontaneously rise up and wash me away. Floating adrift for eternity in the Mediterranean is far preferable to drowning in the awkward silence that has descended on this deck. That syrah color has consumed Richard's entire head. Bijou is intensely focused on her Uno hand, looking very much like she wants to be anywhere but here.

"Hello?" Veronica's voice blares out from the phone speaker. "Did I lose you? The Wi-Fi on that yacht must be terrible. If you'd only—"

Bijou grabs the phone back from her father and taps the screen, cutting Veronica off abruptly. "Can we get back to the game now, please?" She tosses the phone aside and slaps down a red card. "Your turn, Abby."

I've got three red cards in my hand, but I draw from the pile because I'm too flustered to remember the rules. I'm not even paying attention to the game. I lose round after round, distracted by the memory of Veronica's words. What exactly did she mean by that? Does Richard have a history of "messing around with the help"? Coco said he didn't date, but that doesn't mean he's not having covert affairs with his employees. Am I just the latest in a long line of tutors who fall head over heels for him? Because apparently it never ends well.

The mood is awkward around the table, our earlier playful banter replaced with single-word sentences. After what feels like a hundred years, Bijou finally gets to five hundred points, and this Uno game is mercifully over.

"Well, this was fun." I hop to my feet, eager to get the hell out of here.

"Shall we go to the dining room for lunch?" Richard asks. "The chef said he was making bouillabaisse."

Bijou pulls a face. "Ugh, gross. I'll pass."

She walks away and disappears into the cabin, leaving me and Richard alone on the deck. When he turns to me, his brown eyes are white hot, and for a split second, I don't really care if I'm merely another notch in his bedpost. I want him.

But as soon as the initial wave of desire recedes, I realize exactly how much I could be risking. And I don't just mean my job. I mean my heart. This thing I feel for him, it's more than a physical attraction or a superficial crush. It is real and it is deep, and I cannot give in to it only to be cast aside when this summer is over. Coco said he's too hyperfocused on his work to have a relationship. So why would I risk everything when I already know what the outcome will be?

"You know," I say, "I'll pass, too."

"You don't like bouillabaisse, either? I didn't realize it was such an unpopular dish. I would've asked him to make something else. Anyway, I'm sure there's plenty of other food in the kitchen."

"No, it's not that. It's . . ." How exactly should I finish this sentence? Do I come right out and admit that my heart is too fragile for this? That simply being in his presence is a special kind of torture, knowing I can never taste his lips?

"If this is about what Veronica said, I can explain."

"Don't. Really, it's none of my business. And anyway, it doesn't matter."

"It does matter, and—"

"No." The word splits the space between us like an axe blade splitting a log in two. "Look, Richard, I think maybe I've given you the wrong impression."

His face falls, just like Bijou's did when Veronica brought up her failure. "What do you mean?"

"I mean you and I have been getting too familiar. Don't get me wrong—I've been having fun hanging out with you, but it's beginning to feel a little bit . . . unprofessional. You're a parent and I'm a tutor, and I think we need to establish some firmer boundaries."

"Boundaries." He clears his throat and stares down at the floor. "I'm sorry, I didn't realize—"

"You have nothing to be sorry for." I smile, as if that makes this moment any less uncomfortable. Any less painful. "It's just . . . it's better this way."

When he looks up, his expression is so raw and so wounded that I have to turn away immediately. If I don't, I might change my mind, and that would hurt even more in the long run. I totter across the deck and race down the stairs, eyes fixed on the floor in front of me so I'm not tempted to glance over my shoulder. I don't trust myself.

I practically run back to my stateroom, where I collapse facedown on the bed, panting and sweaty. My headache is back with a vengeance, my eye sockets throbbing and sore. The steady hum of the yacht's motor is soothing, but somewhere deep in my brain, I can still hear the contemptuous cackle of Veronica Vale.

The longer I lie here, my face smashed into the pillow, the more I fear I've read this situation all wrong. One offhand comment from Richard's ex-wife sent me on a downward emotional spiral. But the truth is, I don't know if I can trust what she said. I hardly know anything about her.

When I first got this job, I did some internet research on the Vales, but back then my focus was on Richard. Now it's time to do a deep dive on Veronica. I grab my phone and type her name into the search box. There are tens of thousands of results. Most of them are gossip websites, the same ones that always report on what a callous cad Richard is. They take a more compassionate angle with Veronica, understandably. She's a woman wronged, harrowed and humiliated by her ex-husband. Article after article details her heartache in the wake of the divorce and her struggle to find herself once more.

Her Wikipedia page is short yet complimentary. Her Instagram is highly curated and heavily filtered. There's a write-up in Radar about her extended stay in Los Angeles this summer, how she's doing a "guest appearance" on a new *Real Housewives* spin-off, accompanied by behind-the-scenes set photos in which she's perfectly posed and preened. These are way more flattering than those scowling ones the tabloids post of Richard.

While Richard and Veronica are plastered all over the internet, it appears Bijou is mostly shielded from the public eye. Aside from some complaints about child support early on in her divorce proceedings, Veronica doesn't mention her daughter at all. I find a few mother-daughter photos from family-friendly events in New York City, but no personal details are ever included. Even the paparazzi seem to leave Bijou alone.

I scroll for a solid hour, clicking links and scrutinizing pictures, yet at the end, I feel no closer to understanding the truth. Of course, it's not like the internet is a fount of reliable information, especially these gossip websites. It's all hearsay from strangers who've probably never even spoken to the Vales. I need to talk to someone in the know.

Luckily, that someone has a room right across the hall.

Coco answers the door in sweatpants and glasses and an extra-huge T-shirt that comes down to her knees. I'm so used to her looking sophisticated and pulled together. The shock must be apparent on my face because she says, "I'm off today, okay? I'm taking advantage of our day at sea to get some writing in."

"Oh, I'm sorry to bother you. I can come back later."

She leans on the doorframe. "No, don't worry about it. I'm at a good stopping place. What's up?"

I scratch the back of my neck, trying to think of the best way to phrase it. "I have some questions about Veronica."

"My favorite subject. Come, this could take a while."

She pulls me into her room, latching the door shut behind us. It's a mirror image of my room—same furnishings, same decor—except it's a lot messier in here. Clothes are strewn around the floor; papers and books are piled high on the chair and the nightstand. She sees me taking it all in and says, "Don't judge, I'm an artist."

"I'm not judging, I swear. It's just that you're always so orderly and organized, I expected your room to be the same way."

"I'm orderly and organized when it comes to planning events and keeping schedules because that's my job, and I do it well. Otherwise, all bets are off." She shoves aside her pillows and blankets to clear a space for us to sit on the bed. "Now what can I tell you about Veronica? Keeping in mind that I can go on about this woman for hours."

"Well, earlier today, I was playing Uno with Bijou and Richard when Veronica called, and I overheard their conversation." I tell Coco about the snarky yacht-chartering comments and the way she's already planning for Bijou's college applications.

"Then Veronica made this snide remark to Richard," I continue. "She said he shouldn't mess around with the help, because nothing good ever comes of it."

Coco rolls her eyes. "Oh, Lord."

"Does he have a history of hooking up with his employees or something?"

She barks out a bitter laugh. "There was only one employee he ever hooked up with: Veronica."

"I don't understand."

"Veronica's talking about herself. When Richard first launched Vale Venture Capital, she was Richard's personal assistant. The way I understand it, it all happened really fast. They started dating soon after she was hired; then like two months later she got pregnant, so they eloped."

"Oh. Wow. How long were they married?"

"For about six years. I started working for him right after they split. During their marriage, she only allowed him to hire male personal assistants. Can you believe that?"

I shrug one shoulder. "I can kind of understand that. I mean, he cheated on her, didn't he?"

"No!" Coco scowls, then clucks her tongue at me. "Didn't I tell you not to believe the shit you read on those websites? She's the one who cheated on *him*, sneaking around with some oil tycoon. I think she thought that guy was gonna leave his wife for her, but she thought wrong. When Richard found out, he was heartbroken and filed for divorce."

That side of the story has been conveniently omitted from all the gossip rags. "How do you know all of this? Did he tell you?"

133

"Not directly, but it was all documented during his divorce proceedings, which I helped him deal with. Those dragged on forever because Veronica was trying to take him for all he was worth."

This is *a lot* to wrap my head around. "That's the complete opposite of what the press says."

"I told you they were liars."

"But . . . why? What's their motivation for making up all these stories?"

"Well, my theory is that Veronica plants it all. After the divorce was finalized, she hired a PR team, and that's when photographers started following Richard around all the time. I think they were trying to catch him in a compromising situation, but they didn't find any because . . . well, you know Richard. So when they didn't get any real dirt, they started making it up."

"That is the most bonkers revenge plot I've ever heard."

"I don't think Veronica does it for revenge. I think she does it to stay relevant. Like I said, she's thirsty for attention, and the gossip rags give it to her—but only if it has to do with Richard. They don't care about her otherwise. Why would they? She hasn't accomplished a single thing independent of him."

How incredibly sad that her entire identity is wrapped up in being Richard Vale's ex-wife. Realistically, though, could she ever establish an identity independent from him? Probably not. Richard's a billionaire; he's the one with all the power in this relationship. Veronica will forever live in his shadow. In a way, she's simply doing what she must to claim some of that power for herself.

But it doesn't make it any less sad for Richard. He doesn't deserve this public derision. He's a good guy. "Why doesn't he fight back? Get his own PR person."

"Oh, believe me, I've told him to. He says he 'refuses to play that game.' I don't know if he thinks he's above it or what, but he says he doesn't care what anyone has to say about him." She throws up her hands in frustration. "Hey, he's a grown man. If he wants the world to think he's a philandering scumbag, that's his business."

Coco's got a point. Though I, for one, couldn't handle this kind of intense scrutiny. People following you around with cameras and publishing lies about your life—it sounds like a nightmare. I enjoy being an anonymous nobody.

"There's one thing I don't understand," Coco says. "Why was she telling him not to mess around with the staff? Like, how did this topic even come up?"

"Hmm. I don't remember." I very much do remember. He was talking about what an excellent tutor I was. I believe the exact words he used were *thoughtful* and *supportive* and *intelligent*.

"Well, what staff was she referring to?" She narrows her eyes. "I know she didn't mean me. She used to think I was making a play for Richard until I made it very clear to her that he is not at all my type. Like, at all. So who was she talking about?"

Every blood vessel in my face expands and fills to capacity. "I don't know. I think maybe she was just referring to the help, in general."

"You sure about that?" Her lips spread into an evil smile. She's loving this. And frankly, there's no sense in pretending she doesn't already know.

My tongue trips over the words as they fall from my lips. "He was talking about me in sort of a flattering way, with regard to my tutoring skills, and so I suppose she probably might've been referring to me."

"See? Even Veronica could tell he's got a crush on you." Her sly grin grows ever wider. "Be real with me: You have a thing for him, too, don't you?"

"Kind of." My voice is barely a whisper, like I'm afraid he might be able to hear me all the way from the other end of this gigantic yacht.

Coco's smile softens, the slyness transforming to affection. "Well, if you want something to happen with him, you know you'd better make the first move."

"That wouldn't be a good idea." For a lot of reasons. Most notably, the potential for a broken heart. I'm too cowardly to admit the depths of my feelings for him, so instead I say, "I could get fired from the tutoring agency."

"The tutoring agency will never have to know." Coco leans in and takes my hand in both of hers. "Look, it's up to you, but you could do a lot worse than Richard. If you're scared of what the gossip rags will say, don't be. He may not care about what they say about him, but he never lets them say a word about Bijou. That's why you'll never see her mentioned on any of those websites; he protects her. I know he would protect you, too. He's a good guy."

So I've heard.

There's no denying that I *do* want something to happen with him. Specifically, I want to be wrapped in his embrace, to feel the quiver of his heartbeat beneath the palm of my hand, to discover the taste of his lips. It almost happened last night, after the sun went down. All day long, alternate endings to the evening have been playing out in my head, each one culminating in a kiss.

But I just told Richard we need firmer boundaries. That he's a parent and I'm a tutor, and our familiarity was unprofessional. So if I ever want that kiss to happen, I'm going to have to tell him I was wrong.

CHAPTER THIRTEEN

I am a coward.

It's not that I'm afraid to admit I was wrong. I'm certainly not above apologizing or walking back my previous statements if it means I have a chance at being with Richard.

But I keep wondering: What if he realizes Veronica's right, that it's not a good idea to mess around with the help? I could pour my heart out to him, tell him exactly how I feel, only to be swiftly and painfully rejected.

So instead of going to find Richard and having a serious heart-to-heart, I've decided to hole up in my room for the rest of the afternoon. The Mediterranean whizzes by outside my window as we race along toward Saint-Tropez, nothing but water as far as I can see. I try to read a novel, but my focus is too scattered, and I wind up tidying my closet and my dresser drawers. When that's done, I text Arpita: What's going on?

A few minutes later, she replies, The real question is, how'd your date go last night????

Ugh. I forgot I told her about that. Reluctantly I admit, I didn't go.

She sends me a thumbs-down emoji, and I feel like a loser. I should've gone. I could've enjoyed a nice, uncomplicated evening with a nice, uncomplicated Australian guy whom I'd never see again. But no, I had to stick around and flirt with the boss, and now I'm trapped at sea, alone in my room, hiding out for hours on end because I can't bear to look him in the eyes.

Eventually, I get hungry, but rather than risk running into him on the way to the kitchen, I eat whatever snacks I've got hanging around my room, including an expensive container of Mallorcan almonds I'd meant to bring back as a souvenir for Arpita.

Like I said, I'm a coward.

By the time we arrive in Saint-Tropez, it's after nine o'clock, the lights of the harbor glowing dusky pink. From my window, I can see the promenade is bustling with activity, people dining in open-air restaurants and strolling along the waterfront. Perhaps I'll head out, have a glass of wine in one of those sidewalk cafés. A bit of liquid courage might be exactly what I need.

I'm staring at my open closet, willing an outfit to assemble itself before my eyes, when my phone buzzes with an incoming call from my mom. In a shocking turn of events, I'm happy to hear from her. Our talks are often frustrating, but I know she loves me unconditionally, and right now I am really craving the comfort and familiarity of her voice. Or maybe I'm desperate for a reason to keep avoiding Richard. Either way, I swipe to answer the video call.

"Hi, Mom!"

"Hello, sweetie. You look like you're in a good mood."

"I am."

"Still having fun out there in Mallorca?"

"Actually, we just arrived in Saint-Tropez. And yes, I'm having a *lot* of fun."

I launch into a lengthy description of this past week's exploits, including Bellver Castle, the sunset cruise, and the beach club (sans the vomit-pool). She nods politely as I'm speaking, but her eyes are sort of glazed over. She's humoring me, I can tell.

When I'm done regaling her with tales from the Mediterranean, she says, "That's wonderful, sweetheart. And have you given any more thought to filing an appeal with the dean?"

This is what she called for. Not to hear about my international adventures, but to nag me from halfway across the world. "No."

"Well, you should figure it out soon. You'll be home before you know it."

She's right about that. These past two weeks have gone by in a flash. I suspect the next four will slip away swiftly, and then it'll be back to the grind. No more leisurely lunches in town squares. No more sun-soaked stretches of beach. I won't have time to read escapist fiction either, not with all the hours I'll have to devote to scouring science journals in the hopes of identifying a research topic that will sustain my interest for the next four to seven years. The very thought of it makes my stomach cramp.

"You know, Mom, I've been thinking a lot about school and . . . with everything that happened, maybe I'm not destined to become a college professor."

She clucks her tongue. "Honestly, Abigail, that's ridiculous. Stop with the negative self-talk."

"It's not negative self-talk. I just feel like I might be on the wrong path."

"You've been on this path for years, and you've never questioned it before."

"Well, things change, right? I mean, I applied for the PhD program when I was only twenty-two. That's sort of young to be making a lifetime commitment, isn't it?"

"When I was twenty-one, I was engaged to your father."

"Okay. But surely your life hasn't been one straight line, has it? I mean, haven't you made any wrong turns?"

Her gaze drifts past the phone camera, as if she's staring off into her past. "No wrong turns, but there was a turn I think I may have missed."

"Oh?" I hope this isn't about some long-lost love she wishes she'd chosen over Dad. That would break my heart for so many reasons.

"I always wanted to get my college degree."

139

This breaks my heart, too. Even though she's never said this out loud before, I've always suspected it. It was evident in her reverence for Dad's job in higher education and the way she persuaded me to get a PhD, too. Like I would be making up for her lost opportunities.

"Why didn't you?"

"My parents were poor, and I didn't see it as an option. It was simply expected that after high school, I'd get a job."

"But you could've gone later in life."

She shrugs. "Well, after I married your father, I was the breadwinner while he was studying for his doctorate. Then you came along, and I didn't have the time or the energy to devote to a degree program. Not that I'm complaining, I'm grateful for you every day. It just never happened for me. That's all."

"What would you have studied?"

"Art history." It's stunning how quickly she answers. "I always dreamed of working in a museum. Curating exhibits or managing collections."

This doesn't surprise me. She's been a patron of the Rochester Contemporary Art Museum ever since I was a kid. "It's not too late, Mom. Get your degree now. There are plenty of colleges near you; you can go part time."

"Don't be ridiculous."

"Why is it ridiculous?"

"Because it'll cost a lot of money and take a lot of time. I'm too old for that kind of thing now. What's the point?"

"Your happiness. That's the point."

She rolls her eyes, as if her happiness isn't something worth discussing.

"I'm serious, Mom."

"I'm serious, too. You cannot let this setback stop you from—"

"—achieving my goals. I get it. You said that last week, too."

"Clearly, it bears repeating, since you're still spouting this nonsense about giving up."

I open my mouth, ready to argue, but quickly realize it'd be a waste of my breath. The only words Mom wants to hear right now are *You're right*, and since I can't bring myself to say them, I settle for "It's late. I should go."

After this emotionally draining phone conversation, my desire to go out for a drink has faded. I crawl into bed, and I turn out the lights and wait for the blissful peace of sleep to whisk me away to unconsciousness.

Sadly, sleep never comes. I try yogic breathing and one of those meditative body scans, but none of it calms me down. My body's practically vibrating with nervous energy as I question every life decision I've ever made. Am I really on the wrong path? If this whole fiasco with Nick had never occurred, would I have been happy to continue on my way? Or have I always been ignoring this deep-seated discontent I'm feeling right now, this desire to make a U-turn and choose another direction? I don't want to be like my mother, missing a turn and regretting it for the rest of my life. Not making my happiness a priority.

There's no sense in lying here, staring at the ceiling, stewing in my own self-doubt. I throw back the covers and slip out the door, then shuffle down the hallway until I'm outside. The salty air on my face feels invigorating, and I head downstairs to scan the main deck for signs of life. A heaviness settles in my stomach, the weight of disappointment. Secretly, I hoped to find Richard here, sitting on the sectional, just like our last late-night meeting. Maybe I could've drummed up the courage to confess my feelings to him in the dark.

I move to the edge of the deck and lean against the railing, looking out over the vast blackness of the Mediterranean Sea. Only four more weeks of this. Moments are slipping through my fingers like grains of sand.

"Abby."

The tiny hairs on the back of my neck stand at attention. I spin around to see Richard standing in the doorway. He looks at me like I'm a grizzly bear and he's deciding whether to play dead or run away.

"Richard."

He clears his throat. "I'm sorry to interrupt. I can go if you'd—"

"No. Please stay. I want to talk to you."

I take a step toward him, but he doesn't budge. "If it's about what Veronica said, I told you I can explain."

"It's not. And I don't need an explanation. I just wanted to tell you that I didn't mean what I said before. About us getting too familiar."

"No, you were right," he says. "There should be firmer boundaries between us. I'm your employer, for crying out loud. This needs to be strictly a working relationship."

"Does it?" My hands are shaking and my stomach is clenched, but I can't back down now. "I only said that because I was afraid . . ." I trail off, not willing to admit what it is I was really afraid of. What I'm still afraid of. Getting my heart broken.

"Look, it's my fault," he says. "I should've taken the hint when you decided not to come kayaking with us last weekend."

"What? No. I stayed behind because I thought you needed some alone time with Bijou. I knew you were trying to repair your relationship, and I didn't want to get in the way. And I'm glad I did because look how far you two have come in the past week."

"You weren't in the way. You never are. The problem was that my mind was always elsewhere, which you thankfully brought to my attention." He rakes his hand through his hair and heaves out a frustrated sigh. "Not that I wasn't already aware of it. I know it's been a problem for a very long time."

"But you're trying to fix it now."

"Now I'm trying, yes. But my relationship with Bijou isn't the first relationship to suffer on account of my work. Obviously, things between me and Veronica aren't amicable. I'm sorry you had to overhear that conversation earlier. That comment about the help—"

"It's fine, you don't have to explain it. Whatever happened in the past is in the past."

"It's not in the past because she still hates me, and frankly, I under-stand why. I was an inattentive father and a failure as a husband. I wasn't there when they needed me. It got to the point where I drove Veronica into—" He stops, breathes in and out, and starts again. "I drove her away."

"You can't blame yourself."

"Yes, I can. If I'd been less consumed with my work and more con-cerned with her feelings—with *their* feelings—then maybe we wouldn't be in the mess we're in now. This tension between us, it can't be good for Bijou. But I keep on making the same mistakes." He fists his hand in his hair, wincing like he's in physical pain. "I'm sorry for dumping all of this on you. Talk about overstepping boundaries."

"Don't be sorry." I take two more steps toward him, closing the gap between us. "I'm here to listen."

I'm barely breathing as I hold out my hand, waiting for him to accept my offer. An eternity passes before he finally does. His touch is soft, tentative, matching the tone of his voice. "I feel so much pressure. To be a good father, a good provider, a good leader. The pressure to lead doesn't bother me as much as the rest of it does. Work is the one place I never seem to fail. But being a good person . . . that's my weak spot."

"How can you say that?" I try to catch his eye, but he's gazing down at our hands. His hesitant fingertips graze my palm with slow, tender strokes.

"Because it's true. I want to be a good person, I really do."

"You already are one." I grasp at his fingers, lacing them through mine. His grip is firm now, more self-assured, as if he was merely wait-ing for me to take the lead. "You're conscientious and fair, and you want to do what's right. When you make mistakes, you acknowledge them. When you fail, you try again. You're a good person, Richard."

Finally, he looks up at me. The lights of Saint-Tropez shine brightly in his dark eyes, the glimmering coastline reflected back with all the warmth and intensity of this balmy summer night. I'm mesmerized by the depth of his stare, by the rhythm of his breath, by the slow-motion parting of his lips. His next words come out hushed and husky. "You make me better."

His voice resonates through my whole body. I feel it in my muscles and my sinew and my bones. When he leans in, my stomach bottoms out. It's like I'm peering over the cliff at Cala Varques all over again. I know this could be dangerous, but I'm drawn to it all the same. And even though I'm terrified, I close my eyes and take the leap.

His lips taste salty, like the sea. I want to swim in them, let them carry me away on an undulating wave, show me places I've never even dreamed of seeing. I breathe him in, savoring the spice and sweat of his scent. He slides his arms around me, his palms finding the small of my back as I press my hips against him. I can feel the measured throb of his heartbeat against my quivering chest.

Kissing him is an adventure. I'm flying and falling and feeling completely weightless. My pulse is pounding, adrenaline coursing through my veins. His mouth fits mine so perfectly I never want this to end.

When it does, we're both breathless. Richard cups my face in his hands, his eyes burning right through me. "Abby," he whispers. "You are absolutely perfect."

CHAPTER FOURTEEN

The rush of adrenaline is quickly replaced with a cold-blooded panic.

"We can't tell Bijou."

Richard furrows his brow. "Why not?"

"Because this is your special daddy-daughter trip, and the focus needs to stay on her. Not . . . whatever it is that's happening between us." What *is* happening between us? All I know is I had this overwhelming urge to kiss him, and now that I did it, I'm not sure what comes next. I didn't plan that far ahead.

He doesn't seem to share my concern. "Is what's happening between us somehow bad?"

"No, but it's a distraction. You've only started to heal your relationship with her. She needs to know she's the center of your attention right now."

Not to mention, I don't want word getting out about this. If Bijou finds out, she'll inevitably tell Veronica, who will no doubt bring this information to Dianne's attention, at which point I'll be fired. Or worse, I could wind up in the gossip rags. Coco said Richard would protect me, but what if he can't? It isn't worth the risk.

Besides, this was only one kiss. There's no sense in making a whole *thing* about it.

"I suppose you're right," he says. His hands tighten around my waist, and the warmth of his touch is so inviting, I realize that I actually want to make a whole *thing* about it. I just want to do so privately.

We kiss again, and my entire body lights up. I'm aware of every inch of my skin, every beat of my heart. My world has gone from shades of gray to vibrant color. In this moment, it almost feels like it's worth risking everything.

A sound comes from inside the cabin, a dull thud like someone dropped a heavy object or slammed a door. In an instant, we're six feet apart, staring in different directions, as if we weren't just desperately clawing at each other's clothes. After a few seconds of silence, I hazard a glance through one of the windows, but there's nobody around.

"What do you think that noise was?" I ask.

"I don't know. Maybe a crew member?"

"Or maybe it's Bijou."

We stand still, listening for signs of movement, but all I hear are gentle waves lapping against the hull of the ship and my own blood rushing through my ears. We're alone, and that's good, but I've got a thin sheen of sweat on my brow. Maybe I'm not as ready to risk everything as I thought.

"I should go to bed," I say. "I've gotta be up to tutor in a matter of hours."

"Right." He flashes his half smile. "See you in the morning?"

I'm tempted to give him a goodbye kiss, just a small peck for the road. But there's a good chance a peck will lead to something more, and if I get started again, I may never want to stop. So instead, I say, "See you in the morning," and head upstairs.

Back in my stateroom, I collapse into bed, dizzy and boneless. Despite my ecstatic state, I drift into a pleasant slumber with joyous and brightly colored dreams. When I wake up the next morning, sunlight's streaming through my window. I'm smiling before I even lift my head off the pillow. It's going to be a glorious day in Saint-Tropez.

I grab my phone off the nightstand and check the time: 7:15. Hard to believe I woke up before my alarm, especially considering how late it was when I finally turned in last night. Sensory memories return in a rush. The salty taste of Richard's lips, the pressure of his palms on the small of my back, the rhythm of his heartbeat against my chest. I could lie here reliving it all day, but I've gotta get up and get moving. Bijou and I start geometry today.

She's already waiting for me in the office, five minutes before our session is scheduled to start. "You're early," I say, booting up my laptop.

"Oh, you know me," she says. "I just can't wait to learn math."

"Well, you're in luck, because we have a fascinating lesson all about rectangular prisms." I giggle at my own corny joke, but Bijou doesn't crack a smile. "Everything okay?"

She chews on her thumbnail, then says, "I'm sorry about what my mom said yesterday."

I hesitate before I answer. "I don't know what you're talking about."

"Don't lie. My mom made those weird comments about the help, I know you heard. I'm really sorry."

"You have nothing to be sorry for. This is one hundred percent not your fault."

"I told her she was being mean."

Uh-oh. I hope Veronica doesn't know I was listening in on their conversation. "Really, it's fine. I don't want to cause any problems."

"You didn't cause any problems—it's all her. So what if my dad likes you?"

My face is on fire. "He doesn't like me."

"Sure he does."

I don't want to know why she thinks that. And I'm done with this conversation.

"Okay, enough chitchat!" I clap my hands so loudly she jumps. "It's time to get started. Three-dimensional shapes, here we go!"

She rolls her eyes as she opens her laptop, but at least she drops the subject, and I launch straight into a discussion of lines versus planes.

Though it got off to a rough start, the rest of the morning rolls along smoothly. As usual, Bijou masters new concepts with ease. After an hour, she's already learned how to calculate the volume of a rectangular prism, and we've just moved on to surface area when there's a soft knock at the window.

The sight of Richard's face sends a tingle through my whole body. As he slides the door open, I bite down hard on my lower lip. It's a painful, visceral reminder to keep things professional in front of Bijou. No casual flirting or moony stares.

"Hope I'm not interrupting," he says.

"Of course you're interrupting," Bijou says. Thankfully, her tone is playful. "What's up?"

"I was wondering how you'd feel about going to an amusement park this afternoon. Ride some rides, play some games, eat some cotton candy."

"Uh, I'd feel amazing about that." She turns to me with a wide grin. "Abby, you have to come."

I do love cotton candy. Thrill rides, not so much, especially tall ones with fast drops. But since I overcame my fear of cliff jumping, maybe I'd actually enjoy a spin on a roller coaster now. Besides, Bijou wants me to go, and Richard assured me that I never get in the way. Though that was before we kissed. Now I might be more of a distraction.

"Abby?" he says. "You in?"

I'm doing that overthinking thing again. You know what? I really want to go, and as long as I avoid eye contact with Richard, I'm sure everything will be fine.

"Yeah," I say, "that sounds like fun."

"Great!" He smiles, and my heart goes pitter-patter. "We'll leave right after lunch. It's only a twenty-minute drive from here. I'll ask Coco to arrange for a car."

Richard's lips are so perfect. The bottom one is full and luscious, and the top one has the sexiest Cupid's bow. But it's not the appearance of his lips that make them perfect so much as what he *does* with them. What he did with them last night. What I want to do with them now.

"What's wrong with you two?" Bijou's voice disrupts my lip fantasy, and I suddenly realize Richard and I have been engaged in a stare of the moony variety. Exactly what we weren't supposed to be doing.

"Nothing," I say at the same time he clears his throat.

"I'll let you get back to your studies," he says, then hastily slips out the door.

"Okay, where were we?" I scan our notes, grasping for some reminder of what was happening before Richard walked in the room.

"See? I told you my dad likes you."

"Stop."

"Why?"

"Because we have a lot to cover today. We're working on coordinate geometry now, which is what your dad is most concerned about. And we can't leave for the amusement park until you know how to find the volume of a fractional cube."

"What's a fractional cube?"

"Exactly. Let's get cracking."

The rest of our session goes quickly as we walk through the remainder of our lesson, and by the time we're done, Bijou is a master of three-dimensional shapes. The three of us eat lunch together in the dining area on the main deck. I eat with my eyes pointed down, fixed on my plate. That way, if I start fantasizing about some other part of Richard's body, it won't be so obvious.

Then we hit the road. Our driver is a brawny man named Pierre. He's quiet and brooding, and when he escorts us through the turnstiles and into the amusement park, I realize he's not just a driver but a bodyguard as well. I forgot that they need protection when they're in public. Funny how easy it is to forget these are some of the richest people in the world.

Pierre isn't in our faces or anything. He doesn't even talk to us. He simply hangs back, omnipresent but unobtrusive. Still, it's hard to forget he's there, and for me, that's a good thing. I'm on my best behavior knowing someone's always watching us.

Which means, of course, that I'm avoiding eye contact with Richard. Thankfully, there are plenty of other things to focus on here. Azur Park is a whirlwind of neon lights and clanking gears and exhilarated screams. When we first arrive, Bijou makes a mad dash for the Crazy Mouse, a rickety roller coaster with spinning cars pulled straight from one of my worst nightmares. Upon closer inspection, it's not *that* much taller than that cliff I jumped off of, and it has the added bonus of a safety harness (I hope), so even though I'm shaking in my shoes, I follow her onto the ride.

I don't regret it. I don't regret the carousel, either, or the log flume or the fun house. I do, however, regret getting on the Frisbee, a huge circular pendulum that spins around as it swings back and forth, eventually turning us all upside down. As we disembark, my head is pounding, and I can barely stand up straight.

"Are you okay?" Richard's eyes brim with concern. When his hand grazes the small of my back, I feel even more off balance.

"Yeah, I think I just need a break from rides for a minute."

"Let's play mini golf," Bijou says, and leads us to the prehistoric-themed course at the far end of the park, where the eighteen holes are surrounded by waterfalls and statues of dinosaurs. We invite Pierre to play, but he turns us down with a silent scowl. In the end, Bijou kicks both our asses, with Richard lagging in a distant third place.

As we return our equipment, I venture a tease. "What happened, Richard? I thought businessmen were supposed to be virtuoso golfers."

"I guess I'm not that kind of businessman." He rests his golf club on the counter, and when he turns around, his gaze lands directly on mine, his brown eyes burning with desire. This was exactly what was not supposed to happen. Now my skin is tingling and my thoughts are scrambled. My muscles have melted into gelatin; I'm afraid I may collapse into a puddle on the ground.

"Can we get cotton candy now?" Bijou's voice snaps me out of my stupor. She starts pulling us toward the snack booth, completely oblivious to our little lapse in judgment.

The three of us get sugared up and hit the bumper cars, riding them twice before heading to the arcade, where Richard makes up for his defeat in mini golf by knocking down three milk bottles in one powerful throw. His victory scores Bijou an oversize plush unicorn, which she hugs tightly as we go for a spin on the Ferris wheel.

It's dark outside by the time we walk back to the car. My feet ache with each step, and Bijou's eyelids are heavy. "I'm so tired," she says. "I don't know how I'm gonna get up for tutoring tomorrow."

"We can move it to later in the day, if you'd like," I say.

"No, you can't," Richard says. "I booked a tour to Provence tomorrow afternoon to see the lavender fields. It's a bit of a drive, so we'll need to leave promptly."

Bijou raises a skeptical eyebrow. "Lavender fields?"

"Trust me, it'll be fun. There's a farm with baby animals, and then we're going to drive around the town on e-bikes."

At that, she perks up. "E-bikes? That *does* sound fun. Abby, you're in, right?"

"Absolutely." I answer without missing a beat. Today was the best day I've had this summer, by far.

When we return to the yacht, Bijou runs ahead of us, eager to get back to her room and check her texts. "There's some drama happening with her friends in New York," Richard says. "I'm not sure what because she won't tell me. It sucks—I thought she was finally opening up."

"Don't worry, that's normal," I say. "Even though my dad and I were super close, there were still certain things I didn't discuss with him."

"Like friend drama?"

"Yes."

"And boyfriend drama?"

"You know, I didn't have much boyfriend drama until . . ." I almost say *until now*, because this is the most exciting romantic entanglement I've ever had. My dating life has been one fleeting, meaningless fling after another. The most serious boyfriend I ever had was a guy I met during my first year of grad school, a postdoc in the biology department. We both shared a passion for science; sadly, that was the only passion we shared. Our affair was perfectly pleasant, but perfectly boring.

With Richard, it's impossible to be bored. He infuses each moment with excitement, with the thrill of discovering something new. Being with him is an adventure, whether we're jumping off cliffs or watching the sunset, riding a roller coaster or sharing a secret kiss.

As if sensing my thoughts, he leans in close, his voice a whisper no one else can hear. "Meet me at midnight?"

"Absolutely."

CHAPTER FIFTEEN

It's hard to keep up a secret affair when you're confined to a boat. Even though this is one of the largest yachts on the planet, it offers surprisingly little in the way of privacy. Richard and I have declared our staterooms off limits for romantic encounters—his is next door to Bijou's, mine is across the hall from Coco's, and neither of us is interested in getting caught doing a walk of shame. And we can't very well start making out in the middle of the deck again, where anyone could see us through the cabin windows.

So that night, we tiptoe around in bare feet, searching for a spot that's somewhat secluded. Richard leads the way while I trail a bit farther behind to create an air of plausible deniability should someone wander by. He brings me to the glass-top bar where we shared that bottle of red.

"This isn't exactly private," I say.

"Not here. Over there." He points past the bar, toward a narrow corridor against the far wall that I never noticed before. It's dark and constricted and completely out of view. No one would ever find us there. My skin prickles all over as I envision us tucked away in that secret hiding spot, our bodies pressed together tightly because there's nowhere else to go.

I grasp his hand urgently and pull him toward the corridor, eager to feel his hands on my hips and his breath on my neck. The moment we're inside, I spin around, ready to wrap him in my embrace. But as

I'm lifting my arms, my elbow bashes against the wall, sending a sharp pain down the length of my forearm all the way to my tingling pinky.

"Are you okay?" he asks.

I nod, biting my bottom lip to keep from screaming.

He leans over to inspect my injury. "It doesn't look like you're bleeding."

I'm sure it'll be one hell of a bruise, though. No matter. Not even a broken elbow can deter me from this pursuit. With my arms squished firmly against my sides, I run my fingers through his curls, gently coaxing his head back so I can kiss him properly.

He looks at me, eyes blazing, and as he stands up straight, he bashes the top of his head against a pipe that's protruding from the ceiling.

"Shit!" He grabs his head in his hands and squeezes his eyes shut. Instinctively, I try to comfort him but wind up bashing my elbow again. This time, I can't hold back my scream.

"Are you okay?" he asks.

"Yeah. Are you?"

"Yeah." His voice is strained. "But maybe we should do this somewhere else."

Seeing as my elbow is rapidly swelling, I can't argue with that. As we emerge from the corridor, Richard touches my elbow. His fingertips feel soft and soothing against the tender flesh, which is already turning a light shade of purple. "We should get some ice on that before it gets any worse," he says.

"It's fine, really."

"Please. It'll only take a moment." He ducks behind the bar, where he pulls a linen napkin from within a drawer. He scoops a small amount of ice from the freezer and sets it inside the napkin, then balls it up and twists the ends together to create a makeshift compress. Then he cups my elbow in one hand and uses the other to hold the ice against the bruise. "Is that okay?"

I've never been handled this carefully before, never been doted on so thoroughly. It's more than okay. It's exquisite. And it makes me want him more intensely than ever. "Yes. Now let's find a place where we can be alone."

We investigate a few other possibilities. There's a hatch beneath the helipad that leads to a small, uninhabited room. It seems promising until we take a deep breath and discover the inside stinks of fish. After that gut-churning experience, we consider the onboard gym, which I didn't even know existed until now. It's highly unlikely anyone would stumble upon us here at one in the morning, but there's no room for us unless we want to lean against the weight rack or straddle the stationary bike.

My elbow is throbbing, and this ice pack is dripping cold water all over the front of my shirt. I'm feeling discouraged, until Richard snaps his fingers. "I've got it: we can use the tender!"

"What's the tender?"

"Come. I'll show you." He curls his perfect lips into a devilish smirk, and as I follow him into a small room at the front of the yacht, the throbbing in my elbow seems like nothing compared to the throbbing between my thighs.

Turns out the tender is a small boat, stored in a tidy little garage beneath the cockpit. "They use it when they're anchored at sea," Richard explains. "So far all the marinas we've visited had berths large enough to accommodate us, so we haven't had to deploy it yet."

"It looks like it's never been used." I run my hand along the sleek mahogany hull. There isn't a scratch or a speck of dust.

"The crew keeps it in good shape. Just in case."

I glance at him over my shoulder. "In case of what? A *Titanic* situation where we need to escape via lifeboat?"

His laugh is a low rumble that resonates throughout my whole body. He takes the dripping ice pack from me and tosses it into a corner.

Then he points to a step stool beside the tender, offering his hand to help me climb aboard. "Women and children first."

The inside is immaculate, with two swiveling captain's chairs and a long curved bench upholstered in cream-colored leather. I sink into it, leaning back against the soft, supple cushions. "Who knew a dinghy could be this luxurious?"

Richard slides in beside me, his arm already finding its rightful place around my shoulders. His dark eyes twinkle in the dim light of this room, his lips ease into a satisfied smile. He looks calm, content, like there's nowhere else in this world he'd rather be at this very moment. I feel the same way.

"Are you comfortable?" he asks.

"Very."

Our hands engage in a slow, sensuous dance. I stroke my thumb across the calluses that line the fleshy part of his palm. He traces soft circles on the inside of my wrist. Finally, he brings my fingertips to his lips and presses a lush, lingering kiss to each and every one.

"This is really just like *Titanic*," I whisper.

He stops midkiss and scowls at me. "Are you comparing this beautiful moment to one of the worst nautical disasters in history?"

"No, I mean the scene in the movie where they're in the car in the garage and Rose is kissing the tips of Jack's fingers."

"I've never seen it."

"How is that possible? It's so romantic. Easily one of my top five greatest movies of all time. I watch it at least once a year."

"Then I'll just have to watch it so I can understand you better." He resumes kissing my fingertips. Each touch of his lips sends a shudder up my spine. "So what else happens in that car with Rose and Jack?"

"They get naked and steam up the windows."

"Oh really." His eyes turn to hot coals, burning with such passion that it starts to feel a little steamy in here, too. I know what he's thinking, but sex in a dinghy doesn't sound particularly sexy to me, no matter how luxurious it may be.

"I'm not quite ready for that level of steam yet. I hope that's okay."

"Of course," he says, without hesitation. "I'd never want you to do something you don't want to do. I'm happy just to have this moment alone with you. To have you all to myself. If all you want to do is talk—"

"I want to do more than talk," I say.

So we do more than talk.

The tender becomes our meeting place for the next few nights. I feel like a teenager again, though my teenage years didn't involve a romance that was anywhere near this all-consuming and intense. I'm sure some of that intensity is spurred on by the fact that we're sneaking around. At times, the secrecy can be stressful, but admittedly there's something scintillating about having to keep things so hush hush. Forbidden fruit and all that.

My life isn't all midnight make-out sessions, though. It's also grand adventures during the day. There's the trip to Provence, where the rolling fields of brightly colored lavender take my breath away. There are the private windsurfing lessons in Hyères, where I surprise myself with both my core strength and my determination. There's the pristine Île Sainte-Marguerite, where we hike among the sweet-smelling eucalyptus trees and bask in the natural beauty of the forest. It's all so magnificent, each experience more awe inspiring than the last.

I'm so lost in the wonders of the South of France that I'm worrying less and less about my life in New York. I don't have to push the bad thoughts out of my brain, either; I just don't care about them so much anymore. It's as though I've reached a turning point, where I'm not as concerned with the future as I am with the present moment. Instead of fretting about what comes tomorrow, I'm enjoying what today has to offer.

It's all going so well until Thursday night.

I'm lounging in bed, reading another book in the hunky, horny alien series—there are over twelve of them!—and waiting to attend my midnight rendezvous with Richard, when my phone buzzes. It's an email, the weekly newsletter from Philip, so I mark it read without even opening it. Nothing in there is relevant to me right now, seeing as I'm thousands of miles away from campus. Plus, I'm really happy in this blissful bubble I've created overseas. There are still a few more weeks before I have to even start thinking about real life again.

I return to my world of sci-fi romance, only to be interrupted by a second buzz five minutes later. It's another mass email, this time someone responding to the newsletter. *Reply all* is the work of the devil.

After the fourth reply, though, I'm a little concerned. Newsletters don't normally elicit this kind of reaction, so I pull up my inbox and skim the replies. They're from other professors and postdocs in the department, all of them offering a variation on the same theme: "Congratulations, Professor Bauer!"

My heart's in my throat as I open the newsletter and scan for any mention of Nick's name. I find it in the first paragraph:

> We're pleased to announce that Professor Nick Bauer has been shortlisted for a $250,000 grant from the National Science Foundation related to his recent groundbreaking research on dark energy.

That groundbreaking research isn't Nick's; it's mine. At no point is my name even mentioned in this email, not even as a contributing member of the team. Not only has he taken all the credit for my work, but now he has the potential to make a whole lot of money off it.

My hands are shaking as I screenshot the announcement and send it off to Arpita with a CAN YOU BELIEVE THIS???

Almost instantly, my phone buzzes in my hand. It's another email, this time from one of my lab mates. I open it, naively hoping he might hop to my defense by telling everyone that *I* was the real mastermind behind this project. But no. It's merely another ass-kissing message of congratulations. He even followed up with a party hat emoji. Each fleck of digital confetti is a grain of salt in the wound.

My phone buzzes again, and thankfully this time it's Arpita: Unfortunately, I can believe this. I'm so sorry. Are you okay?

Oh, I'm fine. Just plotting my revenge.

Remember, the best revenge is success.

No, the best revenge is seeing your opponent go down in flames.

What are you planning, Abby?

When I don't respond right away, she calls me. Her face is scrunched up with concern. "Don't do anything rash, okay?"

"Everyone is congratulating him," I say, as my phone buzzes with yet another email. "I'm dying to reply all and tell them exactly what kind of thieving jerk he is."

"Under no circumstances are you going to do that."

"Why not?"

"Because it'll make you look petty and bitter."

"Maybe I am petty and bitter."

"No, you're not. You're above this."

"Above what? Receiving credit for all the hard work I've done?"

"Of course not." She sighs. "But I don't think you're going to get anywhere by writing an angry email. They'll see you as the dramatic, hysterical woman and no one will take you seriously."

"You think I'm being dramatic?"

"No! I'm saying *they'll* think you're being dramatic. I'm on your side here, don't get mad at me. This is just how things are. Politics, remember?"

Right: politics. The hierarchy, the dishonesty, the corruption. The fact that I need to silence my voice for the sake of an older man's ego. "Well, if this is *just how things are*, I don't want to be a part of it anymore."

"You don't really mean that."

"Yeah, I do." Or maybe I don't. Maybe I'm simply being *dramatic* and *hysterical*. But in this moment, I feel like I never want to set foot in the physics building again.

"You've worked way too hard to let these jerks push you out of the program. And if you do that, they win. Don't let them win. Stop reading these emails. You're supposed to be taking a break right now, so go enjoy your time in France. What'd you do today, anyway?"

What *did* I do? I'm so flustered by this unsettling news that I can't even remember what I was doing a few hours ago. My happy little bubble has burst.

Finally, it comes back to me. The Île Sainte-Marguerite. Lush greenery and the smell of eucalyptus. "I went hiking on this beautiful island."

"That sounds amazing. Update your Instagram, will you? It's been over a week since you've posted anything."

"Okay." I haven't posted anything because I haven't been taking any pictures. I've been so caught up in each moment with Richard it never occurs to me to stop and snap a photo. A photo can't capture the true essence of these experiences, anyway. The scent of lavender, the sound of the sea, the sensation of my heart beating inside my chest; these things are magical and ephemeral, just like this whole summer.

"I'm really sorry, Abby," she says, "but I have to go. I'm meeting some Tinder guy for a drink in ten minutes. But call me if you need anything, okay?"

"I'll be fine. Good luck on your date."

She crosses her fingers in front of the camera. "Thanks. I'll need it."

The call ends, and my screen reverts to my email inbox. Four new congratulatory messages have come in during my brief chat with Arpita.

I'm tempted to send my own message, one that's far less congratulatory in nature. In my head, I draft a dozen different versions, my blood pressure rising higher with every imaginary insult I craft.

But I never type any of them out. Instead, I swipe them off my screen and immediately turn off my email notifications. Arpita's right; I don't need to concern myself with this right now. I've got more important things to attend to, like my scheduled midnight meeting with Richard.

I arrive five minutes later than usual. When I climb into the tender, he looks relieved to see me. "There you are. Thought you were standing me up."

"Sorry, I got caught up in something going on at home."

"Everything okay?"

"Not really." I melt into the seat beside him and bury my head in his chest. He tucks his hand beneath my chin, gently lifting my face so he can look into my eyes.

"What is it?"

"My old adviser just got short-listed for a really prestigious grant, using the research he stole from me. And of course he didn't give me any credit."

"That's horrible; I'm so sorry." He frowns, gently stroking my cheek with the pad of his thumb. "Do you think it's time to go to the dean? Maybe even the provost, at this point."

"I don't think it would be a good idea. If I was going to do it, I should've done it already. Now it'll just look like I'm moneygrubbing. Besides, I wasn't good about keeping a paper trail, so I have no evidence to back up my claims." I heave out a sigh, but it doesn't provide any relief from the heavy weight that's resting on my rib cage. "This is all my fault. I should've been smarter about how I handled everything."

"Don't say that." He seems genuinely offended that I'm blaming myself. "You're incredibly smart. None of this is your fault. It's the fault of the person that betrayed you. And he shouldn't get away with it."

"But he's going to get away with it. No one's willing to stand up for me. The entire department is congratulating him, even the people who know he stole my research. I'm completely alone in this."

He narrows his eyes, like he's zeroing in on a target. "Let me speak to my lawyer. You can bring this to court, if need be."

I wrap my arms around him and press my face into the crook of his neck, breathing him in, completely immersed in gratitude for his support. His willingness to defend me when I am completely defenseless. "Thank you. I appreciate the offer, more than you know. But precedent in cases like these doesn't favor the student. And even if I were to win the case, I'd still lose."

"What does that mean?"

I sit back so I can look him in the eyes. "It means I wouldn't be welcome in that department anymore. I'm already walking on thin ice, as it is. They even denied me a summer teaching assignment just to punish me for not keeping my mouth shut. Getting lawyers involved would not improve my reputation as a troublemaker."

"You're not a troublemaker. You simply tell the truth. I love that about you."

I can feel my cheeks flush. "You do?"

"Of course. You're brutally honest, but you don't throw daggers. It's so different from what I'm used to. It's exactly what I need. I love your voice, Abby. Don't ever let anyone silence it."

The press of his lips against mine is electric. It flips a switch somewhere inside me, turning my self-doubt into a bright beam of confidence. I lose myself in the moment again, reveling in the soft caress of Richard's fingers on the back of my neck, the firm yet gentle pressure of his tongue against mine. New York, with all its problems, is thousands of miles away. How can I ever feel bitter when life is this sweet?

CHAPTER SIXTEEN

The next day, we have plans to go to a ropes course in a forest near Cannes. The old Abby would've said no to crossing wobbly suspension bridges dangling precariously between the treetops, but the new Abby can't wait to strap on a helmet and get climbing.

After tutoring Bijou, I go back to my stateroom to change into closed-toe shoes—a necessity for today's excursion—and find a text message waiting for me from Arpita: How are you doing?

> Turned off my email notifications just like you
>
> told me to, so I'm feeling much better!
>
> How was your date last night?

> Sorry. Better luck next time?

I think I'm taking a dating hiatus for the rest of the summer.

It's rough out there.

What about you?

> Any romantic encounters since you stood up that poor Aussie?

I haven't yet mentioned the whole hooking-up-with-the-boss thing to Arpita. Honestly, I'm a little afraid to; when she (rightly) accused me of having a crush on him, there was a definite note of negativity in her voice. But I'm having the time of my life, and he's such a great guy—I'm sure once I tell her all about it, she'll be happy for me.

> Do you have time to chat?

Five seconds later, her face fills my screen, her eyes alight with curiosity. "What is it? Tell me, tell me. Did you have some tawdry affair with a fellow traveler?"

"I wouldn't describe it as tawdry." *Tawdry* implies sleazy and cheap. That's not what Richard and I have, at all.

"You used a condom, right?"

"We haven't had sex yet." Will we? I hope so. Just not in that dinghy. I want my first time with Richard to be someplace that's a bit more comfortable, more special. If only we could get off the yacht for a couple of hours without anyone finding out about it. Would a few early-morning hours in a hotel be considered tawdry?

"Hello-o?" Arpita says, and I realize I've zoned out on the logistics of planning a potential sexual encounter.

"Sorry, I got distracted."

"Yeah, I could tell." She makes a face like she's annoyed, but it quickly turns to a good-natured smile. "Who is it? Some local Frenchman?"

I shake my head, biting back a squeal. It feels like my organs are going to burst right through my skin. Up until now, I haven't told anyone what's happening with Richard, not even Coco. I'm too afraid of it getting back to Veronica.

But Arpita's my best friend, my confidante, my support system through the good times and the bad. There's no need for me to be nervous. So I pull the phone in close to my mouth and whisper, "It's Richard."

She squints at me, like she hasn't heard me right. "Did you say *Richard*?" When I nod, she says, "As in Richard Vale?" I nod again, and her mouth falls open. "He's your boss, Abby."

"He's a really great guy."

"I knew you were lying when you said you didn't have a crush on him." She shakes her head. "This is a bad idea."

"No, it's fine. We're being very discreet."

"Of course he wants you to be discreet, he's the 'Billionaire Playboy,' remember? He's probably hooking up with, like, ten other women at the same time."

"Actually, it was my idea to be discreet. And the whole playboy image isn't true. The gossip rags are all lying."

"That's what he wants you to think."

"It's not like that." How do I begin to explain the situation? An unhealthy marriage, a bitter divorce, a war waged in the tabloids. It's all so messed up. If I were Arpita, I'd be wary of Richard, too. "I wish you could meet him. Then you'd see that—"

"Abby, you need to be smart about this."

"I am being smart! Look, aren't you the one who told me to have a hot girl summer? You even reminded me to bring condoms."

"Yeah, for a fling with a Frenchman, not for banging your boss!" She sighs and pinches the bridge of her nose. "Beyond that, doesn't Dianne forbid you from fraternizing with the parents of the kids you tutor?"

"Geez, Arpita, can't you just be happy for me?"

"I'd be happy for you if I wasn't afraid this was going to end with you being incredibly sad."

"Well, I'm not sad. I'm the happiest I've been in a really long time. And now I have to go. There's a car waiting."

"Wait, don't leave while you're mad at me. I'm sorry I shit all over your happy time."

"It's fine." It's not fine, but I don't like being angry at my best friend, and I don't want an unsettled argument to cast a shadow over the rest of my day. "I know you're worried, but don't be. I'm a big girl, and I'm having a wonderful time."

We end the call with smiles on our faces, but our tense conversation leaves a sour sensation in the pit of my stomach. I try my best to ignore it as I tie my shoelaces and head off to the parking lot toward the boxy Mercedes SUV that's bringing us into the wilderness. Pierre's in the driver's seat and Bijou's in the back, but Richard's nowhere to be seen.

I climb in beside Bijou. "Where's your dad?"

She shrugs. "I dunno. I haven't seen him all morning."

"I hope he's feeling okay."

"He's probably stuck on a work call or something."

"He can't be." That unpleasant feeling in my stomach is getting sharper. Like the tip of a knife blade digging in. "He told me he's taking off of work for the rest of the summer."

She rolls her eyes. "Yeah, right."

"He is, though. The three of us have been hanging out all week, and I haven't seen him check his email once."

"Just because we don't see him doing it doesn't mean it's not happening," she says.

I can't argue with that, particularly in light of the things I've been doing lately that no one else can see. "Does it bother you, the idea that he might be working?"

"No. It hasn't been getting in the way of us doing stuff together, like it did before."

"Good," I say, though her downcast expression belies her words. I check the clock on the dashboard. Her father is five minutes late. "Are you sure about that? Because you look sort of sad."

"That's not what I'm upset about." She rests her head against the window, staring out at the marina without elaborating on what's actually upsetting her.

I get it. Being twelve is hard. I'm sure having a billionaire for a dad makes it easier in a lot of ways, but some twelve-year-old problems are inescapable. Like friend drama, which Richard suspected she was dealing with.

"Well, if you want to talk about anything," I say, "I'm here to listen. No pressure, though."

"It's totally not a big deal." She sighs, still gazing out the window. I give her space to feel her feelings, and eventually, she decides to share them. "I miss my friends, that's all."

"Missing your friends is a big deal."

"Yeah, but I'm on a yacht in Europe having an amazing time. Complaining about how I miss my friends makes me sound ungrateful."

"First of all, the fact that you have this sort of self-awareness shows me that you are not ungrateful. Second of all, it's okay to be sad about missing out on something even if you're doing something else that's really awesome."

"My best friend is having a big party tonight," she says. "I just wish I could be there."

"I'm sorry. That sucks." Yes, we're sitting in a luxury SUV in the South of France, heading into the forest for a ropes course, which will inevitably be followed by a gourmet dinner at an exclusive restaurant. It'd be so easy to dismiss her feelings as those of a selfish, spoiled child. But when you're twelve, your entire world revolves around your friendships. Every party feels like a pivotal moment in your social life. Miss one, and you might as well not exist.

"Your dad told me you have a video chat with your friends every Saturday night," I say. "Is that still happening tomorrow?"

"Yeah." She lifts her head off the window and turns to me. "It's gonna start earlier than usual. We'll have a lot to talk about after the party. I'm not the only person who's missing it, so all my friends in New York are gonna fill the rest of us in on what happened. And they promised to keep us updated on any important stuff by text tonight."

"That's great. Something to look forward to, right?"

She nods and smiles softly. "Right."

"And look, the trip is already half over. We'll be home before you know it." That knife in my stomach plunges deeper. I don't want to think about returning to New York. Because that means figuring out "what's next." And I'm not just talking about my career.

Richard and I haven't discussed a future together. For all I know, what we have is nothing more than a vacation fling. It feels like a whole lot more to me, but what would the day-to-day reality of dating a billionaire look like? Would I be forced to dodge photographers on the streets? Would he be so preoccupied with work that I'd never see him? Our lives are so different. I can't fathom how they could fit together in any real way.

"You're right," Bijou says, bringing me back to the present moment. "I feel a lot better now. Thanks for letting me vent, Abby."

"Anytime. And remember, your feelings are always valid, okay?"

"Okay." She relaxes into her seat, reclining against the headrest. "You always know the right thing to say. I love having you here."

"Well, thank you. I love being here."

"And you're, like, so good for my dad, too."

Uh-oh. "What do you mean by that?"

She rolls her eyes. "Duh. It's obvious you guys are a thing."

Please tell me she hasn't seen me and Richard sneaking into the dinghy in the middle of the night. I sputter nonsensical syllables before

I'm finally able to string together a coherent sentence. "I'm not sure what you're talking about."

"You don't have to lie, Abby. The way you two look at each other? You're so in love."

"We are not in love." We're nowhere near mentioning the L-word. Miles away from it, in fact.

"Deny it all you want," she says, "but you totally are. You guys need to kiss already and get it over with."

Okay, so she hasn't seen us kissing. That's good. Even so, it irks me that she's figured us out. I thought we were being so discreet. Are we really that bad at hiding it?

"I'm totally cool with it," she continues. "Since he met you, my dad's been so much more fun. He actually smiles now, which never used to happen before. And he asks me questions, and he listens when I talk. It's like you made him into a better person."

The air rushes from my lungs in a surge of relief. Maybe it's not such a bad thing that she knows. The three of us are having a great time, after all, getting along and enjoying each other's company. This should be a cause for celebration, right? Except it's also really terrifying.

As if reading my mind, Bijou says, "Don't worry, I won't tell my mom."

"I can't ask you to keep a secret from your mother."

"I keep plenty of secrets from my mother, Abby. Besides, if I tell her, she'll just say mean things. It's none of her business."

Suddenly, the back door flies open. Richard ducks his head inside, smiling, completely oblivious to the heavy discussion we've got going on. "I'm so sorry I'm late. Time got away from me."

"It's okay," Bijou says. Her calm demeanor is a stark contrast to the eye rolls she gave him when he showed up late for our trip to Cala Varques. What a difference a couple of weeks makes.

"Merci, Pierre," Richard says as he closes the door. "Allons-y!"

Pierre gives an irritable grunt before pulling out of the parking lot. Richard turns around, slinging his hand across the headrest. He opens his mouth to say something but stops short when he looks at our faces. Bijou's wearing this wicked smile, and I'm sure my cheeks are all sorts of flushed.

"What's wrong?" he asks.

"Nothing." My voice is way too high pitched to be believable. Bijou's not backing me up, either. In fact, it looks like she's actually enjoying this.

"I know you're hiding something. Tell me what it is." Now I feel bad. Richard looks upset, but not in an Angry Dad kind of way. It's almost like he's got FOMO because he's not in on our secret.

"She knows," I say.

"Knows what?"

"That you two are a thing," she says.

He frowns at me. "Did you tell her? I thought you didn't want her to know."

Now Bijou frowns at me. "Why didn't you want me to know?"

"Because I thought it would complicate things. I didn't want to be a distraction or get in the way of your time with your dad."

"You're not in the way."

"I keep telling her that," Richard says.

"Well, now it's out in the open," I say, throwing my hands in the air. "Your dad and I have a thing for each other. Are you happy?"

"Yes, in fact. I'm very happy." She crosses her arms against her chest, seeming quite pleased with herself for figuring us out. "Now you two can stop pretending. You're bad at it, anyway."

"Are we? I thought we were doing okay," he says.

"I thought so, too."

Bijou scoffs at the both of us, which frankly feels the tiniest bit rude. But when Richard slides his gaze toward me, our eyes lock with a force so strong I can feel a magnetic pull in the base of my spine.

No wonder Bijou knew. It's impossible to hide an attraction of this magnitude.

Still, we limit our PDA to longing stares; I'm not quite comfortable holding hands or hugging in public just yet. Not that there's much time or opportunity to throw ourselves at each other while we're navigating this ropes course. We spend the next three hours scaling cliff faces, navigating obstacle courses, and zip-lining across a river. It's as thrilling as it is exhausting, and by the time we get back to the yacht, it takes every ounce of energy I have to shower off all the dirt and sweat before I crawl into bed.

Just for a quick nap, though. Richard and I have plans to meet at midnight again, and I want to get some rest beforehand. I set an alarm for eleven o'clock so I'll have plenty of time to pretty myself up before our rendezvous in the dinghy. But there's still a wink of daylight filtering through my curtains when I'm awoken from a sound sleep by a knock on the door. Probably Coco. It's a Friday night, after all. She's probably got VIP passes.

I roll out of bed in my SpongeBob pajamas and answer the door midyawn. Then I slam it shut again when I see Richard on the other side.

"I take it you're not happy to see me?" His muffled voice sounds from the hallway as I fumble out of my ratty PJs and into something a little less embarrassing.

"No, no, I am. I just wasn't expecting you! Give me one second." While tugging on a pair of shorts, I catch a glimpse of myself in the mirror and oh my gosh, what is going on with my hair? I pull it back into a messy bun, throw on a tank top, and race back to open the door. "Hello again."

"Hello." He looks me up and down, his eyes lingering on my nipples, which I've just noticed are extremely visible through this white tank. "You know, I love this outfit, but you didn't have to change out of your SpongeBob pajamas just for me."

I want to fall through the floor. Arpita has been telling me to get rid of those PJs for at least six months. They're faded and pilly, and I've had them since my freshman year of college. But I can't bear to part with them. "Those are my favorite pajamas. I know they're stupid, but they're super comfy."

"They're not stupid. I love SpongeBob." He leans in, surprising me with a searing, sensuous kiss. My whole body responds to the taste of his lips, the scent of his skin. I press myself against him, sinking my fingers into the thick hair at the nape of his neck. But the second his hand cups my breast, I back away. I'm so used to hiding in the shadows; it feels strange kissing out in the open like this.

"Slow down," I say. "Where's Bijou?"

"In her room, texting her friends. I'm sure she'll be there all night. I'm bored and lonely, so I thought you could come down to the saloon with me and keep me company."

"Do you think that's a good idea? I mean, I know Bijou knows about us, but I'm not really comfortable doing . . . you know"—I waggle my eyebrows—"out in the open."

"Oh, of course not. We can save"—he waggles his eyebrows right back—"for the dinghy later tonight. I have something else planned now. Come, I'll show you."

I take his outstretched hand and gleefully follow him down to the main deck, where he leads me into the dimly lit saloon. A wall of windows offers a view of the rapidly setting sun, and as we sit beside each other on the sofa, he gestures to a bottle of wine on the coffee table. "May I pour you some?"

"That would be delightful, thank you." I glance around the room, taking in the opulent decor. There are crystal vases filled with fresh flowers and brocade throw pillows on every chair. An enormous Persian rug covers most of the hardwood floor. And, of course, there's the huge flat-screen on the wall. "This is the biggest TV I've ever seen."

"A hundred inches. I thought it would be perfect for a movie night. Interested?"

"Definitely. What do you think we should watch?"

"Well, I have an idea, but stop me if you've seen this one before." He picks up the remote and taps the power button. Instantly, the screen lights up with a familiar sequence of scenes: an ocean liner docked in a harbor, hundreds of passengers waving from the balconies; an ominous close-up of an undulating wave; the word *Titanic* in bold white letters.

"Oh, yay!" I squeal with joy. "I haven't done my yearly rewatch yet, so this is perfect timing."

"Good. You don't think it's bad mojo to watch a boat-disaster movie while we ourselves are on a boat, do you?"

"Of course not. There are no icebergs in the Mediterranean." I pat his knee affectionately and plant a soft kiss on his cheek. "You're going to love it. Trust me."

We sink into the plush seat, snuggling together and sipping our wine, as the story of Jack Dawson and Rose DeWitt Bukater unfolds on the massive screen before us. I must've seen this movie at least a dozen times, but it's never any less moving. I still hold my breath as Jack saves Rose from falling overboard, still sneer when Cal treats her like one of his possessions. Richard seems engrossed in the story, silently watching while he wraps his arm tightly around my shoulders, holding me close.

During the iconic moment where Jack and Rose stand at the bow of the ship, arms raised as if they're flying over the Atlantic, I get a little misty eyed. I can't help it; it happens every time I watch this scene. I glance sideways to get Richard's reaction to find he's not watching the movie. He's watching me.

"I see why you like this movie so much," he says.

"It's romantic, isn't it?"

"Yeah. And you remind me so much of Rose." He twines his fingers in mine, and our hands look so much like those of the lovers on-screen that it makes my stomach do backflips. "You're strong and adventurous, and you never back down from a challenge. To borrow Jack Dawson's words, you're 'amazingly astounding.'"

My body temperature rises under the warmth of his stare. No one has ever made me feel this special before. This wanted.

"Then you're my Jack," I say. "You bring out the best in me and never let me doubt myself. You've showed me there's a whole world beyond what I knew existed. And you make me excited to see what else is in store."

Our mouths meet in a soft, searching kiss. His lips taste like wine, and his hands feel like heaven as they skate up the sides of my body. He leans back and drinks me in like the sight of me is an intoxicating brew.

"I never expected this to happen," he says. "Who would've thought I'd fall head over heels for my daughter's math tutor?"

"Who would've thought I'd fall for my boss?" I smile and nuzzle my head against his shoulder. "You are so different from how I thought you'd be."

"How did you think I'd be?"

"I don't know. Probably more serious, more severe. Definitely not as fun as you actually are. I had this image in my mind of you always hunched over and scowling."

I giggle at how ridiculous it is, in hindsight, to think of this gorgeous, confident, humble geek as the grumpy, skirt-chasing jerk the tabloids made him out to be. Richard doesn't laugh along with me, though. In fact, he's completely silent.

I lift my head to find those perfect lips of his drooped in a frown. "I'm sorry. Did I upset you?"

"No. It's just . . . was it those websites? Is that what gave you these preconceived notions of me?"

"Kind of. I didn't realize they bothered you so much." Coco told me he doesn't care what these tabloids say about him, but maybe he actually does.

"They don't bother me." He answers in a rush, then thinks about it and adds, "I mean, it doesn't feel great knowing the whole world sees me as something I'm not, but I've learned to ignore it."

"Why don't you fight back?"

"It's not worth my time or my effort. People believe what they want to believe, you know? They don't care about the truth."

"I care about the truth." I press my palm to his cheek and gaze into his deep-brown eyes. "And the truth is you're a wonderful man."

He covers my hand with his own. "Well, your opinion is the only one that matters to me."

I'm not sure how long we sit there, lost in each other. Richard's probably missing some crucial plot points in the movie, but I'll catch him up later. It's not as crucial as this present moment right here. Us, together, alone.

Suddenly, the door to the saloon flies open, and Bijou comes striding inside. She halts abruptly when she sees us on the couch. "Sorry, didn't mean to interrupt." Then she looks at the television and shrieks. "Oh my god, are you two watching porn?"

To my abject horror, we've progressed to the scene where Jack sketches Rose in the nude. Kate Winslet's bare breast fills all one hundred inches of the screen. Richard and I simultaneously leap for the remote and talk over each other, desperate to explain how *not* pornographic this movie is.

"This is an epic romance, one of the greatest movies of all time!"

"Historical fiction at its finest."

"It won eleven Oscars, including the one for Best Picture!"

She winces, wholly unconvinced. "Whatever. I'm gonna get some ice cream."

"Ice cream sounds good!" Richard says.

"It does!" I agree, and we follow Bijou awkwardly into the kitchen. Anything to reassure her that we weren't watching an X-rated movie.

As we pull containers of vanilla and chocolate from the Sub-Zero freezer, Richard says, "I actually wanted to talk to you about something, B. We were originally slated to leave for Capri next Friday, but Coco told me there was a mix-up at the marina, so we'll be heading there Monday instead. That means this is our last weekend in France. I haven't made any plans yet, but is there anything special you wanted to do before we leave?"

Bijou shakes her head, plopping a giant scoop of ice cream into her bowl. "Not really."

"You sure you don't want to go to Paris? It only takes an hour to fly there. We could go shopping or see the Palace of Versailles."

"No, I've already done all that with Mom. But you should definitely take Abby. I know she really wants to see the Eiffel Tower."

His eyes slide to mine, suspicious. I'll bet he thinks I put her up to this. I lift my hands, declaring innocence. "This was not my idea."

"It's true," she says, smiling with pride. "I thought of it myself."

He furrows his brow. "We're not gonna go without you, Bijou."

"Why not?"

"For one thing, I cannot leave you alone on the yacht while I go to a different city."

"I wouldn't be alone. I'd be with Coco."

"I've gotten in trouble in the past for leaving you with Coco while I travel."

"Well, this is different, because I'm asking you to do it. Plus, I'm sure she'd be happy to hang out with me so that you two could have some alone time in Paris. You and Abby deserve a proper date. Obviously." She gestures in the direction of the living room.

Richard's cheeks flush pink. "I'm here to spend time with *you*."

"Well, I can't spend time with *you* tomorrow. I'm gonna be online all day with *my* friends. Probably all night, too."

"Why?"

"We have a lot to talk about," she says. "So you two should go to Paris. We can all hang out together on Sunday."

With that, she grabs her bowl of ice cream and a silver spoon and marches out of the kitchen.

Richard stares at the empty space where Bijou was just standing, his mouth hanging open. I'm frozen in place, still as a statue. Do I want to go to Paris? Of course. My heart is pounding at the prospect of getting to see the City of Light with the man who lights me up inside.

I hold my breath as Richard looks at me. His teeth graze his lower lip, his eyebrows quirk up. "Do you want to?"

"Yes." The word falls from my lips in a frantic exhale, and all the pent-up tension releases from my body.

He flashes that half smile I love so much. "Then let's go to Paris."

CHAPTER SEVENTEEN

It's possible Coco's more excited about this trip to Paris than I am. The next day, she knocks on my door, waking me from a sound sleep. When I open the door, she's already smiling and immediately asks, "What are you wearing tonight?"

"I don't know yet," I say, through a yawn. "I'm barely awake."

"It's almost one in the afternoon."

"I know, I overslept." I'm usually an early bird, but this morning I needed to get some extra shut-eye so I'm fresh and peppy for tonight.

I can't believe I'm going to Paris! And I can't believe I'm going to be there with Richard. The two of us alone—truly alone—for the very first time. Although maybe Pierre will come with us, too. The details are blurry; I asked Richard what he's got planned, but he insisted on keeping it a secret.

"I promise you, it will be a beautiful surprise," he said, then silenced any follow-up questions with a kiss that left me limp and breathless.

I'm reliving that kiss right now, remembering the flavor of his lips and the feel of his hands on my hips, when Coco waves her hand in front of my face, bringing me back to the present moment. "Earth to Abby."

"Sorry." I blink, clearing away my daydreams. "What were you saying?"

"I was saying your wardrobe is dismal." She's standing in front of my open closet, scowling like it's a picked-through sale rack at the Gap.

"That dress you wore to the club that night would've been perfect, but it still smells like cigarettes."

"Yeah, I never got it cleaned." I pull out a flowery cotton dress. "What about this?"

"Schoolmarmish. You need something elegant yet sexy." She holds up a black, lacy, off-the-shoulder top. "This is a good start. I have a pink skirt that'll go perfectly with it. Now what about shoes?"

I pick up my rhinestone slides. "Will these work?"

"Absolutely not. You need heels. Sexy ones." She tosses the shirt at me. "Put this on. Let me go see what I can find in my closet."

Ten minutes later, I'm standing in front of my full-length mirror in a tiny pink skirt and sky-high stilettos while Coco circles me with a discerning eye. She smooths a wrinkle out of the skirt and smiles. "Perfect. You're going to blow him away."

"Why are you so invested in this date?"

"Because you're the best thing to happen to that man in a long time. He better not mess this up, I swear." She turns her attention toward my face. "Your hair looks great the way it is, all long and loose, but I think you need some dramatic eye makeup to complete the look."

"I'm terrible at doing eye makeup. The last time I tried to follow a YouTube tutorial, I looked like a reject from Cirque du Soleil."

"Don't worry. I'll take care of it." She disappears to her room and returns a moment later with a giant makeup case. She sets it up on a side table, then directs me to sit on the love seat and starts working her magic.

While she layers foundation on my cheeks, I ask what's going on with her most recent short story submission. She answers matter-of-factly. "They rejected it."

"Oh. I'm so sorry. Are you submitting it elsewhere?"

"I already have. The second journal rejected it, too. No big deal, though. Just another day in the life of a writer."

"You don't seem fazed."

She laughs as she picks up the blending brush. "Do you know how many rejections I got in the last year alone? Take a wild guess."

"Ten?"

"A hundred and twenty-seven. That's one every three days. I did the math. Every three days, some stranger is telling me my writing isn't compelling or my voice isn't unique or that the piece I've been working on for two years just 'isn't ready yet.'"

"That sounds demoralizing."

"It's only demoralizing if you allow it to be. So a bunch of editors don't like my work. So what? Their opinions don't define me. And I don't need their approval or acknowledgment to keep going."

"Don't you ever feel bitter?"

"Feeling bitter doesn't serve me. Remember my motto?"

"If it doesn't serve you, let it go."

"Exactly. Does a rejection get me down? Yeah. So I give myself a minute to be upset about it, and then I move on. I don't gain anything from wallowing in bitter feelings."

She's got a point. I certainly don't gain anything from wallowing in the bitterness I feel toward Nick and Philip. All the same, I can't seem to let the feelings go. Every time I picture their faces, I can taste the bile rising up from my stomach, burning the back of my throat. Then I find myself fantasizing about telling them off and storming away, saying goodbye to the physics building forever. Would that make me a quitter? According to my mom, yeah. But if grad school isn't serving me, shouldn't I let it go?

Then again, if I quit, that means Nick gets away with it, and the bad guys win, exactly like Arpita said. So do I stay and keep fighting, simply on principle? My throat burns just thinking of it.

As I silently contemplate the trajectory of my life, Coco finishes my face. When she holds up a mirror, I gasp in amazement at my reflection. "I look incredible. It doesn't even look like me."

"It looks exactly like you. Just flashier."

"Thank you so much, Coco." I give her a hug, careful not to smoosh my freshly contoured cheek against her shoulder. "I owe you big-time."

"Don't be silly, I'm happy to help." She puts away her makeup and snaps her case closed. "The car is coming in about a half hour. Try to chill out until then. You've got a big night in Paris ahead of you."

"Do you know what the plan is?"

"Yes, and I'm not telling. You're going to love it, though." She heads toward the door and disappears.

I try my best to follow her advice and relax for the next thirty minutes, listening to some soft piano music and sipping a cup of chamomile tea. It doesn't calm me down. I'm too amped up, brimming with anticipation and shaking with nerves. When I'm not brainstorming witticisms and practicing seductive expressions in the mirror, I'm imagining potential catastrophes and making contingency plans. I want everything to be perfect, even though I know it's impossible to plan perfection.

Finally, I close my eyes and take a few slow, deep breaths. Eventually, my thoughts slow down, too, reduced to a single image projected on the movie screen in my mind: me, Richard, the Eiffel Tower. Our lips pressed together and our bodies locked in an embrace. That's all I really want from this evening. That's my idea of perfection.

Richard meets me out on the main deck. His eyes travel the length of my body as I move toward his outstretched hand. "You look absolutely stunning," he says.

"You're looking quite dapper yourself." In fact, he's drop-dead gorgeous in his expertly tailored gray suit. The top two buttons of his crisp white button-down are undone, and there's a pink pocket square tucked into his blazer that matches my skirt to a tee. Coco's name is written all over that detail.

He takes my hand, and my whole body quivers. Not merely from the sensation of his skin, but from the knowledge that we no longer have to hide our affection. No more sneaking around in dark corners after midnight. This is for real, this thing between us.

Our fingers remain entwined as we walk to the car, where Pierre is waiting beside the open back door. "Merci beaucoup," Richard says, to which Pierre responds with his standard grunt.

It's a quick ride to the airport, where we bypass the main departures terminal for a smaller building dedicated to private aircraft. The whole experience is somewhat surreal: no waiting around on long lines, no invasive body scanners. We're simply deposited at the entrance, where Pierre stays behind and a concierge escorts us to our plane.

On board, we settle into cushy leather seats that face each other, so we both have unobstructed views out the window. A flight attendant—our only flight attendant, who addresses us by name—offers us chilled champagne and salted almonds. When we're ready to take off, there's no need to stow our tray tables or raise our seatbacks. The pilot comes out to say hi, informs us the flight time will be just under an hour and that she expects we'll encounter smooth air the entire ride.

Five minutes later, we're soaring through the clouds. As we sip our bubbly, Richard says, "I forgot to tell you: I finished *Titanic* this morning."

"Oh! What'd you think?"

He gives a little grimace. "To be honest, I thought the end was more depressing than romantic."

"What?"

"I expected Jack and Rose to end up happily ever after, but instead she kills him and chucks his frozen body into the Atlantic."

Oh no. He is not going to insult the memory of Jack and Rose. "Okay, first of all, she didn't kill him: he died of hypothermia. And second of all, she didn't 'chuck' his body anywhere. She had to dislodge him from the door in order to fulfill the promise she made to him. Which was to survive, no matter what happened."

"Well, that's the thing. There was plenty of room on that door for the both of them. If she'd just scooted over and made space for him, they both could've survived."

"Actually, you're wrong." I set down my flute, trying not to smirk too smugly. "You're not the first person to make that unsubstantiated claim, which has been debunked repeatedly by numerous scientists and mathematicians. See, it's not about space—it's about buoyancy, which is the force that allows an object to float in liquid. In this scenario, buoyancy is determined by the volume of the door, the density of ice-cold salt water, and the force of gravity. For simplicity's sake, let's call that number N.

"Now, for Jack and Rose to float safely, N must be greater than their combined weight plus the weight of the door itself, but the weight of the door can vary wildly depending on the material of which it was made. Historians have concluded that the door was almost certainly constructed of oak; in fact, even the door used in the filming of the movie was made of oak to preserve authenticity. Sadly, oak is an extremely dense wood, and therefore would've been far too heavy to support both of them at the same time. Jack made the ultimate sacrifice for love. Tell me that isn't romantic."

Triumphant, I grab my champagne and take a long, satisfying sip. Richard's mouth is hanging open as he says, "Wow. That's impressive."

"It's basic physics." I shrug my shoulder, feigning nonchalance. "No biggie."

Those hot coals are glowing in his eyes again. He leans forward, slides his warm palm up the side of my exposed thigh, and growls, "I love that delicious brain of yours, Abby."

Our mouths meet in a succulent kiss, his lips soft and salty, his tongue hungry and hot. The only thing keeping me from unbuckling my safety belt and straddling Richard's lap is the flight attendant sitting in the jump seat ten feet away. Too bad this plane doesn't come with a privacy shield.

Not that I'm complaining. If we turned around now and headed back to Saint-Tropez, this would still be the best date of my life. Fortunately, though, we keep going until we touch down in Paris, where a new driver is waiting to collect us. His name is Hugo, and he's friendlier than Pierre, welcoming us to the city with a warm bonjour.

"You have a special evening prepared, yes?" he asks, making eye contact with me in the rearview mirror as we pull out of the airport.

"Yes," I say, then slide a sly smile toward Richard. "At least, I think we do."

"We do." He brings my hand to his lips and presses a tender kiss against each of my fingertips. An electric current travels up my arm and down my spine, making me shiver.

The first stop on our whirlwind one-night stand in Paris is the river Seine. Richard's hired a small boat to take us on a private tour. It's oddly reminiscent of our luxurious dinghy. "We only have a few hours here," he says. "I thought this would be a great way to get a feel for the city in such a short amount of time."

"It's perfect," I say. The steward pours us more champagne as we float along the water, passing one famous landmark after another. The Notre-Dame Cathedral, in the midst of renovations. The Musée d'Orsay is on the right bank, the Louvre on the left. We pass beneath the Pont des Arts with all its locks, each representing an unbreakable love.

"Paris is more beautiful than I ever imagined it would be," I say. "Every building is like a work of art."

"It's a shame we won't have enough time to visit Montmartre tonight." He presses a kiss to the back of my hand. "Next time."

"Next time?"

"On our next trip to Paris."

"And when will that be?"

"Whenever you want. For you, my schedule is wide open."

My stomach flutters at the thought of a future with Richard, one where we travel to Paris on a whim. Private jets, luxury accommodations, VIP everywhere we go. Maybe he doesn't mean it. Maybe it's just the champagne talking. But this moment is so magical I'm choosing to believe that every word he says is true.

He whispers, "Turn around," and the moment becomes even more extraordinary.

I've seen countless photos of the Eiffel Tower in my lifetime, but when our little boat pulls up beside it, I'm awestruck. Photos don't do justice to its magnitude. There's an energy emanating from the latticework, well over a hundred years of history in its iron plates and beams. Being in its presence makes me feel both unfathomably lucky and incredibly small.

Richard stands behind me and wraps his arms around my waist. His breath is hot in my ear as he asks, "What do you think?"

"I think I might be dreaming." This summer has been one pinch-me moment after another, but this moment right here is straight out of a fairy tale.

He kisses my earlobe, and I feel it in the tips of my toes. "You are very much awake," he says. "And the night is still young."

When our cruise is over, the car whisks us away to the eighth arrondissement. We pass the tall Egyptian obelisk in the Place de la Concorde, then zoom down the Champs-Élysées, turning left before we reach the Arc de Triomphe. The car pulls up in front of a five-story Haussmann-style building with a stone facade and a mansard roof. At the entrance, five wide steps lead to a double door flanked by colonnades, one of which displays a sign for the Shangri-La Hotel.

Richard got us a hotel room.

My blood runs hot, fire flooding my veins at the thought of what's going to happen tonight. Suddenly, I feel ravenous, and as we step into the lobby hand in hand, I'm ready to devour him whole.

He approaches the doorman. "Bonsoir, monsieur. Je suis Richard Vale et j'ai une réservation pour deux."

I had no idea Richard could speak French so well. And with such a flawless, sexy accent. I cannot wait to get him alone.

"Ah, oui," the doorman says. He leads us to an elevator bank, where he mutters something to a bellhop, who nods and says, "Bien sûr," before ushering us into the elevator and pressing the button for the top floor.

"Are we going to the penthouse?" I ask. Of course he would get the penthouse suite. When Richard makes plans, he always goes all-out. We're VIP, everywhere we go.

"The roof," he replies. "There's a Michelin-starred restaurant up there with beautiful views of the Eiffel Tower."

"Oh." I'm so surprised that my voice falters, which makes me sound ungrateful, so I try once more with enthusiasm. "That's so amazing!"

If he can sense my disappointment, he doesn't let on. Not that I'm *at all* disappointed in a gourmet Parisian dinner with rooftop views. I was merely expecting a different kind of meal, but I'm more than satisfied with actual food.

The host seats us at a table on a private balcony, completely secluded from other diners, so when we sit down, it feels like the city belongs to us and us alone. The Dôme des Invalides glitters in the distance, the Seine ripples directly below. The Eiffel Tower feels close enough to touch.

"I'm in heaven," I say, as a server brings us yet another bottle of champagne.

"This was the first place I thought of when you said you wanted to see the Eiffel Tower," Richard says.

"Have you been to this restaurant before?"

"Yes. Under far less romantic circumstances, I assure you. It was for a business meeting. Two years ago, we started investing in a small French start-up that aims to crowdfund job training for people experiencing homelessness. So far they've helped over a thousand people in France find new careers and completely turn their lives around. Our goal is to bring this model to other countries, including the United States."

His eyes light up as he talks about this start-up, the passion he has for his work evident in his sweeping hand gestures and mellifluous tone of voice.

"Their main office isn't far from here, actually," he continues. "I'd toyed with the idea of dropping in on them during this trip, but after you and I had that conversation about taking time off to focus on Bijou, I decided against it."

"I'm glad to hear that. You know, Bijou's convinced you're still working when she's not around."

He clears his throat and studies the linen napkin folded neatly in the center of his plate. "Well, I'm doing small things here and there. Responding to emails, reviewing documents, attending the occasional conference call. But only when she's otherwise indisposed. There's a full four hours each weekday when she's busy with you, so I don't see the harm in it."

There really *is* no harm in it. It doesn't bother Bijou. So why is it bothering me? "You really can't take the time off of work? You said you trusted your team."

"I do. And I *could* take the time off, but frankly, I'm more comfortable this way."

"Because you like being in control of what's happening in the office?"

"Yes, and because helping to build these businesses genuinely makes me happy. I don't *have* to work; I *want* to work. But I don't want my life to revolve around it. Not anymore. I want other things, too. Like time with Bijou. And time with you. Not just here, but in New York, and in Paris, and anywhere else we might travel together."

He reaches across the table and threads his fingers through mine. Somewhere inside my chest, a bottle of champagne goes pop. The cork ricochets throughout my rib cage as a million tiny bubbles fizzle and crack around my heart. This isn't just a vacation fling. We have a future together.

But the bubbles go flat when I think about all the other aspects of my future, all the trouble that's waiting for me back in New York.

There are so many question marks, so few answers, and I have so much unresolved bitterness in my bones.

"I admire your passion for your work," I say. "I wish I had that same sort of deep drive and desire to keep going. I'm so unhappy that I keep daydreaming about giving up on my degree."

"Who can blame you? You've been betrayed by your adviser, all your hard work stolen out from under you."

"The weird thing is, I'm not sure that's the only problem. I mean, it was certainly the catalyst for all these confusing feelings, but if I take an honest look at the last four years of my life . . . I was never really happy. I've always sort of been hiding from the truth."

"Which is?"

"I don't want to be in grad school." It feels good to finally say it out loud. Scary, but mostly really, really good. "I don't know that I've *ever* really wanted this."

"Then drop out." He says it so casually, like it isn't a monumental, earth-shattering decision that will rock my world to its core.

Plus, I can't stop thinking about what Arpita said. "If I do that, then the bad guys win."

"No, *you* win. You get to follow a new path, chase a new opportunity. It's a chance to find something that really makes you happy." He squeezes my hand to emphasize his words. "And you deserve to be happy."

He's right about that. I do deserve to be happy. I'm just not sure how to make that happen. "What would I do, though?"

"Only you can answer that question. My only advice? Don't overthink it. It'll all end up the way it's supposed to."

He presses his lips to the back of my hand, kissing away any lingering doubt I may have had about the existence of destiny. Who knows what joy I might discover if I simply close my eyes and take the leap? Yes, the future is full of question marks, but I don't need to have all the answers right away. Sometimes it's better to let things unfold naturally while remaining open to the possibility of pleasure. After all, I never imagined that a miserable meeting with Philip would lead me on the winding road toward this magical moment in Paris.

And it truly is magical. As the sun goes down, the lights of the city flicker on one by one. First, the windows in the buildings, then the lanterns in the streets. Finally, the Eiffel Tower glows golden against the dusky sky.

It's an extraordinary backdrop for an extraordinary meal. We order the tasting menu, which is ten courses of pure indulgence. Each plate is small, but our palates are more than pleasured with dishes like salty caviar, ripe tomatoes, roasted quail, mushroom risotto, French cheeses, and a delightful sorbet.

When dinner is over, I'm satisfied but not overly full. As the server clears our silverware away, my head is swimming from sensory overload and one too many glasses of champagne.

"Now what?" I ask, curious about his plans for the rest of the evening. Maybe we'll go for a stroll through the Tuileries Garden or pop in on a cabaret show.

Richard takes my hand again, candlelight flickering in his eyes. "I don't want to be presumptuous," he says, his voice low and smooth like velvet. "But I reserved a suite. Here, in this hotel. In case you'd like to have some alone time."

"Yes." I practically leap out of my chair. "Alone time sounds wonderful."

It's a struggle to keep my cool as we walk to the elevator. It's been less than a week since we first kissed, but I feel like I've been waiting an eternity for this moment. Sneaking around was exciting at first, but I'm tired of hiding in dark corners, hoping no one will see. I want to touch him and taste him and hold him without fear. I want all of him, in private, immediately.

Desire consumes me as he taps his electronic key card to the door. A beep and a click, and we're stepping inside. The suite is luxurious, with silk brocade drapes and gilded panel molding. French doors open up onto a wide terrace with panoramic views of the city, from the Sacré-Coeur to the Grand Palais. Straight ahead, the Eiffel Tower performs a glittering light show, like a thousand camera flashes going off at once.

I barely register any of it, though. At this moment, we could be in an empty windowless room, and I'd still be floating on air. All I need is what's standing before me. This imperfect man in his perfectly tailored suit.

I grab him by his lapels, crumpling the fine fabric in my clenched fists. When I pull him toward me, there's no need for words. There's only the crush of our mouths and the heat of our breath, the feel of his fingers tracing fire up my thigh.

CHAPTER EIGHTEEN

The next few hours are fantastical and dreamlike. I have no idea what time we leave Paris or touch down in Saint-Tropez. All I know is we return to the yacht at some point before sunrise, my legs deliciously weak and my lips beautifully bruised.

Richard and I part ways on the main deck. "Thank you for everything," I say.

"No, thank *you*."

We say goodbye with a kiss. It's a brief, chaste kiss—especially compared to the way we kissed last night—but it feels good to openly acknowledge our relationship. No more hiding. No more secrecy.

Back in my room, I close the curtains, climb into bed, and sleep for hours. Part of me feels bad for spending the whole day in bed—it's our last day in Saint-Tropez, after all; I'm surely missing out on seeing something amazing—but my body doesn't give me a choice. I'm worn out, in the best possible way.

When I wake up in the late afternoon, a note's been slipped under my door:

I want to know everything but not today

because I'm writing. HMU tomorrow.

—C

That's too bad. I'm dying to debrief, spill all the details of my journey through Paris, from the private jet to the luxury suite. I suppose I could always call Arpita, but we haven't spoken since Friday afternoon, when she told me dating Richard was a bad idea. I doubt she'd be too thrilled about this news.

Instead, I wander outside to find Bijou and Richard lounging by the pool. He looks unbearably handsome in his board shorts and aviators, his bare chest glistening in the sunlight.

"Hey there," I say, pulling up a chair beside them. Richard smiles, and I nearly melt into my seat. "How's it going?"

"Great," Richard says, slipping his glasses up onto his head. "Bijou was just telling me about all the things she wants to do when we get to Capri."

"There's this place called the Blue Grotto," she says, boiling over with enthusiasm. "It's basically this massive flooded cave. To get there, you have to take a rowboat and then duck your head to enter."

"Wow. That sounds cool."

"Yeah. And I wanna go cliff jumping again. Is that cool, Dad?"

"Of course, B. What about you, Abby? Are you interested?" Richard's eye contact feels indecent. The last time he looked at me that way, he was hovering above me, his damp curls falling in his face.

I look down at my lap, hoping my flushed cheeks don't betray my thoughts. "You know it."

She tells us about a chairlift we can take to get to the top of a mountain, and a gelateria in town that serves over forty different flavors. Eventually, I can look at Richard without going red in the face. The three of us talk and laugh and make plans for the week ahead, and it all feels very natural. Like I belong here.

I'm on a high for the rest of the afternoon, a feeling that lasts well into the night, when Richard and I meet at our usual spot in the tender. But as we lie side by side in the dim light, a sense of unease descends on me. I have fallen for this man, hard and fast, and our time on this trip is quickly coming to an end. He's made vague references to a shared future, but did he really mean them? Or were they champagne-fueled promises that he'll forget the moment we leave this fantasy world behind?

"I need to talk to you."

Richard props himself up on one arm, glancing down at me with a crease of worry in his forehead. "That doesn't sound good."

"No, it's not bad. At least I hope it's not. I just need to know something." I pause, struggling to find the right words. "Yesterday, you said you wanted me in your life, not just here but in New York, too. Were you serious about that?"

His eyes soften. "One hundred percent."

"Is it realistic, though?"

"Why wouldn't it be?"

"You and I come from two such disparate worlds, you know? And you're so committed to your work I'm afraid there won't be room for me in your life."

He sees right through my attempt at subtlety. "Abby, I promise you, I am not the same person I used to be, and I will not make the same mistakes I made in my marriage. I will create space in my life for you. I will be there when you need me. You make me feel more alive than I ever have before, and I do not want to lose you. I can't."

I reach up and pull him down to me, relishing the weight and warmth of his body against mine. And as our mouths meet, I realize I've never felt more alive, either. And I've never been happier.

The next morning, I sneak back to my stateroom before the sun comes up, hoping to catch a few hours of sleep before tutoring starts. But before I close my eyes, I make the grave mistake of checking my phone.

There's a text from Arpita—OMG!—along with a link to one of those gossip websites. I know before I open it that whatever is in here will ruin my mood, but I can't stop myself. I hold my breath as I tap the link, and when I read the headline, I gasp in horror: VALE RENTS HOTEL BY THE HOUR FOR PARISIAN RENDEZVOUS WITH NANNY.

Directly below those big bold letters are two photos of me and Richard. In the first, we're on the steps of the Shangri-La Hotel, hand in hand. It's the moment we arrived, when he spoke to the doorman in perfectly accented French. I'm beaming beside him, my hair glossy and my skirt smooth, completely oblivious to the fact that there's a photographer lurking somewhere behind us.

In the second photo, I'm equally oblivious but far less composed. My eye makeup is smudged and my skirt is rumpled, and I'm sporting what can only be described as "sex hair." It's dark outside, and Richard's arm is wrapped around my shoulders as we exit the hotel and walk toward the car that's waiting for us at the curb.

My brain must be malfunctioning, because I can't seem to read the rest of the article. Half the words blur together, and the ones I can discern don't make sense. I'm not the nanny. And it wasn't a "top secret sex getaway" like it states in the first paragraph. It was a beautiful evening, a special and meaningful date in the City of Light. There's no mention of our cruise on the Seine or our rooftop dinner. The whole experience has been reduced to a few hours in a hotel room, like we're engaged in some tawdry affair.

As I'm staring at the photos, my phone buzzes in my hand. Another text from Arpita: Call me when you're up. I'm still awake.

I don't feel like being chastised again for having an affair with my boss, but I also don't feel like being alone right now, so I dial her up.

"Hey," she says, drawing the word out slowly and carefully. She's got this guarded expression, her big brown eyes wide and wary, like she's not sure how to handle this situation. If she says, "I told you so," I will absolutely snap. "How are you?"

"I don't know." Truly, I don't. I feel as if I've stepped off the Frisbee again, my head spinning from the rapid change of altitude. Moments ago, I was flying high, dizzy with delight. Now I'm plummeting toward the ground with my stomach in my throat.

"You look really upset," she says. "I'm sorry. I shouldn't have told you about the article. I was so shocked when I saw it I sent you that text without thinking."

"No, no. I'm glad you told me. I wouldn't want this information floating around out there completely unbeknownst to me." Although it's not like I can do anything about it. Maybe blissful ignorance would've been better.

"I didn't realize you were going to Paris," she says.

"It was a last-minute thing. Richard took me there because he knew I wanted to see the Eiffel Tower." I don't mention how we ended up at the hotel. Suddenly, it all feels so shameful. Tawdry, even.

"Look, it's one stupid article on one stupid website that I'm sure no one ever reads. The only reason I found it is because I set up a Google Alert for Richard's name. Your name isn't even mentioned; it's just a couple of grainy photographs. As far as the internet is concerned, you're an anonymous nanny."

"Exactly what I've always wanted to be known as."

She gives me a pitiful smile. "Memories are short these days, and people are easily distracted. I promise you, this will not be a big thing at all. Just . . . you know . . . try to be careful from now on."

She's probably right. There's no mention of my name, and if you don't know me, you might not be able to tell that it's me in those photos. Dianne might recognize me, but she also might not even see this. It's a socialite gossip blog, not the *New York Times*. She's got her hands full with her business, and I doubt she's set up a Google Alert for *Richard Vale* the way Arpita has. All in all, the situation is not great, but it's not the end of the world.

As soon as we end the call, I do a quick Google search of my name, just to be sure nothing else is lingering out there. Thankfully, I'm not the only Abby Atkinson in the world, and it turns out none of us are newsworthy. I scroll through a bit and eventually find my website, the one hosted by the physics department. When I click the link, the page is woefully empty. Current teaching assignments: none. Current research lab: undefined. I may as well not be listed there at all.

I delete my name from the search box and type in *Richard Vale*. As expected, hundreds of thousands of results are returned. Currently, I'm only interested in news items, so I sort them by date, in descending order. The first one is the article I've already seen. When I read the words *HOTEL BY THE HOUR*, my stomach lurches, and I scroll past it quickly to avoid reliving the trauma.

The past couple of weeks have produced a dearth of Richard Vale content. Probably because he's been lying low on the yacht, and when he does go out, he's always with Bijou, who has clearly been marked as an off-limits topic by these gossip rags. Since he left New York, there have only been two articles published that mention his name, both from this same sleazy website: the one with the pictures of us in Paris, and another titled VERONICA VALE LOOKS FAB & GLAM IN WE-HO WHILE TAPING NEW REALITY SHOW.

Lovely. I'm the nameless nanny who doubles as an hourly escort, while Veronica is a fabulously glamorous Hollywood star. I scan the text for Richard's name and find it mentioned exactly once, in the second paragraph, when Veronica is referred to as "Richard Vale's ex-wife, who is bouncing back from heartache with a breakout role on the new *Real Housewives* spin-off." All these years later, is she really still "bouncing back"?

As the sun comes up, I stare out the window, contemplating my terrible choices. At some point, the boat's engine roars to life, and I watch the city of Saint-Tropez recede as we slowly back out of the harbor. Eventually, it disappears completely. France is now just a memory.

We'll be sailing to Capri until sundown, which is good, since there are no paparazzi cruising around on the open seas. At least, I don't think there are. Either way, I can't hide out in my stateroom any longer, because it's time to tutor Bijou. So I gather my courage, slap on a fake smile, and get ready to start the day.

I'm sitting in the office, still fake smiling, when she walks through the door. At the sight of me, she stops abruptly and scowls. "What's wrong?"

"Nothing." The word snakes out through clenched teeth. I'm not fooling anyone.

"You look like you're about to cry. Did something happen?"

I clasp my hands together so tightly my knuckles ache. "I kind of wound up on this website."

"Which one, Radar?" She asks it so nonchalantly. Like ending up in the tabloids is a customary nuisance, similar to jury duty or a heavy-flow day.

"No. A blog called NYC Social Scandals."

"Oh. Their readership is, like, terrible." She sits down at the desk and boots up her laptop.

"How do you know that?"

"My mom knows the stats for every gossip column out there. She has a spreadsheet where she tracks every time they mention her. It's embarrassing."

"Does it upset you? I mean, that these gossip columns write about your mom." I almost add "and dad," but think better of it. Maybe she's unaware of the terrible things they say about him.

"Not really. I mean, it's annoying how obsessed she is with it. But it's not like anyone important reads what's on those stupid websites. My friends definitely don't. And my dad says it's all lies, anyway, people making stuff up for advertising money, so whatever. Don't worry about it."

"Oh." Well, Bijou's certainly well adjusted. I wish I could be that blasé and unemotional about the whole thing, but every time I blink, those photos appear behind my closed eyelids. Me, gazing at Richard with longing and admiration. Me, hours later, leaving the hotel with rumpled hair and a wrinkled skirt. I'm painted as nothing more than a sex toy. Another meaningless conquest for the Billionaire Playboy.

"If it really bothers you," she says, "I'm sure you could ask my dad to get it taken down."

"I don't think that's possible. He doesn't own these websites."

She cocks her head and gives me this skeptical look. "My dad's a powerful guy, Abby. When he speaks, people listen."

Maybe she's right. Maybe I could ask him to talk to that website, get the photos taken down. Coco said he never lets them print anything about Bijou, so he must hold some sway.

On the other hand, maybe I'm being dramatic and hysterical. It's one measly lie, on one measly website. This'll probably all blow over in a matter of hours.

CHAPTER NINETEEN

It does not blow over in a matter of hours. On the contrary, it blows up.

When I return to my room after tutoring, I'm finally feeling sort of okay about everything. Then I check my phone, which I really need to stop doing, because nothing good ever comes from it. Like the text from Arpita that says, **Whatever you do, do not google your name.**

Does she honestly think I won't google my name now? I can't hit the search button fast enough. Though I regret it immediately, because a new story was posted about an hour ago, titled ABBY ATKINSON: 5 FAST FACTS YOU NEED TO KNOW ABOUT RICHARD VALE'S LATEST HOOKUP.

Suddenly, I am no longer the anonymous nanny. I am now a public figure. My full name is printed here—Abigail Jane Atkinson—along with photos swiped from my Instagram account, which they've conveniently linked to. They've got my age here, and the fact that I was born in Rochester, New York, and currently live in Astoria, Queens. My whole life is on display for the entire world to see.

Except it's not *really* my whole life. It's distorted bits and pieces of it, assembled into a search engine–optimized listicle. They finally figured out I'm a tutor, not a nanny, but fortunately they don't mention Dianne or her agency by name. They do, however, quote an unnamed former client who describes me as "extraordinarily bright but perpetually dissatisfied." What does that even mean?

The article calls me a "money-hungry vixen" who "seduced and devoured" Richard Vale. Halfway through, when they say I'm a "PhD student in physics," my mouth goes dry. A mystery "source from grad school" has a whole lot to say about me, like that I'm a "loudmouth" who is "out of my depth" and "not committed to my program." They allude to a "departmental scandal" in which I "falsely accused a greatly respected professor of theft, in an act of deluded desperation."

I know I should shut down the browser window. There's no need to keep torturing myself like this. But for some stupid reason, I read the article until the very end, digesting all the half truths and quotes from anonymous sources who jumped on the opportunity to tear my character to shreds.

With shaky thumbs, I text Arpita: What the actual fuck?

She calls me immediately. When I answer, she says, "I told you not to google your name."

"I cannot believe this," I say, my voice quivering. "It has everything about me. My name, my socials. All the shit that happened in school."

"Who do you think the unnamed source was?"

"Probably some grad student. Maybe even one of my lab mates. I'm sure they were looking for extra cash, and these sites always pay for information."

"That's good."

"Good?"

She shakes her head apologetically. "I mean it's good that it's not Nick or Philip."

"Does it even matter who it was? If the grad students are gossiping about my affair with Richard, I'm sure word's gotten around to the faculty, too. Now I'm not just a troublemaker but I'm also a gold-digging skank."

"Oh, by the way," she says, "you might want to lock down your Instagram account."

"What?" I pull up my profile to find hundreds of likes and comments, and a follower count that has tripled in size. I can't process this right now, so I set my profile to private and shut down the app. "I'm going to murder someone."

"Don't do anything rash."

"You keep saying that, but it's not like sitting on my hands has gotten me anywhere. I can't keep letting people trash my reputation. I need to defend myself."

"Well, maybe Richard should be defending you. He's the one with the power in this situation. The tabloids will listen to him. Besides, he's the whole reason this happened. Go tell him to fix it."

Is there any fixing this? What's done is done. Even if Richard could get the post taken down, these words have already been consumed by who knows how many people. And once a rumor starts to spread, there's no reining it in.

I still want to talk to him, though. I want the warm reassurance of his embrace, his soothing velvety voice in my ear. I want him to tell me that everything will be all right, because he'll stop the tabloids from coming after me, the same way he stopped them from coming after Bijou.

I end the call and go off in search of him. Since we're at sea today, it's probably safe to assume he's working, so I head straight to his office. As I climb to the top deck, wind whips my hair around my face. It's the first blustery day we've experienced on our journey, which seems fitting for my turbulent mood. I knock at the door, and when he doesn't answer, I knock again, this time harder. Finally, he slides it open and peeks his head out, a wrinkle of annoyance running the length of his forehead. The moment he sees me, the wrinkle disappears and he smiles.

"Hey," he whispers, then points to his earbuds, which I haven't seen for quite some time. "This call is almost over. Come in."

I've never been inside this office before. It's strikingly similar to the one I share with Bijou, the same plethora of gadgets and supplies. It's a bit bigger, with only one desk instead of two and a separate seating area, presumably for conducting business meetings at sea. Richard gestures to a comfy-looking chair, and I take a seat while he paces around the room, engrossed in his call.

"Well, I understand what you're saying, Nat, but I'm afraid that's not going to work . . . I said, no." He speaks with authority, the pitch of his voice plummeting on that last syllable to form a hard and decisive *no*. I envision him saying the same thing in the same way to whoever runs that gossip rag. That settles my nerves a bit.

A few minutes later, he removes his earbuds and sets them on the desktop. "I'm so sorry about that," he says.

I stand up and move toward him. "Don't be. I'm sorry to interrupt you."

"I'm happy for the interruption." He wraps his arms around my waist, and as he leans in for a kiss, I forget why I came here. The feel of his mouth on mine erases all other thought. But it's a momentary amnesia, because as soon as he pulls back and looks in my eyes, he can tell something's wrong. "Are you okay?"

"Not really. They wrote about us. About me."

"Who's 'they'?"

"The tabloids."

He hisses dismissively. "Oh, just ignore that trash."

"But they found us in Paris. There were pictures and everything. They said we were on a top secret sex getaway, that you paid for our hotel room by the hour." A sick sensation settles in my stomach as I recall the headline.

"Huh." Richard seems more pensive than undisturbed, his hands still clasped against my lower back. "I wonder how they knew to look for us there. Maybe they had an informant. That Hugo guy seemed a little too friendly, didn't he?"

"That's not all, though. There's this whole other article." My voice catches on that last word, so I pause, take a deep breath, and try again. "It's all about me. They posted pictures from my socials and talked to people I know. Past tutoring clients, people from grad school. They said awful things."

"Oh, I'm so sorry, Abby." He slides one hand up between my shoulder blades and presses me in for a hug. It's warm and reassuring, exactly what I was hoping for. A symbol that whatever may come to pass, he's always got my back. I press my ear to his chest, his voice deep and resonant as he asks, "How are you feeling?"

"Violated. Disrespected. Humiliated."

"I understand. The first time the tabloids came after me, I was furious."

"Yeah. I'm feeling furious, too."

"Don't worry," he says, heaving a sigh. "Everything will be all right. Eventually, you'll get used to it."

"Get used to it?" I pull away and look up into his eyes. "What do you mean by that?"

"I mean, you'll learn to ignore it, like I do."

"My whole life has just been dissected in the public eye. That's kind of hard to ignore."

"It's a gossip site. No one important reads that garbage."

I take a step backward, cutting off physical contact. "Maybe they do, maybe they don't. But regardless, it's going to live on the internet forever. When someone searches for my name, this insulting article is the first thing they'll find."

"And then they'll see that it's published on a disreputable website, and they won't give it any credence." He gives me this incredulous look, like I'm being completely unreasonable. "Why do you care so much about what strangers on the internet are saying about you?"

"I think a better question is, How can you *not* care?"

"Because it's not the truth!" He throws his hands in the air. "People believe what they want to believe, remember? These people don't know the real me. They don't have the power to define who I am."

"Well, it's a little different for me. I can't shake it off and get on with my billion-dollar deals as if this article doesn't exist. I'm not a high-powered businessman—I'm a loudmouthed graduate student, as they've so politely pointed out. They've made me appear incompetent and irresponsible, and if Dianne sees it, she's going to fire me."

"I'll talk to Dianne. She'll understand."

"There's nothing you can say to her that'll make it better. I've breached my contract with her, just by being with you." He flinches. Had he not been aware of that rule against fraternization? "Besides, it's not only this job. What about future jobs I apply to? No one wants to hire someone with this kind of mess attached to their name. How will I explain it away?"

"I don't know. I feel like you're mad at me for something that's completely out of my control. I didn't hire those photographers to come chasing after us in Paris."

"No, but you can ask the website to take down this story. You can tell them to leave me alone."

"I cannot do that." He has the nerve to laugh, as if there's anything remotely funny about this situation. As if there isn't something he can do.

"Why don't these tabloids ever say anything about Bijou?"

"Because I threatened them with a lawsuit."

"Exactly. So you do have some control over this."

"Bijou is a child. You're an adult. I can't call my attorney every time a tabloid says something negative about my girlfriend."

That's the first time he's called me his girlfriend. I'd be overjoyed if I weren't incandescent with rage. "Why the hell not?"

"Because then they'll know they got to me, and I refuse to play their game."

"It sounds like you're already playing." The echo of my angry voice reverberates around the office. I take a deep breath, recenter myself, and in a calmer tone, I say, "This isn't some game, Richard. This is my life."

He shoves his hands in his pockets and stares at his bare feet. For the first time since I've entered the room, I notice he's back in his videoconference attire, all business on the top and party on the bottom. He looks just like he did when I first laid eyes on him, the awkward geek who stole my heart.

I want him to fight for me. I want him to *want* to fight for me. But more than anything, I simply want him to swallow his pride and tell the world exactly who I am. That I'm not some nanny he's using for a secret sex romp, but a hard-working, intelligent, independent woman. A woman he cares about.

"You don't have to get a lawyer," I say. "I'm not asking for you to start any legal battles. Just issue a statement. Please."

The muscles in his jaw clench and release. He's still looking down, thinking it over. I wish this wasn't such a difficult decision for him to make. The answer should be crystal clear.

Finally, he lifts his gaze. I don't like what I see in his eyes.

"Look," he says, clearing his throat, "like it or not, I'm a high profile man. I didn't ask for this, but it is what it is, and you knew that going in. If you want to be with me, this is something you'll have to learn to live with."

Learn to live with. Like it's a minor inconvenience to be secretly photographed and publicly trashed. Maybe his skin is thick enough to avoid getting wounded by these kinds of slings and arrows. Or maybe it's that mine is exceptionally thin. Either way, I can't walk around knowing people think of me as the desperate, deluded woman whose only accomplishment was banging a billionaire. I'll forever be known as the sex-romp nanny, the same way Veronica's singular claim to fame is that she's Richard Vale's ex-wife.

I came on this trip to try to find myself. Instead, I've gotten hopelessly lost in this man, in this VIP adventure, in this fantasy of a passionate romance. This summer has been like a dream, but suddenly I'm wide awake, asking myself what exactly it is I'm fighting for. Richard and I don't make sense. Three weeks from now, we'll be back in New York, and while he's settling comfortably into his luxury home in Manhattan, I'll be . . . doing what, exactly? Going back to a school that doesn't want me there?

What I shouldn't do is waste any more energy on this pointless relationship. I may have felt like what we had was more than a vacation fling, but I was wrong. A fling is all it is. All it was. Now it's time for me to get back to myself and back to reality. Boundaries up.

"I think we need to stop what we're doing."

"Stop fighting? I agree."

"No, stop this." I point to him, then to me. "It was a mistake."

His eyes go wide, and for a second I think he's going to take it all back, to admit he was wrong, to say he'll tell the world about us, about me. Then he frowns like a petulant child. "Don't allow a gossip column to break us apart, Abby."

"Bullshit. You said I should never let anyone silence my voice, but that's exactly what you're doing here."

"I'm not silencing your voice; I'm protecting our truth by not acknowledging these lies. I know what we have. It's stronger than this."

"Then why can't you say that publicly?"

I hate myself for wanting him to say that he will. But he doesn't. So I spin around, and I march out the door. And though I feel an acute sense of loss, at least I know who I am. I'm not Richard Vale's girlfriend, and I'm not a sex-romp nanny. I am Abigail Jane Atkinson, and I am no longer silencing my voice to protect another man's ego. Better to be a troublemaker than a doormat.

CHAPTER TWENTY

The second I get back to my stateroom, I fire off an email to the editor of this gossip rag. My fingers fly across the phone screen as I chastise them for invading my privacy and publishing lies that damage my reputation. I explain that I don't exist for entertainment purposes, that I'm a real human with real feelings, and that I don't deserve this kind of treatment. Hitting send feels like a victory. Not just for me, but for anyone who's ever been the target of vicious rumors.

But when I receive their response, the sweet taste of victory turns sour.

From: Editor at NYC Social Scandals
To: Atkinson, Abigail
Subject: Your Message

Ms. Atkinson,

We found your story compelling and we sympathize with all the victims of the Billionaire Playboy. Would you be willing to partake in an exclusive interview? We'd love to hear more about how Richard Vale wronged you.

All best,
The NYCSS Team

It's as if they didn't read my email. I never said anything about being Richard's victim; *they* were the ones who wronged me here. I hit the reply button, ready to lay into them, but halfway through another angry draft, I trash it. Writing back would be a waste of my energy. These people don't care about me or my feelings. They don't care about my side of the story, either. They only care about crafting salacious narratives to draw in the clicks.

By the time we pull into port, it's after dark. I go to sleep feeling disempowered and completely out of control. I'm plagued by vivid dreams where I'm stranded at sea in shark-infested waters, my life raft rapidly deflating. When I wake up, I'm drenched in sweat, and my head aches from grinding my teeth.

On a positive note, no new Google Alerts have appeared overnight, neither for my name nor for Richard's; there must've been nothing new to report while we were at sea. I wonder if the paparazzi know where we are. From what I gather, Capri is a hot celebrity hangout, so they must have a presence here. Maybe I just won't go out today.

I roll out of bed, pull back the curtains, and gasp at the view. Colossal white cliffs covered with bright-green trees, colorful buildings dotting the foothills. The photos I've seen don't do it justice. There's no way I can stay inside when there's so much beauty to explore on this island.

Bijou's blissfully unaware of what went down between me and her father yesterday, so when I show up to our tutoring session, she's bouncing off the walls with excitement about today's plans. "Dad's taking us to Mount Solaro," she says.

"Awesome." That's the mountain she told us about, the one where you take a chairlift to reach the summit. I want to check it out myself, but I think I'll wait until tomorrow so I don't risk running into them.

"You don't seem happy about this," she says. "Is it because it's, like, two thousand feet above sea level? I thought you got over that whole fear-of-heights thing."

"I did." I stare at my laptop, typing nonsense words simply to avoid looking her in the eye.

"Then what is it?"

"I'm not going with you guys today."

"Why not?" Her voice is tight with worry, and when I finally look at her, my heart shrinks at the sight of her furrowed brow.

"Because I don't want to be seen in public with your dad." I conveniently leave out the part about us getting in an argument and breaking up, but that seems like extraneous information at the moment.

"Is it because of that website?" When I nod, she says, "Didn't you ask him to get it taken down?"

"It doesn't really matter." *To your father, anyway.* "If they take that one down, another one will pop up somewhere else."

"So what, you're like never going to be seen in public with him again?"

That's the plan, but I can't quite bring my lips to form the words. Instead, I settle for a diplomatic "It's a very stressful situation. I already talked to your dad about it."

"But my dad isn't the only person here. What about me? I like when you come out with us; we always have such a good time together."

"I know. I always have a good time with you, too." Memories of the past few weeks glide through my mind like pictures in a slideshow. Hiking in a pristine forest. Riding roller coasters until we're dizzy. Playing Uno and eating gelato. Jumping off cliffs into the great unknown.

But that's not why I'm here with these people on this yacht. I'm not their friend, I'm the math tutor, and our session was scheduled to begin fifteen minutes ago. "We're running late," I say. "Let's get started."

She sucks her teeth and opens her laptop. "Fine. What are we working on today?"

"Quadrilateral problems on the coordinate plane."

"Isn't that the last unit?"

"Second to last. We'll finish all your lessons by Friday, but there's two weeks left until we head back to New York, so I think I'll put together some review sheets. Maybe we can stage some mock tests."

"Or maybe we could do nothing?"

"I don't think your dad will be okay with that."

"I don't really care what my dad thinks." She scowls, her attitude alarmingly reminiscent of the early days of this trip, when she and Richard were constantly at odds.

I ignore that little jab, and we get down to business. As usual, she flies through her problem sets, exhibiting excellent understanding of the material. When our four hours are complete, we part ways. While she goes off to join her dad at Mount Solaro, I'm planning to head to the south side of the island to explore the small harbor at Marina Piccola. I refuse to hole up in my room and be sad about what happened. My relationship with Richard was fun and intense and wholly unexpected, but now it's over. Time to move on.

Of course, I don't want to end up back in these gossip rags, either. And though I know I'm probably being paranoid, I can't help but wonder if there are photographers hiding out in the bushes surrounding the harbor, waiting for me to show my face. What other lies will they print about me?

So before I leave, I track down Coco, who's eating lunch in the dining room. "I need your help."

"What did he do now?" Her voice is shaded with annoyance. When I ran into her at breakfast this morning, I told her about our fight, how I decided to cool things off between us. She said she was going to yell at him, but I asked her not to. He made his position clear. There's no point in dragging this out.

"Nothing," I say. "I want to go explore the city, but I'm afraid of being recognized. Do you happen to have any big sunglasses or floppy hats I can borrow?"

"I have both. Come with me." She slips out of her chair and leads me to her stateroom, where she hands me my new disguise kit with a heavy sigh. "I knew he was gonna mess this up."

The walk to Marina Piccola is nothing short of breathtaking. I cross winding roads and climb a hundred stairs, taking in views from the Gulf of Naples to the Tyrrhenian Sea. Along the way, I stop at a pizzeria for lunch and savor a huge lemon slush ice that I know Bijou would love.

I plan to tell her about it, but when she plods into the office on Wednesday morning, she's in no mood to have a lighthearted chat about Italian desserts. "Dad told me you broke up."

"Yeah. We did."

"I told him he had to apologize to you."

"Bijou, I appreciate that, but it's complicated."

"No, it's not. My dad's a jerk, and he needs to say he's sorry."

Frankly, it's hard to argue with that. "I don't want to put you in the middle of this."

"I'm already in the middle. We've been hanging out for weeks. Do you suddenly want me to pretend that never happened? Because I can't, and I'm not. I told my dad I'm not going anywhere with him until he apologizes to you."

"So you didn't go to Mount Solaro yesterday?"

"Nope."

"Bijou, no." This is awful. They've come so far in their relationship, healed so many old wounds. And now I've gone and destroyed it all by hooking up with my billionaire boss. "Please don't let me ruin your trip with your father. I honestly wouldn't be able to live with myself."

"You're not ruining this trip. You're the best thing about it. Everything sucked until you came along. My dad barely paid attention to me; we didn't do anything fun. You make him a better father, Abby. And I like having you around."

Her voice is so soft and her words are so sweet that I suddenly feel so guilty. Like I'm letting her down by sticking to my guns.

Then I remind myself that *I'm* not the one letting anyone down here.

"You should go out with your father. Being with him in Italy, this is a once-in-a-lifetime opportunity. Who knows if you'll ever have this chance again?"

She rolls her eyes, like I've said something supremely cheesy. I can understand why she might think that way. She's only twelve, never experienced real loss, not that I'm aware of, anyway. At the very least, she's never had to grieve for one of her parents. She probably doesn't comprehend how short life is, how it can be snatched away at any moment. I hope she doesn't have to understand that for a very long time.

Somehow, we manage to slog through our geometry lesson. Bijou's attention is scattered, and I'm not performing at my best, either. Good thing we're ahead of schedule so we can repeat this lesson tomorrow.

When we're done, I spend the afternoon at Mount Solaro. The chairlift to the summit looks absolutely terrifying, much farther above sea level than the cliffs in Mallorca, with a safety bar that doesn't feel particularly safe. Standing at the loading bay, I wonder if anyone's been injured on this thing. It seems awfully easy to slip out from under that "safety bar" and fall to one's death.

I'm doing that overthinking thing again, so I stop, close my eyes, and visualize myself gliding up the side of the mountain, basking in the glory of Capri from on high. Then I open my eyes and I take a seat.

My palms hurt from gripping the armrests, but the ride is peaceful, the views exquisite. Emerald trees, ruby rooftops, a vast expanse of sapphire sea. At the top, I feel triumphant, reminded that fear isn't necessarily something you conquer but something you confront time and again. Drinking in this beautiful panorama, I can't help but believe my father would be proud of me right now. He'd have loved this view from the top of the mountain, too. It makes me sad to think Bijou won't see it.

I have to convince her to come here with her dad. These days are precious and fleeting, and I'm angry at myself for getting in the way of their time together.

The next morning, I'm all set to give Bijou a stern talking-to about the impermanence of life, but Coco intercepts me on the way to the office.

"Tutoring's canceled today," she says. "You gotta go pack your bags."

All at once, my heart stops beating, like it's encased in a block of ice. "Am I being fired?"

"No," she says. "I'm sorry, I didn't mean to scare you. We've *all* gotta go pack our bags. We're going home early."

"What? Why?"

"Richard's company is trying to close a deal, and they've hit a snag. He said he wants to be there in person to smooth things over. We're sailing to Naples tonight, then hopping a flight to New York first thing in the morning."

"Is Bijou okay? She must be devastated that the trip is over so soon."

Coco raises her eyebrows. "Honestly? I think she's happy to go home. She misses her friends."

That's good, I guess. Still, Richard said he was going to commit this time to her, and now he's ending their trip two weeks ahead of schedule so he can run back to work, putting his business before his family like he always has. Does he really care that little about repairing their relationship? Maybe Bijou isn't the one who needs the stern talking-to.

Before I can second-guess myself, I'm racing up the stairs, my clenched fist prepared to bang on Richard's office door. To my surprise, he's standing outside on the top deck, forearms resting against the railing as he studies the horizon.

"Richard."

He turns to face me with dewy eyes, the corners of his perfect lips drooping down. He looks less like a high-powered businessman and more like a sad little boy. I dig my fingernails into the flesh of my palm, the pain distracting me from the desire to reach out and take him in my arms.

"I have no choice," he says, already aware of why I'm here. "The deal is sinking and I need to save it."

"What about Bijou?"

"Bijou won't even look at me, so what's the point in being here? She hates me, you hate me—"

"I don't hate you. I just wanted you to defend me."

"Defend you how? There is no defense in a gossip war. If I issued a statement, the tabloids would have a ball putting their own spin on it. If I fought them in court, they'd come out swinging with blind items. It's a race to the bottom, one I'm not interested in running. The fact is, people are going to have their opinions about you. They're going to say what they want to say and think what they want to think, and there's damn little you can do about it. Which is why I've had to learn to live with it."

His voice is strained, like it's on the verge of cracking. I have to tamp down the urge to reach out and comfort him. As much as he likes to pretend that these tabloids don't bother him, I know the truth. But even if he can't control the rumor mill, he can certainly control how much effort he puts into his relationship with his daughter.

"You can't give up on this time with Bijou."

"Bijou doesn't want to be with me. And I can't give up on work. Once you lose a deal, it's gone forever, and I will *not* let that happen. My job is the one place where no one has ever questioned my character or my competency or my commitment. It's the one place I've never failed. And I can't fail now. I refuse to."

His voice is suddenly firm and strong, his eyes unyielding and grim, and I realize there's no point in arguing with him. His work is his whole world, his final proving ground. If he didn't change for his ex-wife or his own daughter, what makes me think he'd change because I ask him to?

"Okay," I say. "I'll start packing."

He looks down, hesitating for a moment before clearing his throat and smoothing his shirt, collecting himself to project the pretense of a coolheaded businessman. "We can continue her math lessons back in New York. She'll be living with me for the next two weeks, until Veronica returns from LA. I'm on the Upper West Side, by Central Park, if you're comfortable working there."

Am I comfortable working there? I'll be relegated to the dining room table, like I am with the rest of my tutoring clients. I'll never sit beside him on the couch or share a late-night glass of wine in the kitchen or spend the night curled up in his bed. It'll be like this thing between us never happened. No, I'm not comfortable with that.

"Well, Bijou's been flying through her lessons so quickly, we don't have much left to do. I can finish it up in one more session, maybe even on the plane ride home."

One final lesson on the plane ride home. It's really all over, isn't it? My summer of self-discovery has come to an end, and I don't feel any closer to knowing who I am or what I'm going to do next.

"Actually," he says, "if you wouldn't mind, I'd like to keep you on for the full six weeks. You can move on to some introductory seventh-grade math, so Bijou can start the new school year ahead of the game. It'd be nice to give her a leg up. Help build her confidence, you know?"

There is nothing I want less than to spend more time in Richard's orbit. Just looking at him now, I feel a gravitational pull that throws me off balance and compresses my heart. But do I really have a choice? I signed a six-week contract, and ignoring the fact that I've already breached it, I don't have an alternate source of income. Good thing I like working with Bijou. Hopefully, Richard will be too preoccupied with work to be hanging around the house, reminding me of everything I've lost.

"Okay."

"Take the weekend to settle back in at home, and you can come by on Monday. I'll have Coco send you my address."

I guess this is how we'll communicate from now on. Through his assistant.

He shoves his hands in his pockets before retreating to his office, and I head back to my room to pack my bags.

CHAPTER TWENTY-ONE

I've abandoned that alien romance series. It's too unrealistic. Not the part about the aliens—it's a big universe; there could very well be hunky, horny life on other planets—but the part about the romance. No way do I believe two beings from such disparate backgrounds would come together to find their happily ever after.

Instead, I've discovered a new favorite genre of fiction: twisted psychological thrillers. Especially the ones where spiteful characters get revenge on a backstabbing villain who did them dirty. There's nothing more satisfying than seeing a bad guy get their comeuppance.

Yes, I'm currently consumed by the notion of revenge. I'm bitter and petty and seething with rage. How can I not be, when life is so profoundly unfair?

I devour not one, but two, thrillers on the plane ride back to New York. It's late Friday night when I finally drag my suitcase up the three flights of stairs to my apartment. I knock on the door in case Arpita's home, but when she doesn't answer, I let myself in. It looks exactly the same as it did four weeks ago. Same threadbare green couch, same pile of papers on the coffee table. A familiar smell lingers in the air, our cheap vanilla-scented candles mingled with grilled meat from the kebab shop on the ground floor. Nothing's changed, but everything's different.

On that bleak note, I open my bedroom door. It's musty in here; four weeks of disuse have left the air stuffy and stale. Opening the window doesn't do much to freshen things up. It's eighty-five degrees and muggy tonight, with the kind of thick city humidity that clings to your skin. I miss the fresh air of the Mediterranean, the way everything smelled like lemons and the sea.

I text Arpita: I'm home. Sleeping now. Then I collapse into bed, tired from travel and heavy with regret.

When I wake up, I'm completely out of sorts. With my eyes closed, it's like I'm back in my stateroom, with the tree-covered cliffs of Capri right outside my window. A moment later, the shrill blare of a car horn followed by the shrieking swears of an angry pedestrian remind me I am indeed at home in New York.

I emerge bleary eyed into the living room, and Arpita leaps from the couch with her arms open wide. Her hug is a salve for my stinging wounds. "I missed you so much," she says. "How was the flight home?"

"Fine. It was long, but we flew private so at least it was comfortable."

She rolls her eyes. "Of course Richard Vale owns his own plane."

"No, he chartered one." Richard doesn't own anything that you'd expect a billionaire to own. No yacht, no plane, no helicopter. As far as I know, he has no plans to fly into space. For all his wealth and all his accomplishments, he's a fairly unassuming guy. A good guy.

But he's also a powerful guy. And like he told me, people in power are always looking out for number one.

"Tell me everything." She takes me by the hand and leads me to the couch. "Why did you leave so early? Was it the tabloids? I haven't gotten any more Google Alerts, but maybe I missed something."

I haven't told her yet. She doesn't know about the argument I had with Richard or why he decided to cut the whole trip short. When I found out we were leaving, I sent a quick text to tell her I was returning early, that I was fine but I'd explain it all when I got home. So now I explain.

At the end of my long story, she doesn't chide me or say "I told you so." She simply disappears into the kitchen and returns with a canned margarita for each of us. She always knows exactly what I need.

"I'm sorry things didn't work out the way you wanted them to," she says. "But it's good to have you home."

"It's good to be home," I say, and I mean it. This two-bedroom walk-up is no luxury superyacht, but it's a safe haven. A space where I can be myself with all my flaws and failures, without anyone watching or judging or jumping to conclusions. Just me and Arpita, chilling, sipping cocktails from a can.

We spend the rest of the day watching TV and falling slowly into drunkenness. I go to sleep in the same clothes I woke up in.

When the sun rises on Sunday, I know exactly where I am before I even open my eyes. The heat is oppressive; my bedsheets stick to my skin. There's no more running away. Time to face reality.

I grab my phone and pull up my email, which I haven't checked in over a week. A quick scroll through my inbox shows a few more congratulatory messages to Nick and this week's department newsletter, all of which I delete unread.

Aside from that, there are two other emails. The first is from Dianne, sent late last night:

From: Ruggiero, Dianne
To: Atkinson, Abigail
Subject: Vale

Hi Abby,

Richard's assistant told me about your early return from Europe and how you'll be supporting Bijou at his home for the remaining two weeks of the contract. This works fine for me.

Looking toward the future, though, I'm afraid I can't keep you on my roster. It's hard for me to write this, because you're such a fantastic tutor and I know you really care about the kids, but the whole "sex romp" scandal is not a good look for the agency. I've already had a couple of concerned parents bring it to my attention. I hope you understand that I need to protect our reputation. This is why there's a rule against fraternizing in your contract.

Thank you for all your hard work through the years. I wish I had better news for you. I'll be happy to provide references if needed.

Best,
Dianne

This news isn't surprising, but it still feels like a kick in the teeth when I'm already sprawled out facedown on the ground.

The second email is from Philip, sent on Friday morning, and it's not any less discouraging:

From: McHugh, Philip
To: Atkinson, Abigail
Subject: Urgent Matter

Ms. Atkinson,

I understand you're overseas at the moment. When you return to New York, please let me know. I have an urgent matter to discuss with you, and I'd like to do so in person.

Dr. Philip McHugh, PhD

Wonderful. As if being fired by Dianne wasn't bad enough, now I'm in hot water with Philip, too. I wonder what this "urgent matter" is. Maybe there's some morality clause in the student handbook I've unknowingly violated and he's going to dismiss me from the program. Honestly, that doesn't sound half-bad. Then I wouldn't have to expend any more emotional energy trying to figure out what the hell to do next. The decision will be made for me.

Then again, I can't imagine telling my mother that I've been kicked out of grad school, especially if it's because of this trip she thinks I shouldn't have taken in the first place. Turns out she was right: I was merely running away from my problems. And in the process, I created a whole bunch of new ones.

But I also created a whole bunch of memories. Sweet, beautiful moments when I thought anything was possible. Running through fields of lavender. Swimming in the salty sea. Standing in the shadow of the Eiffel Tower.

I learned a lot of really valuable lessons, too. Like that life isn't a straight path from beginning to end, that I am capable of conquering my fears, and that I'm a strong, smart, badass woman who deserves to be happy.

I press reply and compose a short, simple email to Philip:

> From: Atkinson, Abigail
> To: McHugh, Philip
> Subject: Re: Urgent Matter
>
>
> I'm back in New York. I can meet tomorrow after 1PM if that works for you.

Then I take a deep breath and I call my mom.

"Hello, sweetheart," she says. "I haven't heard from you in a while. What exotic locale are you in today?"

221

I glance around my bedroom, at the stains on the popcorn ceiling and the suitcase that I still haven't unpacked. "Astoria, Queens. I'm home."

"Oh." Her forehead crinkles. "I thought you were going to be gone the whole summer."

"I was supposed to be. My client changed the schedule at the last minute." That's all Richard is now. My client. "How are you?"

"Oh, fine. Good. Nothing new to report." She cocks her head to the side. "What about you?"

"I'm jet-lagged."

She nods, her lips pressed together in a tight line. I know what she wants to ask me: When am I going back to the lab? Have I decided whether I'm going to appeal Philip's decision? Am I finally finished with all this nonsense about giving up? I spare us both the awkward question-and-answer session by cutting right to the chase.

"I don't want to go back to school, Mom."

"Of course not. It's hard to transition back to work after a lengthy break."

"I mean I don't *ever* want to go back to school."

"Because of what happened with Nick? Abigail, don't let this stop you. You're so smart and you've worked so hard—you can find another adviser."

"I know I can. But I don't want to."

"So you're just going to allow these men to force you out of the program?"

"No one's forcing me out. This is my decision, one I've thought about very carefully. I have never been happy in grad school. I didn't even want to apply to the PhD program, but—" That last part slips out before my brain can pump the brakes on my big mouth.

"But what?"

I don't want to tell my mother that I felt pressured to go to grad school because I wanted to make her proud. There's no need to lay a guilt trip on her when she was only trying to help me live my best life, a life she never felt she was worthy of. But there's more than one truth here.

"I wanted to follow in Dad's footsteps. I wanted to honor his memory. But I can't keep lying to myself. This isn't how I want to spend the rest of my life."

Mom runs her hand through her graying hair. After a long pause, she says, "Well, Abigail, I didn't know that. But I think, more than anything, your father would want you to be happy. I want you to be happy, too. And if that means dropping out of grad school, then . . ." She inhales deeply, as if she's drumming up the strength to say what comes next. "Then I support you one hundred percent."

Her words lift a thousand pounds from my shoulders, a weight I didn't know had been sitting there. I may be a grown woman, but I don't think I'll ever be too old to want my mother's approval. "Thank you, Mom. That means a lot to me."

She smiles, and it feels like a hug. "So. What are you going to do now?"

"I'll be tutoring for a little while." By that, I mean exactly two weeks. Once my contract with Richard is done, I've got no other prospects on the horizon, since I've been blacklisted from the biggest tutoring agency in New York City. I'm sure I could find private tutoring work elsewhere, as long as the parents don't google my name. Nobody will want the "sex-romp nanny" hanging around their children. "Other than that, I'm not sure."

"Well, you're a smart woman. You'll figure it out. And you know what? It's good that you're doing this now, while you're still young. You don't want to have any regrets later in life."

Regrets like my mother has. "Mom, it's never too late."

"I know, I know. Don't worry, I haven't forgotten what you told me. I've been thinking a lot about missed opportunities and wrong turns, so I've ordered a few informational brochures. One from Hobart, one from Nazareth, and one from the University of Rochester."

"Are you really going to get your degree? I'm so happy for—"

"Slow down." She holds up her hand, imploring me to stop. "I haven't made any decisions yet. All I did was order some informational brochures."

"It's a start." A promising start. Maybe these next few months will reveal new beginnings for the both of us. New paths to explore, where we'll finally find the happiness we're looking for.

CHAPTER TWENTY-TWO

Finding yourself isn't something you can do on a monthlong trip to Europe. It's an ongoing, never-ending process. I'd love to snap my fingers and discover my life's purpose, the thing that makes me excited to get up every morning. But it's not that simple.

So instead, I start applying to jobs for which I'm qualified and that will pay me a reasonable salary. I basically wallpaper the internet with my résumé, submitting applications for every math or science tutoring position available in the five boroughs. I figure eventually someone will bite, right? Hopefully someone who doesn't know how to google.

As I'm tweaking what feels like my six-hundredth cover letter, my phone buzzes with a text from Coco: Hey. How are you readjusting to the real world?

> You know. It's real.

> What's going on with you?

I heard from Dianne.

She told me she cut you from the agency.

I'm really, really sorry.

> Thanks. But it was my fault.

> I knowingly breached the contract.

Richard wanted me to tell you that

you don't have to come in tomorrow

if you don't want to. He'll still pay you in full.

Well, that's insulting. I'm not going to abandon my obligations, and I'm certainly not going to take Richard's handouts. Besides, I want to check in on Bijou, see how she's handling the whole situation. I text back, Of course I want to come in. Bijou and I have work to do.

She replies with a smiley face and gives me his address. See you tomorrow at 9AM.

Richard lives on Central Park West, a few blocks south of the Museum of Natural History. It takes me forty minutes and two subway lines to get there, and as I approach his building, a slow panic creeps in. What if there are photographers hanging around, waiting for someone interesting to wander by? I wish I had those oversize sunglasses and big floppy hat I wore in Capri.

But when I arrive, there are no photographers. Only a friendly doorman who asks me my name and directs me to the elevator, which whisks me up to the twenty-seventh floor. It's not the penthouse, but it's pretty damn high. Coco answers the door, greeting me with open arms. I go in for a hug, and I'm instantly transfixed by the view over her shoulder. At the far end of the living room, a huge bay window overlooks the park, acres of rolling treetops surrounded by towering buildings. A verdant oasis in the center of the city.

"It's good to see you again," Coco says, then gestures for me to come inside. The apartment is certainly not modest, but it's not over the top, either. It's simply appointed with clean lines and a neutral palette. My heels click against the hardwood floor as we walk through the living room and into the dining room, which also features more magnificent views of Central Park.

Two laptops are open on the long dining table, the same laptops we used on the yacht. There's scrap paper and pencils, a small whiteboard, and some colored markers. Everything's set up to begin.

"Where's Bijou?" I ask.

"I'm right here."

I spin around to find her standing in the doorway to the kitchen, wearing a tie-dye romper and holding a glass of juice in her hand. It's weird to see her here, in the real world, almost like the last month in the Mediterranean didn't even happen. I'm not sure what to say. I settle on "How are you?"

"Good." She shifts her weight from one foot to the other. "How are you?"

"Good." I want to ask how things are going with her father, but I also don't want to pry. He and I aren't a thing anymore, and their relationship isn't my business. I'm simply here to teach math for a few hours before bolting from the borough on the first train back to Queens. Boundaries!

"I'll leave you to it," Coco says, then disappears.

The moment we're alone, Bijou says, "Dad's a wreck without you."

Okay, I guess we're going there. "A wreck how?"

"He's mopey," she says, sliding into the chair at the head of the table. "It's annoying."

Am I a bad person for feeling the tiniest bit gratified that my absence is making him mopey? Obviously, I'd prefer it if he were happy. Ideally, we'd be happy together. But that's not gonna happen, so this is the next best thing. Because it means that he misses me.

"He'll get over it," I say. "What's going on otherwise? Have you seen your friends?"

"Of course. They threw me a big 'welcome home' party on Saturday night. And we're going to the park after tutoring today."

My stomach tightens as I remember the adventures we used to have after our tutoring sessions in Europe. The three of us would take off for the beach or the forest or the lavender fields. Now she's hanging out with her friends in the city, while Richard is . . . working, I guess. That's why we came back to New York, isn't it? So Richard could work.

That's what I should be doing now, too. I wake up my laptop and say, "Let's get started on our review. Then tomorrow we can move on to some introductory seventh-grade topics."

"Do you really think I'm ready for that? I mean, I failed my last semester of math."

"Yeah, and now you're kicking ass. Last semester is history. Seventh grade starts with a clean slate, remember?"

She nods, the look in her eyes nervous but hopeful. I think of the dozens of résumés I sent out yesterday, each one an earnest wish to wipe the slate clean. But is there such a thing as starting over when the internet remembers everything?

I push the thought aside and turn my attention to our review. We power through it with only a couple of quick breaks, and after Bijou aces the mock test I give her, she gleefully runs off to go meet her friends. I want to be angry at Richard for blowing off the end of their daddy-daughter trip, but she doesn't seem too disappointed in the outcome. I guess I'm the only person who's disappointed here.

"Abby."

The tiny hairs on the back of my neck stand on end. I'd know that voice anywhere, low and smooth like velvet. Richard's standing at the far end of the dining table, his hands resting gently on the back of a chair. He's spiffed up from head to toe, from his neatly combed hair to his shiny cap toe shoes. He must be attending his meetings in person now.

"Hello, Richard. It's nice to see you." I'm trying to sound dignified and altogether unperturbed, but the waver in my voice betrays me.

"It's wonderful to see you." He puts extra emphasis on the "wonderful," then his ears go red and he clears his throat. "I'm very sorry to hear you lost your job at the tutoring agency. I tried to convince Dianne to keep you on, but—"

"It was the right decision. I breached my contract."

"Right." His hands tighten around the chairback, knuckles going white. "It was my fault."

"No, it wasn't. It was *my* fault. I knew what I was getting into. And I'm trying to put it behind me now. I've already applied for a bunch of new jobs. Let's just hope my potential new employers don't google my name."

He swallows so hard I can hear it across the room. "I'm sorry about that, too."

"What's done is done."

"But I was wrong not to respect your point of view. Very wrong." He lets go of the chair and drags his hands through his hair. "For so long, I've had my own way of dealing with the attention from the tabloids. It's not that I don't care about what they say. Trust me, I don't like being known to the world as the 'Billionaire Playboy' when that's not who I am. But if I can't control it, then what's the point of worrying? Pretending it doesn't exist, that's always worked for me, but you were right when you said my money blunts the impact. It's easy for me to ignore it and move on with my life, but I didn't appreciate how significant this is for you. I'm sorry for that. I should never have tried to silence your voice."

I appreciate the apology, but it feels like it's too little too late. If he'd acknowledged my feelings to begin with, would we still be on that yacht right now, sailing along the Amalfi Coast? Would we still be having adventures every day and making love every night? How much have we missed out on? My chest tightens with grief as I imagine this alternate future.

"Thanks," I say, forcing myself to snap out of it. "I think the gossip rags have moved on, anyway. I haven't received a single Google Alert since last Monday." A week ago. Has it really only been seven days since we were sailing to Capri? And Paris . . . that seems like a whole other lifetime.

"If anyone raises questions about this during your job search, please direct them to me, and I'll clear everything up."

"Okay." Does he realize that if hiring managers see me referred to as the "sex-romp nanny," they'll almost certainly dismiss me out of hand? Probably not. I'm not sure he's ever actually had to conduct a real job search.

He lingers by the dining table, like he's got something else to say. I have a meeting with Philip on campus in an hour, so I should probably get going. But I don't feel a particular rush to leave. There's a pitiful, masochistic part of me that enjoys being in his presence, even if our relationship is now painfully platonic.

"So," he says, "are you going back to school now?"

"No. I've decided to withdraw."

His smile is a knife slicing my heart in two. "That's great. I'm glad you're following your gut. Time to chase down a new opportunity, huh?"

"Yeah. But I'm not sure what that is yet."

"Didn't you say you always wanted to be a teacher? I could easily see you teaching physics to high school students and actually making it fun. I mean, the way you explained that whole *Titanic* door scene? That was . . . incredible."

Our eyes lock, and the air between us crackles with tension. I can read his thoughts because they're the same as mine. We're both on that flight to Paris right now, soaring through the clouds, sipping champagne, our bodies burning with unmet desire.

But what's done is done. I shake away the memories, ground myself in the present moment. The tension between us evaporates.

"Teaching, yeah. I'm definitely interested, but I'd have to go back to school and get a special credential first. It would take a lot of time. And money, which I'm not exactly rolling in." At the moment, I have no desire to add to my already sky-high piles of student debt.

"You know, if you teach a high-needs subject, like math or science, you can get a fellowship that will allow you to pursue your credential while you're working full time in a classroom. They'd pay all your educational expenses in addition to your salary."

"How do you know about this?"

"Remember I told you that Vale Venture Capital has a philanthropic arm? Well, we've established a scholarship fund for graduates of New York City public high schools who are working toward STEM careers. Through conversations with school leadership, I've discovered how desperately they need good math and science teachers. In my opinion, you'd be a perfect fit."

Well, that sounds like a cool opportunity. I envision myself standing in front of a classroom full of rowdy teenagers, some of whom are eager to learn but most of whom aren't. Kind of like the undergraduates in the introductory physics course I taught when I was a TA.

"Do you know how I can apply for it?"

"I could give you a personal referral, pass your information on to the right people."

Oh. So this would be some sort of backdoor deal. A *hire my ex-girlfriend or you won't get my donations* sort of thing. "I'm not really comfortable with that."

"Why not?"

"I want to get a job because I deserve it. Not because Richard Vale is telling someone to hire me."

"It wouldn't be like that at all, I promise. You'd still have to go through a formal interview, background check, all the standard requirements. There's a chance you might not get the job, but I can tell the recruiters about you and vouch for your qualifications. I know they'd be thrilled to get the referral. The screening process takes a lot of time, and they have difficulty finding driven, dedicated people like you."

There's a part of me that wants to say no. A prideful part that doesn't want to use her billionaire ex-boyfriend's connections to leapfrog the application process. But if I turned down his offer, what would I be proving, and to whom? I'd only be hurting kids who need good teachers. And I'd be hurting myself, too.

"Then I'd love that. Thank you."

"Great. I really hope this works out for you." His mouth quirks up in a half smile, and for the briefest of moments, time stands still. On the streets below this luxury apartment, cars slam on their brakes and pedestrians freeze in place. The whole world is waiting for Richard to say the words I want him to say. That he misses me, that he wants me back, that he thinks we should give us another try.

He parts his lips. I hold my breath.

"Send Coco your résumé at your earliest convenience, and I'll direct it to my contacts at the school board."

My heart deflates like a leaky balloon.

Stay dignified, Abby. Unperturbed.

"I'll do it as soon as I get home."

He nods, eyes on the floor. "See you tomorrow, then."

"See you tomorrow."

My feelings for Richard are a dead end. I make a U-turn, and I walk out the front door.

CHAPTER TWENTY-THREE

It's weird being back in the physics building. I've only been gone for a few weeks, but everything feels so foreign. There's a fresh coat of paint in the lobby, and I don't recognize this security guard. He doesn't recognize me, either, and he scrutinizes my student ID before finally waving me into the elevator bank.

Despite staying those extra few minutes to talk to Richard, I arrive to my appointment ten minutes early. Philip's door is still closed, which means he's probably in a meeting, so I stroll down the hallway in my own twisted version of a farewell lap.

I check the mail room one last time. The only thing in my box is a flyer for a seminar that took place two weeks ago. Next, I stop in the small office I share with three other grad students. It's a hot-desking situation, so I never stored any personal items here, but since no one is around, I decide to search through the drawers just in case there's something I forgot about.

While I'm scanning the contents of a file cabinet, someone knocks on the open door. "Abby, hey."

I look up to find Elliot standing on the threshold to the office. He's one of my lab mates—or ex–lab mates, I should say—who refused to get involved when I accused Nick of stealing my work. I'm surprised he's willing to be seen with me now.

I slam the cabinet drawer closed. "Hi, Elliot."

"What're you doing here? I thought you were in Europe or something."

"Did you read about that in NYC Social Scandals?"

His face turns the color of a pomegranate. "I don't know what that is. I just heard people talking around the office."

"Right." Elliot's looking awfully guilty. I'll bet anything he was the mystery source. Then again, it could've been anyone. Not that it matters anymore. "I have a meeting with Philip in a minute, so I should probably get going."

"Are you here to talk to him about Nick?"

"No, Elliot. Philip already knows that Nick stole my work, and he's made it clear that he doesn't care, so there's really not much else for us to discuss about him."

"You haven't heard, have you?"

"Heard what?"

He glances up and down the hallway, then slips inside the office and closes the door behind him. "It wasn't just you. After Nick was short-listed for that NSF grant, all these other people came out of the woodwork accusing him of academic theft and plagiarism. One person even accused him of falsifying data for his dissertation study. The NSF revoked their nomination, and now he's under formal investigation by the university."

"Wow." I should feel something now, shouldn't I? An evil satisfaction or a sense of justice being served. I mean, I've fantasized countless times about Nick going down in flames, and now it's finally come to pass. I thought I'd be reveling in his downfall. Instead, I feel a whole bunch of nothing.

Elliot, however, is feeling a whole bunch of something. "I'm freaking out."

"Why? You didn't do anything wrong."

"No, but I'm the one who's gonna suffer the consequences. I've spent the last three years in Nick's lab, and we've worked together so closely. Are they gonna come after me, too? And even if they don't, now I've gotta switch labs, find a new adviser . . ." He pushes his glasses up onto his forehead and rubs his eyes until they're raw and bloodshot. "I don't know what the hell I'm gonna do. I mean, he's your adviser, too. Aren't you worried?"

"No."

"How can you not be?"

Elliot doesn't know that I'm quitting the program. Nobody knows, except for my mom and Arpita and, as of a little while ago, Richard. In a few minutes, I'll be handing Philip my official letter of withdrawal, so I'm sure everyone will know shortly after that. Word spreads quickly around this department.

For now, I simply say, "I just think it'll all end up the way it's supposed to."

Then I say goodbye, and I leave for my meeting with Philip. His office door is open now, and he's slouched over his desk, staring at his computer screen with a look of disdain. It's the same expression he had on his face when he told me "science is a collaborative effort." As if I were a stupid little girl who was wasting his valuable time with my baseless accusations. I felt so powerless then, so insignificant in the scheme of the academic hierarchy. Now that hierarchy means nothing to me. And I refuse to sit down and shut up.

"Hello, Philip."

At the sound of my voice, he looks up from his screen, his expression fading from disdain to mild irritation. I wonder if this man has ever smiled a day in his life.

"Ms. Atkinson. Please, have a seat." As I sink into one of his guest chairs, he asks, "How was your trip to Europe?"

"Is this the urgent matter you wished to discuss?"

His rheumy eyes bug out of his head. He's probably not used to lowly graduate students giving him an attitude. Little does he know I don't care anymore.

"No," he says. "I'm here to discuss the matter of Professor Bauer."

"I thought there was nothing more to discuss. You found no evidence of misconduct, right?"

He clasps his hands across his potbelly. "Recent revelations have given us cause to revisit your claim against him."

"Recent revelations. By that, you mean all the other people who've accused him of academic theft?"

"Yes. Unfortunately, we're now forced to question the validity of all his work. Therefore, the university is launching a formal investigation into your claim."

"Didn't you launch a formal investigation when I filed my grievance?"

He furrows his bushy eyebrows. "I did, yes. What I meant to say is we're relaunching it."

I'm sure that's what he *meant* to say, but I'm also sure that's not the truth. It's hard not to feel insignificant again, knowing my voice wasn't important enough to be taken seriously. It wasn't until other, more powerful people spoke out that Philip even bothered to listen. And even now, his motivation isn't about standing up for what's right. It's about covering his own ass. Protecting the reputation of his department.

"What about the publication? Will I receive proper credit for my research?"

"We've already been in contact with the journal in question, and we're working with them to establish correct attributions."

"Good. I'll be happy to finally get my name on that byline. I worked hard enough for it."

Philip looks down at his clasped hands. His cuticles are ragged and red, like he's been picking at them.

"While Professor Bauer is under investigation," he says, "we'll be doing some shuffling in the labs. Professor Sherman has expressed a great interest in having you join her team, as has Professor Zhang. Do you have a particular preference?"

I like Professor Sherman. I don't really know Professor Zhang, but she seems like a nice enough person. I'd be happy to join either of their teams, if I still wanted to be here at all.

There's no sense in drawing this out any further. I reach into my bag and pull out the folder in which I've placed my formal letter of withdrawal. Sure, I could've just emailed it to him, but I enjoy the tactile sensation of sliding the piece of paper from its pocket and slapping it down on Philip's desk with a thump. It's far more *dramatic* that way.

"I'm withdrawing from the program."

I'm not sure what kind of reaction I expected. I think maybe deep down I was hoping he'd apologize for doubting me and beg me to stay. Of course, that's a completely ludicrous expectation. Philip doesn't care about me. This is a competitive program, and I'm sure they could find a dozen qualified candidates to fill my empty space, ones who are willing to respect the hierarchy, to sit down and shut up.

Still, I can't help but feel disappointed when all he says is "I wish you well in your future endeavors." He doesn't even give my letter a cursory glance before setting it on top of a pile of papers at the corner of his desk. Then he turns back to his computer screen as if I no longer exist.

I leave his office feeling very small. Like everything I accomplished within these walls went unnoticed. Like it was for nothing, and these past four years were a complete waste of my time.

But as I walk down the hallway, I start feeling a little bit bigger. In the elevator, bigger still. The more space I put between me and this man, the more confidence I have in myself. His opinions do not define me. And I don't need his approval or acknowledgment to keep going.

I'm free.

When I step out onto the sidewalk, a hot gust of city air hits my face, and it feels as fresh as a breeze from the Mediterranean Sea. I may not know what I'm doing next, but in this moment I believe anything is possible.

CHAPTER TWENTY-FOUR

I spend the rest of the week sending out résumés. By Friday morning, I've applied to sixty-seven jobs. You know how many responses I've received so far? Zero.

Oh wait, I'm forgetting about that one response from a hiring manager who told me I wasn't "a good fit for their culture." Probably safe to assume they googled me. Frankly, it feels better to be ignored than to be outright rejected like that. I don't know how Coco deals with this every three days.

I'm still holding out hope for that teaching fellowship, though. Coco told me I'd hear back either way, so in this case, a nonresponse is not a no. Here's hoping that Richard's referral works to my advantage.

My tutoring sessions with Bijou are going well. She's getting the hang of rates and proportions, and I have a feeling she's going to start seventh grade with an A in math. I can't believe this is the second-to-last Friday we've got together. Only one more week and my summer tutoring contract is complete. I'm going to miss her.

And although it pains me to admit this, I'll miss Richard, too. Although he hasn't been around much lately. I haven't even seen him since Monday. He must be busy with work, closing his big deal. So much for changing his ways.

When I arrive on Friday, Coco answers the door with a huge grin on her face. "Guess what?"

"I got the teaching fellowship?"

With a wince, she says, "Uh, no, I haven't heard anything about that. But look!" She thrusts a daily newspaper in my face, folded open to the gossip pages. The top headline screams: KIM AND KOURTNEY AT IT AGAIN.

"I don't care about the Kardashians."

"No, no. Look here." She points to a smaller heading in the center of the page: VALE THREATENS SUIT AGAINST SLEAZY SCANDAL SITE.

I snatch it from her hands and read the whole piece, which is only two short paragraphs in the middle of the column:

> Richard Vale says enough's enough! He's had it with the dirty deeds of sleazy site NYC Social Scandals. The final straw? Their recent coverage of his romance with Abigail Atkinson, who they shamefully referred to as the "sex-romp nanny." According to Vale's attorney, Atkinson wasn't a "money-hungry vixen"—turns out, the two were involved in a "genuine, caring relationship" earlier this summer, and the statements made about her on their site are "entirely false and egregiously defamatory."
>
> No word on the current status of their love affair, but Vale has made it clear to NYCSS: take down those posts about Atkinson, or be prepared to pay! As of this morning, they've chosen the former, so score one for the Billionaire Playboy . . .

"The posts are gone?"

"Wiped away," she says.

I can't quite believe it. I whip out my phone and pull up the site, but when I search for my name, I get nothing. They really are gone.

Google still shows the links in its search results, but clicking them brings up a 404 error. Soon enough, the whole internet will forget.

"What made him decide to do this all of a sudden?" I ask.

"He's been so mopey, you have no idea. Yesterday, I had enough, so I laid out the truth for him. Told him he had the power to fix this, if he was just willing to put his pride aside. He huffed away all pissy, but an hour later, he asked me to get his attorney on the line and draft a press release to send to all the tabloids. And this morning"—she gestures to the paper in my hand—"voilà."

"But he told me he refused to acknowledge the tabloids."

"Yeah, well, he changed his mind. That man must really love you."

Love. The word rings in my ears and resounds in my bones. It's so loud and so vibrant I'm afraid Bijou can hear it when she walks in the dining room.

"Hey, Abby." Her eyes fall on the paper in my hands. "Oh good, you saw. Now maybe you'll take my dad back so he'll stop being miserable all the time."

Take him back? I didn't realize that option was on the table. I haven't even heard from him since Monday. "I'm sure he's not miserable all the time. Hasn't he been wrapped up in work, trying to close his big deal?"

"I mean, he's in the office all day, but he's always home by dinner. I've been hanging out with him every night."

"That's good. I'm glad to hear you're spending time together again."

"Yeah, well, I couldn't exactly stay mad at him. He's been so sad without you, I felt bad just piling on."

I look to Coco for confirmation. She shrugs. "It's true. He's a mess."

"He wants you back," Bijou adds.

If that's true, then why didn't he say so? He had the perfect opportunity on Monday afternoon, but all he did was tell me to email his assistant. Maybe he doesn't really want me back. His melancholy mood may be less about pining for me and more about feeling guilty for how it all went down.

Or maybe he doesn't want to tell me how he really feels because he's afraid of being rejected. I keep waiting for him to come to me, but maybe I should go to him. Then again, what am I going to do, burst into his office and confess my feelings in front of his coworkers? That might work in the movies, but this is real life, not a rom-com. There's a very real, very horrifying chance that he'd say no, at which point I would have to fake my own death and flee the country to avoid the enduring humiliation of a public rejection. I've already had enough public humiliation for one lifetime.

I'm silently poring over the possibilities, trying to figure out my next move. The problem is, Bijou and Coco are staring at me like I'm an exotic animal on display at the zoo. They're eager for me to do something interesting, to tell them to call Richard up and put him on speaker so I can confess my feelings right this instant. It's too much pressure, too much attention. Besides, it's past nine o'clock.

"Time to get to work, Bijou." They suck their teeth simultaneously, but I'm resolute. "We're gonna graph proportional relationships today."

"Thrilling." She rolls her eyes as Coco snatches the paper back from me and clears out of the dining room. Finally, we can get down to business. I try to focus fully on our lesson, pushing all thoughts of Richard out of my mind, but despite my best efforts, they keep creeping back in. Every momentary silence or bathroom break is fraught with memories of midnight meetings and stolen kisses. My body still remembers the feel of his fingertips caressing my skin, the salty flavor of his lips. What if I could have it all again?

The question plagues me throughout our entire tutoring session. I don't know what to do next. But I do know that life is short, and the idea of being with Richard excites me. If I tell him how I feel, all I risk losing is pride. If I don't, I risk losing out on a beautiful future with the only man who's ever made me believe that life could be an adventure.

By the time our math lesson is over, I've made up my mind. I won't barge in on him at work; that's a bad idea for a number of reasons. I'll simply shoot him a text. Something along the lines of Got a second to chat? Have something important to tell you. That way, if he doesn't respond, I can nurse my wounded ego in the privacy of my own home.

Problem is, I don't have his number. Since we returned to New York, Richard and I have been communicating strictly through Coco. I guess I'll have to get his digits from his daughter. And so the embarrassment begins.

"Hey," I say, as Bijou's shutting down her laptop, "do you think you could give me your dad's phone number?"

She gives me a tentative smile. "Are you going to call him to tell him you're taking him back?"

"He hasn't asked me to take him back. I just want to talk to him, to clear things up."

"Okay." She slaps her laptop closed and tucks it under her arm. "You can talk to him right now."

"Isn't he in the middle of a meeting or something?"

"No. He's right there." She points to the dining room doorway, and I turn around to see Richard striding across the living room, making his way toward us. Suddenly, I'm feeling very dizzy.

"Hello there," he says, unhooking his cuff links and setting them on the dining room table with a plink. "How was tutoring today?"

"Good," Bijou says. "Give me five minutes, Dad—I'm gonna go change."

"Don't take too long. The movie starts in an hour and a half, and we have to grab lunch beforehand."

"Yeah, I know." She heads toward her bedroom, calling over her shoulder, "I'll see you Monday, Abby."

"Bye." My voice is high pitched and as wobbly as my legs. I grab the back of the chair to steady myself before I dare to meet Richard's eyes. "Hi."

"Hi."

I'm at a loss as to what to say next. For the past few hours, I've been rehearsing potential speeches in my head, confessions of deep and constant longing. But I had expected to tell him all this in a phone call. Maybe tonight, maybe tomorrow. Not right now, face-to-face.

"What are you doing home?" I ask. "I thought you were working."

"I took off early so I could hang out with Bijou. The new Avengers movie was released today, and if we wait until tonight, the theater will be packed."

Surely, a billionaire could finagle a private movie screening. But that would be extravagant, which is so not Richard's style.

"But what about closing your big deal? Don't they need you in the office?"

"They can handle it on their own. Bijou's more important," he says. Maybe he has changed his ways, after all. "How's the job search going?"

I shrug.

"No word from the fellowship yet?"

I shake my head.

"I'm sure they'll reach out to you soon. They're wildly understaffed there." He loosens his tie, long fingers digging into the thick knot at his neck. I want to grab the end of it and pull him toward me. There's no need for words when a kiss will tell him everything he needs to know.

Instead, I freeze, my tongue heavy and my throat tight. This moment feels precarious, as if the whole future hinges on what happens next.

He touches the top button of his shirt now, deftly unfastening it with one flick of his nimble fingertips. The collar flaps open, revealing a patch of tan chest, a tuft of dark hair. I wait for him to undo a second button, but his hand hovers in place. When I slide my gaze up to his face, I find his eyes fierce and fiery and firmly fixed on me.

"Did Coco show you this morning's paper?"

My mouth is so dry I have to swallow before I say, "Yes. Thank you. You didn't have to get your lawyers involved."

"Yes, I did. I should've done it a long time ago. As soon as you came to me." He takes a step in my direction, his eyes burning into mine. "I'm sorry I let it go on as long as I did."

"You already said you were sorry. You don't have to keep apologizing."

I don't realize how hard my hands are shaking until he scoops them up and squeezes them tight. "I'll apologize until the end of time if it means you'll give me another chance. I miss you, Abby. I miss your beautiful voice and your delicious brain. I miss your face and your touch and everything about you. I know it's been overwhelming, the unwanted attention, and I can't promise this will be the end of it all. But I promise you I'll never let my pride get between us again. I will always defend you. As long as you want me to."

"I do. I've never wanted anyone more."

"This time, I'll do whatever I can to prove I deserve you."

"You've already proven yourself. Time and again." I press my palm to his cheek. My hand is no longer shaking. "You're a good man, Richard. I hope you know that."

He lowers his head, his lips grazing my earlobe as he whispers, "You make me better."

His voice is a spark that sets a fire within me, every cell in my body erupting into flames. There's no more hesitation, no more uncertainty. I grasp the end of his tie and tug him toward me, closing the gap between us.

Our mouths meet in a frenzy, all this pent-up emotion finally unleashed. One taste of his lips and I'm back in France, champagne bubbles fizzing around my heart. I press myself against him, chest to chest, hips to hips, unable to get close enough. He is mine and I am his. This thing between us is real, real enough to be forever.

"Oh, good!" Bijou's chipper voice snaps us out of our passionate embrace. She's standing in the doorway, smiling brightly. "You two are back together! Now can we get going, please? I don't wanna miss the movie."

She brushes past us, sashaying toward the front door. The side of Richard's mouth quirks up. "Care to join us?"

"I'd love nothing more."

And the three of us set off on another afternoon adventure.

CHAPTER TWENTY-FIVE

Dating a billionaire isn't as glamorous as you might imagine it to be. Yes, there was the whole summer-on-a-yacht thing, but now that the European tour has come to an end, things aren't so over the top anymore. In fact, during our first week as an "official couple," we've been spending pretty much every night on Richard's couch, watching TV and ordering takeout. It's a lot easier to avoid photographers if we don't ever leave the house.

Not that there are hordes of paparazzi stalking the streets, waiting for us to emerge from the shadows. Even if there were, Richard said he'd defend me against any future slander or libel, and I believe him 100 percent. But while I'm still in the midst of this job search, I'd really prefer to lie low.

Hopefully, things will change soon. Like today. Because right now, I'm in downtown Manhattan, standing on Chambers Street in front of the headquarters for my potential new employer. It looks like a courthouse, with an impressive entry portico and wide granite stairway, but it really houses the central offices for the New York City Department of Education. In fifteen minutes, I've got an interview on the fourth floor with Ms. Lillian Lu, the head of the fellowship program.

When I first got the call for this interview, I almost chickened out. How was I going to explain my desire to transition from full-time student to full-time teacher? Fortunately, Arpita talked me out of my panic and helped me prepare. She pitched me practice questions and guided me through the answers. We even went to TJ Maxx together to pick out the perfect interview outfit.

So as I enter the lobby now, I'm feeling confident and composed. It's only when the elevator doors close behind me that my nerves start to fray. What if this interview is merely a courtesy to Richard? They couldn't say no to a referral from such an influential donor, so maybe they're just going through the motions. It's possible Lillian Lu has no intention of hiring me, and this whole afternoon is one big farce.

But when we shake hands in the reception area, she seems genuinely pleased to see me. "It's so nice to meet you, Ms. Atkinson."

"Likewise. Please, call me Abby."

"Come this way." She leads me to a small office down the hall cluttered with metal filing cabinets and overstuffed manila envelopes. She gestures for me to sit in a ladder-back chair and settles behind her scuffed wood desk.

"How was your commute?" she asks.

"Great." It was not particularly great. We stalled at Fifty-Ninth Street for over twenty minutes on account of a flat-screen TV on the tracks, but that's New York for you. Good thing I left my apartment with plenty of time to spare. "It's a straight shot from Astoria on the N train."

"Oh, I used to live in Astoria," she says with a smile.

After some polite small talk about our favorite Greek restaurants, we get right down to business. She examines a printed sheet of paper that I instantly recognize as my résumé. "It says here you were pursuing your PhD in physics for four years but didn't obtain your degree. Tell me about that."

My stomach twists, almost like a reflex. But I knew this question was coming. I dreaded it more than any other, which is why Arpita and I spent the most time working out a response. At first, I was spitting out canned answers, generic word soup you could find by googling "how to spin a career change in a job interview." (Which I did, a lot.) To me, they sounded sensible, but Arpita shot each one down with a sharp *no*.

"You're coming off as insincere," she told me.

"What am I supposed to say? 'After my adviser stole my research, I realized I hated grad school'?" I threw my hands in the air, exasperated. "The truth isn't exactly flattering."

"Flattering yourself is not the point. The point is to be honest about who you are and why you're a good fit for this job."

"How does quitting grad school factor into that narrative? It makes it seem like the past four years have been this pointless waste of time."

She shook her head. "You're framing it all wrong. A lot happened these last four years. You gained valuable experiences, you developed new skills, all of which can be applied in a new career."

"But look at how it ended."

"So? A bad ending doesn't erase all the good stuff that happened along the way. Don't look at your experience as a failure. Look at it as a stepping-stone. You're moving on to a more exciting opportunity, and you wouldn't be here if it wasn't for all the good and bad things that came before."

That's when it clicked. Arpita was right. I'd been so focused on the negative aspects of my time in graduate school that I was ignoring all the wonderful ways in which I benefited. After all, if I hadn't gone to grad school, I wouldn't have wound up on a superyacht in Europe. I wouldn't have met my billionaire boyfriend. I wouldn't be sitting here, interviewing for a job that sounds absolutely perfect for me.

Now, I fold my hands in my lap, and I answer Lillian's question with conviction, emphasizing all the positive aspects of my time as a PhD student. Instead of talking about the struggles I had with the faculty, I explain the research methods I learned and how I apply them in everyday life. Rather than discussing the competitive environment among my classmates, I tell her how much fun I had being a TA.

"Teaching was, by far, my favorite part of being in grad school," I say. "While I enjoy one-on-one tutoring, there's something special about building a classroom culture. Which is why I'm excited about the possibility of teaching high school."

Lillian nods. She seems satisfied with that answer, and frankly, I'm satisfied, too. Every word of it was true. At last, I can look back on that phase of my life without feeling like it was a waste of time.

The interview continues as we discuss my teaching philosophy, the advantages of project-based learning, and the importance of making children feel welcome in the classroom. When she asks me my opinion on grading policies, I explain how it's a double-edged sword: good grades can be motivating, but I never want a student to feel like they're a failure just because they get an F.

Eventually, she pushes her chair back and stands. "Well, Ms. Atkinson, I've really enjoyed speaking with you."

"Thank you. I've enjoyed speaking with you, too." As she escorts me back to the reception area, I confidently say, "I hope I'm a good fit for the fellowship."

"Well, you came very highly recommended by Mr. Vale."

Every muscle in my body tenses at the mention of his name. It's a stark reminder that I didn't get this interview on my own merit. That this might not be the exciting opportunity I've been hoping for but an act they're putting on for their billionaire benefactor. Maybe Lillian even knows about my past reputation as the "sex-romp nanny." Or our current status as a couple.

All I can think to say is "I enjoy tutoring his daughter."

"He said she went from failing her last semester of sixth-grade math to mastering seventh-grade subjects in only one summer."

"Yes," I say. "She's very bright."

"And I'm sure she has a talented tutor." The elevator dings, and the door rumbles open. As I step inside, she says, "We'll be in touch shortly."

"Looking forward to it."

When the door slides shut, I finally feel like I can breathe.

It went well, though. At least I think it did. There were no obvious flails or awkward moments. Then again, I'm not exactly sure what they're looking for. Or if they're actually serious about me. Whatever the case may be, I gave it my best try. I went after it with everything I had. Now I play the waiting game.

Out on the sidewalk, I pull my phone from my purse to find a text waiting for me from Richard: How'd it go?

> Good, I hope. 😘

I'm rooting for you, he replies. Have fun at happy hour. 🤗

Happy hour is in Tribeca, not far from here. There's a break in the humidity today, the breeze ruffling my hair as I walk down Chambers Street toward the tapas bar on West Broadway. I picked the venue; for weeks, I've been dreaming about those fried potatoes I ate in Barcelona, back when I thought one wrong turn determined the trajectory of my life.

When I walk into the bar, Arpita and Coco are already there, sitting at a low table, sipping sangria and chatting. I'd planned to introduce them to each other tonight, but it seems they handled the introductions on their own. I'd been so worried about making friends outside of a grad school environment, but watching these two talk like they've known each other for years makes me feel like it'll all be okay.

"I see you've already met." I take the empty seat across from them, and I pour myself a glass of sangria. "How's it going?"

"Good." They offer me two very polite, very reserved smiles, which is not on-brand for either of them.

"What's wrong?"

"You haven't seen it yet, have you?" Arpita says.

"Seen what?" Instantly, I dive for my purse and pull out my phone.

"Don't look yet," Coco says. "Let's just chill for a minute before we bring the mood down. I wanna hear all about your interview first."

But it's too late. I've already opened my email to find the latest Google Alert for an article titled VERONICA VALE HEARTBROKEN AS RICHARD MOVES ON WITH NEW LOVER. It's a lengthy account of Veronica's anguish, how she feels betrayed and left behind now that Richard and I are a serious item. Not that we've made an official announcement about that, but apparently a photographer caught me leaving his apartment yesterday morning, because there I am, strolling down Central Park West with a goofy grin on my face.

My name is mentioned exactly once, in a fairly innocuous sentence: "Richard's new girlfriend is Abigail Atkinson, a former PhD student." While I'm not thrilled at being described as a "former PhD student"—I'm so much more than that—they don't say anything that could be construed as defamatory or even insulting. Is it an invasion of my privacy? Kind of. But I'm not the focus of the article, either. As I read to the end, it becomes clear this is a puff piece commissioned by Veronica's PR people to promote her new foray into music production. Apparently, she's recording her latest dance-pop album at a studio in Chelsea.

"What happened to her reality show?" I ask.

Coco snickers. "The networks didn't pick it up."

"Of course they didn't," Arpita says. "Who wants to watch a whole season of this woman whining about her ex-husband?"

I chug half my glass of sangria and still feel parched.

"Are you okay?" Arpita asks.

"Yeah. I mean, this isn't great, but it could've been worse."

"I'm sure Richard will take care of it," Coco says. "All you have to do is say the word."

"There's really nothing to take care of." I scan the text again, making sure I didn't miss anything. "They say I'm Richard's new girlfriend, which is true, and this is just a photo of me walking down the street. I don't love it, but if I want to be with Richard, I think this is something I'm just gonna have to learn to live with."

And I want to be with Richard, with my whole heart. It'll be a lot easier if I ignore these tabloids, though. So I pull up my Google Alerts, the ones I set for my name and Richard's name, and I tap the little trash can beside them. When my phone asks me, "Are you sure you want to delete these alerts?" I can't press the yes button fast enough. That's where this news belongs: in the trash.

"Well, that is an extremely mature way of looking at things," Coco says. "I'm very proud of you."

"Agreed." Arpita raises her glass. "I'd like to propose a toast to you and everything you've accomplished this summer."

We clink our glasses and take long frosty gulps of our sangria.

"As long as we're toasting to good news," Coco says, "I've got some to share. One of my stories got accepted for publication today."

"Oh my gosh, that's amazing," I say.

"Congratulations!" Arpita says. "Where's it being published?"

Coco bites her bottom lip and looks about as sheepish as I've ever seen. Then she practically screams, "The *New Yorker*!"

Our responsive squeals of delights make the other patrons in the bar turn in wonder.

"I didn't realize you were trying to get published in the *New Yorker*, Coco," I said. "When I asked you about it, you said you didn't have a goal like that."

"No, I don't have goals. But that doesn't mean I don't have dreams."

"What's the difference?" Arpita asks.

"Goals are plans with action items and deadlines, things you achieve or you don't. Dreams are more like fantasies, wishes from your heart. You can't fail at a dream, because dreams are endless. And when a dream comes true, it's like magic."

We raise our glasses again and this time we toast to Coco, and the magic of her dream coming true. I contemplate my own dreams, but I can't quite put my finger on them yet. They're ambiguous and loosely defined, things like being in love. Having grand adventures. And living my life with no regrets.

CHAPTER TWENTY-SIX

There are two kinds of people in this world: those who step back from the edge of a cliff because they're afraid of getting hurt, and those who take a running leap because they trust the universe will provide a safe place to land.

As I look around my new math classroom, I realize this is it. This is my safe place to land.

School starts on Tuesday, the day after Labor Day. I'm spending this Friday morning setting things up so I can hit the ground running when the first bell rings. There are thirty desks and thirty chairs, organized neatly into five columns and six rows. I've got three sections of algebra and two sections of geometry, and in four out of those five classes, all thirty of these seats will be filled. That's a lot of students, and I'd be lying if I said I wasn't the tiniest bit afraid. But I know I can handle whatever challenge comes my way.

When everything's in its right place, I lock up my classroom and make my way through the echoing hallways to the exit. It's a long train ride home from here; there's no straight shot from Canarsie, Brooklyn, to Astoria, Queens. My commute to work now takes over an hour on two slow trains, but I'm using that time to study for my night courses. If I stick to the plan, it'll only take two years to earn my credential. Then I'll be a full-fledged high school math teacher.

As I walk along Rockaway Parkway toward the L subway station, a dark SUV with tinted windows pulls up to the curb alongside me. When the back window rolls down, I gasp in delighted surprise. It's

Richard, his eyes glimmering with mischief, his lips curled into a devious smile.

"Ms. Atkinson, may I offer you a ride?"

"Why, that would be lovely, thank you." I climb in beside him and close the door. He welcomes me with a kiss that takes my breath away. "What are you doing here?"

"Just wanted to see you." He tucks an errant wisp of hair behind my ear. "Everything set up for Tuesday?"

"I think so."

"Great. So you and I can relax this weekend." He leans over to open a cooler built into the console, revealing a bottle of champagne and two chilled flutes. "And celebrate."

"What are we celebrating?"

"For starters, the beginning of your teaching career. But also, we finally closed the deal."

"Congratulations!"

"Thank you. Soon, Vale Venture Capital will be helping to bring solar farms to communities across the country." His announcement is punctuated with a resonant *thwop* as he opens the champagne, wisps of water vapor curling from the neck of the bottle. "It means I'll be really busy for the next few months as I get to know their corporate culture and ensure our investment is being used in the most efficient way possible."

"That's fine. Between teaching and going to night school, I'll be pretty slammed, too."

"And that's why I was thinking we should spend some quality one-on-one time together this weekend."

As he fills our flutes, my body tingles with the thought of quality one-on-one time. "I like where this is going."

"Oh, you'll really like where this is going once we get there." He nods toward the driver and says, "He's taking us to the airport right now."

"What? Where are we going?"

"It's a surprise. Don't worry—we'll be back on Monday morning so you'll have plenty of time to rest and prepare for the first day of school on Tuesday."

"But I don't have any clothes. Or my toothbrush. Can we swing by my place so I can pack a quick suitcase?"

"All taken care of. Arpita packed you a bag and delivered it to Coco, and now it's sitting safely in the trunk." He hands me a flute. "Sit back. Relax. Enjoy. You deserve it."

We clink our glasses, and as the sweet, fizzy drink hits my taste buds, I can't believe how lucky I am. I'm in love. I'm going on yet another grand adventure. My dreams are coming true, and it's truly like magic.

ACKNOWLEDGMENTS

I owe a huge debt of gratitude to the following people:

Maria Gomez, who has been incredibly patient, unfailingly supportive, and unbelievably kind. Writing this book was *a process* and I am eternally grateful for how much faith you had in me to get it done. Thank you, thank you, thank you.

Angela James, who held my hand through each step of writing this manuscript before carrying me over the finish line. Thank you for all your valuable insight and guidance through every version of this story (both terrible and less terrible) and for helping me (forcing me) to dig deep and write emotional prose when I was feeling like an empty shell. I am so lucky to have had the opportunity to work with you.

Jessica Watterson, who talked me through my tears and reminded me I am not just a writer but an actual human being. Your support means everything to me, and I am beyond thankful to have you in my corner.

Marci and Jessica, who are the absolute best friends any woman could ever ask for.

Diffy and Maple, my rescue chihuahuas, who are the absolute best writing companions any woman could ever ask for.

My son, Andrew, who most definitely distracted me from getting this book done on time (this is the understatement of the century), but I love him more than life itself, so it's okay.

My husband, Emilio, who encourages me to jump off those scary cliffs and always provides a safe place for me to land.

Finally, to the dynamic duo of Lexapro and Xanax, who keep my brain functioning on days when it just wants to give up. If you're struggling, I see you. You're not alone. You can do this. There's no limit to how many times you can start over.

ABOUT THE AUTHOR

Photo © 2022 Josh Mitchell

Kristin Rockaway is a native New Yorker and recovering corporate software engineer. After working in the IT industry for far too many years, she finally traded the city for the surf and chased her dreams out to Southern California, where she spends her days happily writing stories instead of code. You can find her on Instagram at @kristinrockaway and on her website at www.kristinrockaway.com.